# THE BLOOD FOREST

## BOOK THREE IN THE TREE OF AGES SERIES

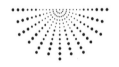

## SARA C ROETHLE

*F*inn peered at the distant coast from the ship's railing, though it was difficult to see through the fog, or was that smoke? The acrid scent in the air seemed too strong to be put off by cook fires alone. She brushed a lock of her long, dirty blonde hair away from her sunburned face, cringing at the feeling of grit beneath her fingers. Her entire body felt covered in a thin layer of salt from the sea.

Iseult stood next to her, gripping the railing tight enough to make the wood creak. She turned to ask him if he thought a bath was in their near future, but kept her mouth shut at his expression.

He was all tension, standing by her side while she leaned against the railing more casually. His black hair, flecked with gray at the temples, was partially held back in its customary clasp, leaving loose tendrils around his face for the sea air to play with. His gray-green eyes were serious, his mouth set in a grim line. He'd been almost relaxed during their time out at sea, but it seemed that had ended now.

Finn turned her gaze back to the distant city. Once they reached land, they'd begin their long journey back to her beginning, where she once stood as a tree. Part of her hoped they'd find Àed there, back in his small hovel, tired from traveling, but she knew it was only wishful thinking. Her aged conjurer friend would not give up on finding them so easily.

She glanced away from the distant city to the other passengers on the ship. At one time, the fast movement while out at sea would have made her lose her last meal, but she'd eventually gotten used to the ship's gentle sway, and now almost found it comforting . . . almost. She could never quite put out of her mind the fact that Sirens dwelled in the sea, waiting to sing sailors to their watery graves.

Finn watched as Iseult's long lost brother, Maarav, and his men manned the sails, guiding the ship steadily toward Migris, where they would dock to meet Kai and Anna. Finn couldn't help but wonder how everyone would get along. She held no warm feelings toward Maarav, and knew he'd likely anger some of the others before long. It was simply in his nature.

She was more worried, however, about how Kai and Anna would behave. Neither of them were particularly good at making friends. Hopefully they'd at least taken good care of little Naoki, Finn's adolescent dragon, though the small creature did present another problem. The people of Migris were terrified of the Faie, and would not take kindly to a dragon in the city. Finn comforted herself with the idea that Kai would think of a way to smuggle Naoki out unseen. He was good at that sort of thing.

Footsteps across the deck preceded Ealasaid's appearance at Finn's other side. Her curly blonde hair had seemed to grow in size the longer they were out to sea, foaming into a snarled mass around her delicate freckled face and pale gray eyes. She wore the same burgundy dress with black accents Finn had first seen her in, causing her to assume it was the girl's only one.

Not that Finn could say much different. She still wore the tight breeches, loose white blouse, and corset she'd been given aboard Anna's ship. Her deep green cloak, beginning to fray heavily at the edges, was secured around her shoulders, shifting gently in the breeze. The people of Migris would likely stare as much at her state of attire as they would a baby dragon, but she was loath to change back into a dress, especially if they'd be riding. Sitting on the saddle wasn't the issue. Her previous skirts had consisted of enough fabric to still cover her ankles, but lifting her leg over the horse always caused a blush. Of course, they'd have to find horses to purchase first, which likely wouldn't prove easy.

Ealasaid stepped forward and leaned her arms against the railing beside Finn. "I've never actually been to

Migris. I've never been to any of the great cities, for that matter."

Finn tilted her head, confused, squinting her eyes against a harsh blast of sea air. "I thought you traveled with Iseult to find me."

Iseult had told her everything that happened while they were apart, including how they'd come to travel with Ealasaid. She knew he'd narrowly missed her in Migris as she sailed away, locked in a cabin on Anna's ship, and had just assumed Ealasaid and Àed were with him.

Ealasaid nodded. "We reached the gates together, but no one was allowed inside the city. Iseult found his own way in, while Àed and I waited with the refugees."

Finn's heart gave another nervous patter at the thought of Àed. Though it was doubtful he'd be waiting for them at the end of their journey in Greenswallow, he might very well be waiting in Migris. He'd parted ways with Iseult somewhere north of the large city, supposedly to search for her on his own. Her only hope was that he had not traveled all the way to the Archtree, only to find it burned to a stump with her nowhere to be found.

"Ah, yes," Finn replied, stuffing her nerves back down, "my travel companion at the time had been able to gain us special entrance to the city. I'd almost forgotten."

The thought of Bedelia brought her nerves right back up. Was she even still alive? Maarav had claimed he'd delivered the potion that would cure Bedelia's illness, brought on by the bite of a Faie wolf, but Finn did not fully trust a single thing he said. He'd stood idly by while Anna kidnapped her, after all. She took a deep breath to settle her anxiety, then nearly gagged on a sudden whiff of smoke in the air, not the pleasant smell of wood burning, or even food, but a sickly sweet stench that made her gut clench.

"Something is wrong," Iseult muttered, drawing her attention.

She followed his gaze to the distant port. It *was* smoke surrounding the city, not fog, though she saw no flames over the city walls. They were still too far out to see anything else.

"Is the city on fire?" Ealasaid questioned.

Iseult nodded. "So it would seem." He smoothed his hands over his clothing, all in shades of his customary black, as if preparing himself for a confrontation.

Finn squinted her eyes in the direction of the city, but could not tell if men still guarded the walls or the dock. She turned her gaze out toward the open ocean, then pointed, "There's Anna's ship. It seems they will arrive shortly after us."

She turned to see Iseult nod. "Yes, if we decide to dock at all. The smoke might mean Migris has been attacked. It may now be inhabited by enemy forces." He frowned at the thought.

Finn knew he was likely thinking of Conall. He'd regaled her of his visit back to the place of his birth, now just a ruined city. It had been taken over and fortified by Conall, a Reiver commanding magic-using refugees.

Reivers were the wild people of the borders, bandits by most accounts. Finn had encountered such a group while she was on Anna's ship. The altercation resulted in disturbing repercussions. She could still clearly picture the man's skin melting from his bones at her touch.

She shook away the memory, focusing on the current situation. She had no desire to encounter Reivers *ever* again. If they inhabited the city, they would simply have to dock elsewhere.

Maarav came to stand at Iseult's other side, leaving his men, Tavish and Rae, to tend the sails. He peered out across the water. "Can't say I like the look of that. I'll not be pleased if my inn is no longer standing."

Finn chewed her lip in consternation. She'd almost forgotten about Maarav's inn, *The Melted Sea*, named after the ocean they now sailed.

"I don't think your inn is necessarily a priority right now," Ealasaid sniped back.

Maarav only chuckled. The pair often seemed to be at each other's throats, but spent more time together than apart. Finn suspected Ealasaid enjoyed Maarav's company more than she let on, though she also seemed constantly irked by the man.

"I'd say it was burned at least a full day ago, judging by the lack of visible flames," Iseult commented. "The remnants of the city will likely smolder for a while longer."

Ealasaid let out a shaky exhale, muted by the sound of lapping ocean waves, more rough now that they were closer to shore. "The whole city?" she asked. "Are you saying the *entire* city was burned?"

Iseult nodded, then gestured toward the sight. "Look at the smoke. That's not the smoke of a single building, or even several."

Unease blossomed in Finn's gut. Migris was only the first stop of many on their journey, but they would still need to resupply. Weeks out to sea had depleted their provisions, and they only had two horses, belonging to Iseult and Maarav. Not to mention that whoever had burned the city might still be in the area.

"Should we still dock?" Finn questioned, searching the sea again for Anna's ship to find it was making steady progress toward the shore. It seemed they planned to dock despite the smoke.

"Aye," Iseult replied. "The nearest ports to Migris are Sormyr, far south, and," he hesitated, "*another* far north." He glanced at Maarav.

Finn supposed he was alluding to the hidden city Iseult had secretly told her about. All on the ship had departed from there, save Finn, who'd been on a ship with Kai and Anna at the time. She couldn't help but be a little jealous. A city completely concealed within a rocky wall, forming a secret cove, sounded like quite a sight, and it irked her that she wasn't supposed to know about it.

Maarav and Iseult turned away to aid the men with the sails, prepared to guide the ship toward the docks, leaving Finn and Ealasaid alone.

"Do you think it was the Faie that burned the city, or was it the Reivers?" Ealasaid questioned distantly, still leaning against the ship's railing. She turned her gaze to Finn. "Or perhaps even An Fiach?"

Finn took a shaky breath and pushed her waist-length hair behind her ear, unsure which option was worse, though it wasn't necessarily any of the three. The Cavari, her tribe, could have been to blame, or perhaps even the Ceárdaman, the *Travelers*, relinquishing their role as watchers to twist the strings of fate.

"Let's just hope whoever it was did not decide to linger," she replied. "And let's hope there are supplies left to find, lest we starve before anyone has the chance to kill us."

Ealasaid's face scrunched up like she might be sick. Finn could not blame her, she was tempted to lose her breakfast herself.

"BLADDERED, CURSED DRAGON," Kai growled, giving a final tug to the blanket.

Naoki perched on the bed, digging her talons into the straw of the mattress. She clasped the other end of the blanket in her beak, refusing to let go, while fluffing up her sparse white feathers to make herself appear larger than she was. He tugged again, making her wings flap chaotically as she tried to maintain her balance, sending loose papers fluttering around the room from the bedside table.

Kai let go of the blanket with a huff. "We can't just go walking about with a dragon out in the open," he explained tiredly. "If you'd just wear the blanket, perhaps we could pretend you're something . . . else."

Dropping her end of the blanket, Naoki craned her long neck to the side, blinking spherical lilac eyes at him. She'd been a handful since they'd parted ways with Finn, Naoki's *mother*, as far as the little dragon was concerned. He'd been forced to keep her in Finn's vacated cabin, lest Naoki attempt to fly away in search of her.

He sighed, then took a seat on the bed beside the dragon. Finn would never forgive him if he managed to lose her friend, not to mention Anna would be furious with losing her collateral.

Naoki made a chittering sound in her throat, then retrieved the blanket and dropped one end in Kai's lap.

He snorted. "It's all just a game to you, isn't it?"

She chittered again.

"Are ye almost done with that dragon!" Sativola called down the stairs leading to the cabins. "We're about to dock, and it looks like the city has been burned."

Burned? Well that didn't sound good. Pushing the blanket aside, he stood, then hurried out of the cabin, shutting the door before Naoki could bound after him. He cringed as her weight hit the closed door, then proceeded to jog down the hallway. He reached the stairs and raced up them two at a time to find Sativola waiting on deck, his massive form partially blocking out the sun.

As soon as Kai was at his side, Sativola pointed a sausage-like finger at the nearby city of Migris. Sure enough, it was giving off large amounts of smoke, and no men could be seen around the gates.

"No signs of life?" Kai questioned, not spotting any, but wanting to verify that whoever had burned the city was not around.

Sativola shook his head, tossing his golden curls to and fro. "None that we've seen yet. Looks like the fire has died down, leaving only the smoldering remains."

Kai snorted. *Smoldering remains.* An apt description for his life at the present, or so he felt. He had no idea where he stood with Finn, and now she was back with Iseult on their little quest. Not to mention Anna's troubles with seeing into the *gray*, the in between places. Her nightmares had only grown worse, sometimes crossing into waking so that she jumped at shadows at the oddest times. Now they somehow had to make it all the way back to Garenoch, and a meadow somewhere beyond that, where Finn used to stand as a tree. It would have all been hard to believe if he hadn't seen too many odd things with his own eyes, including the Faie of the Blood Forest.

"Well at least we won't need to hide the dragon when we dock," Sativola sighed, drawing Kai out of his thoughts.

Kai nodded. There was that, at least. Perhaps he could

just keep Naoki in her cabin, and leave it to Finn to draw her out without a fight.

Thinking of Finn, he scanned the sea for the ship she was on, finding it not far off from his own. He squinted his eyes, attempting to make out the figures on the deck, but they were too far away to see clearly.

Sativola jumped as the door to Anna's nearby cabin burst open, slamming against the exterior wall with a loud *bang*. Anna exited the cabin and approached, looking dangerous in her tightly fitted black attire: breeches, tunic, and corseted vest. Twin daggers, her constant companions of late, swayed at each of her hips. Her straight, black hair, pulled into a tight braid, accentuated her sharp, hawklike features and dark eyes.

"It seems someone has laid siege to Migris," Kai explained as she reached them.

She nodded, her eyes taking on a distant look. "It was the Faie, or something like them."

Kai frowned, waiting for further information.

Instead of answering, Anna glared at Sativola until he raised his hands in surrender and walked away. Turning back to Kai, she explained, "I saw it in a dream last night. I don't know who led them, or why, but many powerful creatures gathered together to conquer the city." She frowned. "They wanted to send a message," she added distantly.

Kai suppressed a shiver. He'd stood witness as the Faie attacked the Ceàrdaman, slaughtering them to break the barrier trapping them within the Blood Forest. He couldn't imagine what the people of Migris must have felt when the Faie descended upon them. Even if some managed to flee, they would not likely last long in the wilds. The roads were already crowded with refugees searching for a safe place to dwell. At least, that was how it had been when they'd departed on their search for the Archtree, over two weeks prior.

"Are the Faie still within the city?" he questioned, hoping Anna had gained more useful information from her dream.

She shook her head. "I do not know, and I didn't say they were Faie for sure, just something like them. Something . . . magical. Perhaps some remain, but I doubt it. They accomplished what they set out to do."

"And that was to send a message?" Kai asked, feeling uneasy as they neared the docks. "What kind of message, and to whom?" This close to the city, he was quite sure there were no signs of life, but he'd prefer to avoid any stragglers who might remain.

"If I knew, I would have said," Anna snapped. "I don't know why I dreamed of it at all. The only thing I can say for sure is that our troubles will only increase from here."

She'd grown flustered as she spoke, darting her eyes around the ship. Was she seeing things again? Kai tried to follow her gaze, knowing he couldn't see what she saw, but unable to keep himself from trying.

Giving up, he left Anna's side to help the other men with the sails. Just a moment before, he'd been thinking his life couldn't get any worse, but if hoards of Faie, or something perhaps even worse, were sacking the great cities, all men would have many more troubles to come.

ISEULT WATCHED as Finn carefully stepped down the slatted plank connecting the ship to the dock. The smell of smoke was stronger this close to the city, coating the chill air hitting his lungs. His gaze lingered as Finn paused to wrap her ratty green cloak more tightly around her, catching her snarled hair in the fabric around her shoulders. She stared down the length of the dock, her feet not moving.

He stepped up behind her on the plank and gently touched her shoulder. She jumped at his touch, then turned her worried gaze back to him.

"There's nothing to be concerned about," he assured her softly. "I will keep you safe."

He looked past her, observing Maarav and Ealasaid already down onto the dock, both watching as Anna's ship drifted into the harbor. Maarav's hired men, Tavish and Rae, also waited below, securing the ship to the large wooden beams of the dock with heavy lengths of rope, in addition to the already lowered anchor.

As Finn nodded and started forward again, Iseult briefly wondered where Tavish and Rae would go from here. He watched Rae, the older of the two, grimly checking each of the ropes they'd secured. Sunlight glinted off his dark skin as he glanced up at Finn and

Iseult as they passed by. He hadn't spoken much on their journey, and Iseult had found himself increasingly uneasy around the man.

Tavish, however, had rarely stopped blabbering. He'd excused his lively demeanor as an accompanying trait to his bright red hair. An idiotic thought as far as Iseult was concerned, though the man's dark brown eyes reflected a certain cunning.

Maarav stepped forward and offered Finn his hand as she reached the dock, but she ignored him. Just as Iseult had found it impossible to trust Rae, so Finn had found Maarav. Though, he couldn't blame her for being wary of his long-lost brother. Iseult was wary too.

Finn stepped onto the dock with him close behind. Roughly sixty paces away, a plank was lowered from Anna's ship. Peering in the direction of the sun, it was difficult to decipher who managed the plank, but judging by the man's massive size, Iseult didn't think it was Kai.

He turned to witness Finn nervously chewing on her lip. Noticing his gaze, she asked, "Do you think there's anyone left in the city? Anyone who might harm Naoki?"

Iseult pursed his lips in thought. He was still skeptical that Finn had actually adopted a *real* baby dragon, though Kai and Anna had both seemed to agree that's what it was. He flicked his gaze to the nearest ruined building, a small shack that would normally store extra lengths of rope and spare planks. "I doubt anyone is left here. Perhaps a few looters hoping to salvage some goods, but our party is large enough that we should not be bothered."

With a nervous nod, she began walking toward Anna's ship. Iseult followed after her, continuously scanning their surroundings for hidden threats. It was unnerving that the city seemed so empty. When they'd first noticed the smoke, he'd thought it likely that Conall was responsible, but now he wasn't sure. If Conall had taken Migris, he would have left men in place to claim it for his people. Now that they were able to observe things more closely, Iseult thought the Faie were more likely to blame. Only the Faie would attack a city simply to lay it to waste, abandoning what could be a useful commodity. It would also explain why any survivors would be hesitant to return. Though most alive had only been around to experience the aftereffects of the Faie War, stories were still told of the horrific occurrences.

Leaving Maarav, Ealasaid, and the other two men behind, Iseult and Finn reached Anna's ship just as Kai was making his way down the plank toward the dock. He seemed tired, and a little thinner than usual, not to mention the pair of angry red gashes across his cheek. Upon closer observation, Iseult noticed more gashes on his hands, and a few tears in his dark green tunic and gray woolen breeches.

Kai's gaze remained on Finn as he finished his descent. Anna could be heard shouting orders up on deck, but was yet to appear at the top of the plank.

"Where's Naoki?" Finn demanded, taking a step

toward Kai. She seemed to have noticed the gashes on his face, taking it as a sign her dragon had been harmed.

Kai narrowed his eyes at her. "Well greetings to you too," he grumbled. "Your dragon is fine. *I*, however, have borne the brunt of her tantrums during this last leg of our voyage."

Finn's expression softened. Iseult's did not.

The trio stood in awkward silence for a moment before Kai gestured toward the plank leading back up to the ship. "I'll leave it to you to retrieve her," he said to Finn. "And you're *welcome*."

Not responding, Finn hurried past him up the plank.

Kai gave Iseult a quick nod in greeting, then turned to walk back up the plank after Finn. A half-second later, Iseult was at his side, boarding the ship. By the time both men reached the deck, Finn had disappeared from sight. Anna stood on the other end of the deck near a pile of supplies, ordering three men around as they carried things out of the main cabin.

Kai sighed, then gestured toward the hatch leading below deck. "Protect any areas you'd rather not have sliced open," he explained. "The little dragon has talons as sharp as any blade." He absentmindedly touched the wounds on his cheek, then led the way forward.

Iseult followed Kai to the hatch, then down a narrow set of wooden stairs. At the bottom, they walked down a short hallway, then turned right into one of the small, windowless cabins. Iseult widened his eyes in surprise as he observed Finn, seated on a small bed, being nuzzled by what appeared to be a baby dragon.

With only the light streaming in from above deck to see by, he couldn't make out all of the creature's details, but he noted a sharp beak, large, round eyes, likely lavender or blue in color, and a sparse sprinkling of glossy white feathers, densest around the edges of the creature's wings. It was making a soft purring noise deep in its throat as its beak rubbed against Finn's face.

At Kai and Iseult's appearance, Finn bundled the creature into her arms and stood, disregarding the sharp talons resting perilously close to her throat. Iseult would have liked to tell her bringing a dragon on their travels was not a wise idea, but her glowing smile forced him to silence. He hadn't seen her smile like that since before he'd told her she was responsible for stealing his people's souls.

"Let's check the city for supplies," he muttered instead, "then we'll move on."

He turned and led the way back out of the cabin, as Kai whispered, "A man of few words, eh?" to Finn behind his back.

Their footsteps followed his a moment later, and soon they were all on the dock, along with Anna and her three crewmen, including the massive one with curly hair he'd heard referred to as Sativola.

They met Maarav, his men, and Ealasaid further down the walkway. Maarav now held the reins of both his and Iseult's horses, brought down from the ship.

Once everyone was gathered together, Iseult repeated his plan.

"What about the ships?" one of Anna's men, with deeply tanned skin and short yellow, hair argued. "We can't leave them behind."

Iseult sighed. He didn't have time for these men. Greenswallow was a long way off, and they needed to arrive there before anyone else discovered the location of the Faie Queen's shroud, buried where Finn once stood as a tree.

"I had hoped to leave my ship in a safe harbor as well," Maarav cut in smoothly. He raked his fingers through his black hair, peppered with a few strands of white, just like Iseult's. "But we must adapt to the current situation. Many of us have places to be inland, and those left can hardly manage to sail two ships on their own. We'll have to leave them, and hope for the best."

"Or someone can stay to guard them," the yellow-haired man spat.

"Are you volunteering?" Kai questioned. "I'm sure a *brawny* man like yourself can hold off an entire army of Faie on your own. We'd be much obliged if you'd watch the ships for us."

The yellow-haired man snarled his dry lips, but didn't speak again.

Iseult took a step closer to Finn, still holding the dragon in her arms with its limbs curled around her. Tavish, Rae, and Ealasaid were all staring at the creature, but said nothing.

"We'll divide into two groups, search for supplies, then meet at the front gates," Iseult instructed.

No one argued. Instead, all glanced warily at the smoldering city, wondering what dangers might still lurk within its walls.

FINN STRAIGHTENED her satchel strap across her chest, trying to balance its weight with the awkward addition of Naoki on her shoulders. It seemed the dragon had grown a bit in their time apart, but still insisted on her chosen perch.

Finn suppressed a grunt of effort. Her legs already felt like pottage transitioning from the ship to dry land, and the added weight made her feel even more off balance. It would not do to topple over and land on one of the corpses, visible now that they'd entered the city.

Iseult prowled at her side, his eyes keen on the surrounding buildings, all showing signs of being touched by fire. At their backs walked Ealasaid, Maarav, Tavish, and Rae. Maarav still held the reins to his and Iseult's horses. The animals remained eerily quiet, as if sensing the ghosts of the dead. Kai, Anna, and Anna's crewmen had taken another route. They would all search for supplies, then reconvene at the city gates to begin their journey.

They now walked in the direction of Maarav's inn, since he'd insisted they check in on the establishment.

Finn didn't know what he was hoping to find, it seemed most everything had been destroyed, but she supposed if he had a cellar some goods might remain.

She quickly averted her eyes from the ground as she stepped around another charred corpse. It wasn't the first body they'd come across, and it surely would not be the last. Many had been killed.

She hurried forward, only to have Iseult reach out a hand to stop her. "Don't look down," he instructed, but the warning came too late. At their feet lay a child, badly burned like many of the other bodies.

She raised a hand to her mouth, afraid she might be sick.

Seconds later, from behind her, Ealasaid gasped. Naoki hissed at the noise, prompting Ealasaid to then let out a surprised yip.

Iseult put an arm around Finn and led her forward. Surprisingly, Naoki did not seem to mind his presence, or else found him more frightening than Kai, and so refrained from hissing at him.

"Are you sure you want to walk all the way to your inn?" Iseult grumbled, looking over his shoulder toward Maarav.

"We need supplies," Maarav replied simply, "and our best chance of finding them is my inn. With any luck, the cellar will be intact."

"I think I'm going to be ill," Ealasaid muttered as they passed another body. "This is far worse than Uí Néid."

"The dead there were freshly killed," Maarav

explained. "It's different once they've been lying around for a while, but you'll get used to it."

Ealasaid snorted. "I'd rather not get used to seeing corpses at all."

Finn attempted to take a steadying breath, but inhaled too deeply. Her stomach convulsed, forcing her to bend forward. The smell of the charred corpses was too much for her, and she found herself expelling what little food was in her belly. Naoki hopped to the ground and chittered nervously at her side as Iseult kept a hand on her back, waiting for the moment to pass.

As Finn's nausea began to wane, she heard someone else retching behind her, and turned to see the red-haired man, Tavish, had also lost his morning meal. The sight somehow made her feel slightly better.

"Perhaps some of us should go ahead to the gates," Maarav sighed, glancing between Tavish and Finn. "Rae and I can gather the supplies on our own. With only two of us, we can ride the rest of the way."

"And what if you encounter whoever killed all these people?" Ealasaid gasped.

Maarav gestured to the desolate streets. "Take a look around you, my girl, no one is left in this cursed place."

Finn crouched to allow Naoki back onto her shoulders, then looked to Iseult for his opinion, secretly hoping he'd agree with Maarav so she wouldn't have to continue looking at the bodies.

Iseult nodded in understanding, then turned his gaze to his brother. "I'll take the women . . . and Tavish, to the gates," he agreed. "But be quick with your tasks, I'd like to be far from this place come nightfall."

"We all would," Tavish muttered, then gestured for Ealasaid to walk ahead of him toward Iseult and Finn.

The four of them changed directions, making their way toward the gates, while Maarav and Rae climbed atop the horses and continued on toward whatever might remain of Maarav's inn.

Finn walked beside Iseult in silence for some time, deep in thought, keeping her gaze upward to avoid looking too closely at any more corpses.

"Do you know what's odd?" Tavish blurted suddenly.

Finn jumped, realizing the man was walking close to her other side, though she noted he was peering around her toward Iseult.

Iseult did not reply, but Tavish still continued, "It's odd that we seem to only be seeing the corpses of towns-folk and the city guards."

"Why is that odd?" Ealasaid questioned, walking a few paces behind them.

"Because in any battle there are casualties on both sides," Iseult answered grimly.

"So you *did* notice," Tavish commented, seeming relieved that he wasn't the only one to find the situation strange.

"Yes," Iseult replied simply.

Finn wished she could be so observant, but she'd been too busy trying to pretend they weren't surrounded by *any* corpses, let alone only those of the townsfolk.

"So what do you think happened?" Tavish continued, once again looking past Finn at Iseult.

"Either the bodies of the opposing forces were taken," Iseult explained, "or the townspeople were killed by a force so great they all died where they stood. Now keep your mouth shut. Dangers may still lurk."

Wide-eyed, Tavish snapped his mouth shut and glanced around warily. Finn couldn't say she was glad for the silence. It seemed to bring out the eeriness of their surroundings. As far as she was concerned, they couldn't reach the gates soon enough.

Naoki let out a sudden *squawk* from her perch on Finn's shoulder. Finn stumbled, but Iseult's hand darted out to catch her arm before she could fall.

Maintaining his grip on her, Iseult glanced around for what had alerted Naoki. Finn looked too, until her eyes caught a hint of movement a few feet away. She pointed, just as Tavish seemed to notice the same movement.

It was the corpse of a young woman, less burned than the rest, but still just as dead. Her limp body was wriggling back and forth, though none of her limbs seemed to be responsible for the movement.

"The dead are coming to life!" Tavish gasped.

"No," Iseult said coolly, then released Finn's arm to step forward.

He withdrew his sword, lowering the tip toward the woman's still wriggling body. At first Finn thought he might use the sharp edge to skewer her, but instead he slid the point beneath her torso, then flipped her body over, revealing a small creature that had been trying to free itself from the trapping weight of the corpse.

It struggled to its clawed feet, checking over its craggy, rock-like skin for injuries with its spherical eyes. One of its bat-like wings seemed to be broken.

"It's a Grogoch," Finn gasped.

The Grogoch jumped at the sound of her voice, then trembled in fear as it looked up at Iseult. Naoki hopped off Finn's shoulder and crouched on the ground, prepared to pounce the Grogoch.

"Wait!" Finn cried, then knelt beside Naoki to halt her pounce. However, Iseult looked just about ready to pounce the small creature himself, and Finn couldn't blame him. They'd met Grogochs before. Not only had many townsfolk danced themselves to death, but both Finn and Iseult had been rendered unconscious long enough for Kai and Anna to kidnap her.

The Grogoch blinked up at her, still trembling.

"What happened here?" she demanded. "Did you sing the townsfolk to sleep so the other Faie could murder them?"

Naoki let out a low growl.

The Grogoch was trembling so violently she thought it might wet itself. "N-no, lass," it sputtered in its humming voice. "I was only here to have a bit of fun, then *they* attacked. I was knocked down and my wing was broken." It gestured pleadingly with its taloned hands at the drooping wing.

"We know these creature's tricks," Iseult muttered. "We should kill it and move on."

"No!" it rasped. "I did no wrong!"

Finn held up a hand toward Iseult, halting his sword arm.

"Tell me what happened," she instructed. "Who attacked?"

"Other Faie," the Grogoch whispered. "Elementals, led by someone powerful. The elementals *never* meddle in the world of humans. They must have been forced."

Something tickled at the edge of Finn's memories. She knew something about these elementals, but couldn't quite place what it was. "Tell me more about the elementals," she urged. "Tell me everything you know and you will not be harmed."

"Finn-" Iseult began to argue, but she silenced him with a pleading look.

"Cannot be killed," the Grogoch explained. "These ones were made of pure fire. Whoever commanded them did not reveal themselves. Many of the townsfolk fled, but others tried to fight. Silly men. Stood no chance."

Goosebumps broke out across Finn's entire body. She knew she'd encountered elementals in her previous life, but could not quite recall the event, just like all her other memories. She knew they were there, buried somewhere deep within her subconscious, but she had no access to them.

The Grogoch was eyeing her suspiciously, as if wondering whether she'd go back on her word.

Several pairs of footsteps sounded behind Finn's back. She turned for just a moment to see Kai, Anna, Sativola, and the other two crewmen jogging toward them, carrying sacks of supplies over their arms, but when she turned back, the Grogoch was gone.

"We should not have let it go," Iseult muttered as the others reached them.

"What are you all standing around for?" Kai questioned upon arrival.

Finn frowned and turned back to Iseult. Their eyes met, and she tried to silently let him know there were things they needed to discuss. He seemed to understand her silent meaning, as he nodded, then turned his gaze to everyone gathered around them.

"Let us leave this place," he instructed. "Hopefully Maarav and Rae will have already made their way to the gates."

Soon Naoki was back on Finn's shoulders, and the party continued onward. Finn hardly noticed the corpses they passed, her mind entrenched in trying to recall her memories.

She was not sure who would be able to command the elementals, but she felt it was critical she find out. If elementals could not be stopped by human means, perhaps they could be stopped by one of the Dair. If they could, she needed to figure it out fast, lest they come for her and her friends next.

# CHAPTER TWO

*a*nna's feet were beginning to ache, but she kept her complaints to herself. After so long at sea, her limbs and mind felt useless. She was surprised with how little she'd *seen* in Migris. After all that had taken place there, she'd expected to be jumping at her usual shadows, but the city had seemed *dead*. All that was left was a bit of magical residue and corpses.

After meeting with Maarav and Rae, the party spent the rest of the day heading east down the Sand Road. Ealasaid and Finn had both spent much of the journey on the two horses, but Anna had refused her turn. She could walk as far, likely *farther*, than any of the men. She had, however, allowed the men to strap their proffered supplies behind the horses' saddles. They had found unharmed food in several cellars, along with a few extra bedrolls, some cloaks, and a bit of coin.

After leaving the horrors of Migris behind, they'd had

no relevant encounters besides a caravan camped on the side of the road. They had been on their way toward Migris when they heard of what happened there, and were preparing to turn around the next day. The group did not know about what Finn claimed were elementals, only that the city had been burned.

While the others had conversed with the caravan, Anna had kept her eyes cast to the side, waiting in the background with Finn while she clutched Naoki, wrapped in a cloak like a baby - an *enormous* baby - to keep her hidden. Anna had at least been grateful for the odd distraction of Finn at her side. She didn't want to know if any of the caravaners were magic users. She already had to see Finn shining like a glittering star. She didn't need to see anyone else.

The only problem with keeping her eyes continuously cast askance was that she'd *see* things in the surrounding forest. Magic-type things. Unlike Migris, the woods were alive with movement. Nothing solid, really, just flickers of light, and numerous gray shapes that seemed to be watching the party as they progressed down the Sand Road.

More problematic still, was the fact that soon it would be dark. She always saw more strange things in the night than in the day, whether she was awake or asleep. She did not look forward to her dreams that evening. The sea had offered a relative feeling of safety. There she only had to interact with a few people, and her direct surroundings. On a ship, she knew the gray shapes she was seeing weren't physically there. In the woods, there was no telling what was real or illusion.

"We should make camp soon," Maarav stated, the black cloak draped over his shoulders fluttering in the icy wind.

Anna clenched her jaw at the idea, though outwardly she agreed with a nod. She would have to rest at some point, and she might as well get it over with.

"Somewhere away from the road," Iseult added, walking protectively by Finn's side. "We are safer where we cannot be seen."

Everyone nodded and muttered their agreement. After what they'd seen in Migris, they all feared what they might meet on the road, but it was also the fastest route away from the coast. A worthwhile risk. That same logic did not apply to sleeping. For sleep, they would hide in the shadows, and hope that the shadows weren't what they needed to be hiding from.

With everyone in agreement, Iseult led the way off the path and into the trees. While Anna would defer to the judgement of very few, she found she had no problem deferring to Iseult. She didn't particularly like the gruff man, but she knew one thing about him for sure. He was a survivor. It was wise to follow survivors if one hoped to remain among the living, especially in times like these.

Kai stuck close to Anna's side as the party made their way into the forest, likely worried about her sanity. She'd kept him abreast of the things she'd seen, and fortunately he believed her, but his worry was evident.

Worry, she could deal with. She was just glad she had someone to confide in. Of course, how could he not support her after all they'd been through?

She flexed her palms, trying to banish her nerves. The trees seemed to be closing in around them, but she knew it was only in her head. Their broad leaves, shaped like large hands, cast eerie shadows in the dying light, but did not actually move.

Her remaining crewmen muttered behind her back about the ships they'd left behind. *Fools*. They hadn't lost out. It was *her* ship they'd left. Though she knew the friend she'd procured it from hadn't charged her full price, it was still a greater loss for her than anyone else. The men didn't know how lucky they were now to be traveling with skilled fighters. She didn't know much about the girl, Ealasaid, but knew Iseult, Kai, Maarav, and Sativola knew what they were doing with their blades. Their party was better protected than most traveling these now forsaken lands.

Now that they were concealed within the woods, Finn let Naoki down to roam around. The little dragon scented the ground and ran circles around everyone's feet, but never strayed too far from her mother. Anna was surprised to notice Iseult smiling at the creature as she took the end of Finn's cloak in her beak and tried to tug her along . . . or perhaps he was just smiling at Finn. Either way, Anna had previously thought him incapable of smiling at all.

Soon they reached an area Iseult deemed secluded

enough, and Anna exhaled in relief. Her feet felt like icy bricks, weighing her down with every step.

There was enough of an opening in the trees for everyone to lay out their bedrolls, with a few fallen logs for seating. She knew they'd found enough supplies within Migris for a hearty supper, though they'd be wise to ration what they had, not knowing where the next batch of supplies might be found. Unfortunately, she had a sneaking suspicion it would be difficult to keep things fair, considering her crewmen already seemed to be arguing with Maarav's as they set up their bedrolls.

"We need to get to Port Ainfean," one of her crewmen said. "We can sail the river Cair, far away from any Reiver ships, then return to the sea when it's safe."

One of Maarav's crewmen, Rae, Anna thought his name was, turned to the other man, Tavish, and muttered that they should head north.

"North?" Anna's crewman blurted. "Why in the name of the Horned One would you want to head north? Nothin' up that way but Reivers."

Maarav's two crewmen met each other's eyes, but did not comment, and instead stood and walked off together, muttering quietly to each other. Soon Anna's crewmen followed, demanding to know the reason for heading north.

Finding Maarav's crewmen suspicious, but seeing little she could do about it in that moment, she turned her gaze to the remaining portion of the group. Ealasaid seemed to be upset about something, and Finn was fussing over her like a mother hen, while Kai and Iseult started stacking wood for a fire.

Ealasaid began to cry, and Maarav took Finn's place, ushering the girl off into the woods to speak in privacy.

Anna shook her head and turned back to her bag of procured supplies. They would all need to be sorted and doled out properly, and *she* was obviously going to be the one to do it, since no one else was offering.

"I'll get some more wood for the fire," Sativola sighed, having finished tending to Maarav and Iseult's horses.

"Thank you," Anna muttered, pleased she wouldn't have to do *everything*.

By the time she'd finished sorting the supplies, Kai and Iseult had a roaring fire going. While the fire might draw unwanted human attention, it would hopefully keep other creatures at bay. Plus, it was absolutely *freezing* in the forest, even though they were still well within the growing season by Anna's estimation.

Leaving the bundled supplies behind, she moved toward the fire, holding her gloved palms outward to warm them. The sun had nearly set, casting odd, long shadows through the trees.

"Where is everyone?" Finn asked, walking toward the fire with Naoki bounding behind her.

"Are you truly so unobservant?" Anna snapped.

Finn frowned, reaching a hand out absentmindedly to pet her dragon friend.

Anna sighed. "Sativola went for more wood, and the other men clambered off arguing about where they want to go from here. Maarav went off with Ealasaid . . . " she trailed off, glancing warily around them. *That* had been quite some time ago.

"Oh wonderful," Kai grumbled, moving to stand next to Anna with his cloak wrapped tightly around him. "They've probably all wandered off to be eaten by errant Faie."

"We should probably find them *before* that happens," Anna sighed, lowering her hands to her sides.

Kai groaned. "Why do I have a feeling this is going to be like the Blood Forest all over again?"

Anna smirked. "Because you're not an idiot."

Iseult didn't speak, but it was clear he was *not* pleased. He offered Finn a hand up from where she crouched near the fire with Naoki. Still holding her hand, he said, "Please, stay by my side at all times."

Kai snorted. "Yes, please do. We all remember what happened *last* time we traveled into a forest filled with Faie."

Anna smirked as Finn's complexion deepened with a blush. Anna had been held prisoner whilst her companions traveled through the Blood Forest to find her, but Kai had filled her in on what she'd missed. Finn had become even more Faie struck than anyone else, taking off on horseback in search of her *family*. She and Kai had ended up lost all night, not finding their other companions until the next morning.

At the time, hearing the tale had been amusing. Now that Anna knew just who Finn's *family* was, she was leaning more toward terrifying. Had the Cavari truly been in the Blood Forest that night, or was it simply an illusion? Hopefully Finn would not see them this night as well, because Anna feared she would have to abandon them all to run the other way.

FINN'S BREATH fogged the air in front of her face. Naoki had chosen to prowl around near her feet, leaving her without the extra warmth around her shoulders. Iseult stuck close to her side, his hand on the pommel of his sheathed sword as his eyes scanned the dark trees around them. Behind them walked Kai and Anna. Finn grudgingly admitted to herself that she was glad the pair was currently safe, but *only* to herself. She'd never say so out loud.

"I believe we've found our first missing party member," Iseult grumbled, drawing Finn out of her thoughts.

She peered past Iseult's pointing finger to see a glint of golden curls in the moonlight. "Sativola!" she gasped, prepared to run off toward the man, but Iseult caught her by the arm.

"We don't know if he's under a Faie spell," he explained. "He may be dangerous."

She nodded, then glanced back at Kai and Anna.

Kai sighed. "I suppose *I'll* be going first then." He walked around Finn, dodging a playful swat of Naoki's talons to approach Sativola, who was happily dancing in the moonlight.

Finn, Iseult, and Anna followed after Kai silently, though Finn doubted Sativola would notice their presence even if they shouted at him. He seemed entirely enthralled with his twirling dance.

"Why is he shirtless?" Anna hissed near Finn's shoulder.

Finn tried not to laugh. They were all in horrible danger, and she should not find the situation humorous, but she couldn't help a small smile. Sativola had given Kai a constant ribbing over becoming charmed by the Sirens when they were out to sea. If they all survived, she imagined Kai would have his revenge teasing the large, masculine man about his half-naked twirling in the moonlight.

"Sativola?" Kai questioned, nearing his friend.

Sativola didn't seem to hear him, and instead continued to twirl.

"Perhaps you should kiss him," Finn whispered, stepping up behind Kai with Iseult at her side. *She* had been the one to kiss Kai to break the Siren's spell, a memory she still blushed at whenever she thought of it. She would not mind if Kai had something to blush at too.

Kai glared back at her. "I imagine one of you ladies should have that *pleasure*."

"I think he'd prefer *you*," Finn teased.

Iseult sighed and left Finn at Kai's side to approach

Sativola. He cocked his fist back, then hit poor Sativola square in the jaw.

Sativola staggered backward, then looked up at Iseult in shock. His nose let out a small trickle of blood, but at least he'd stopped dancing. The shock and anger on his face slowly faded as he took in his surroundings, including Finn, Anna, and Kai standing off to one side. Next he looked down at the curly blond hair on his bare chest.

"What in *Tirn Ail* happened?" he asked, returning his gaze to them.

"Faie," Iseult answered simply. He lifted Sativola's tunic and cloak from the forest floor and handed them to him. With a glance at Kai and Anna, he returned to Finn's side and urged her onward. Naoki chirped and began trotting at her other side.

Sativola joined Kai and Anna, and they continued their search.

They hadn't gone far when Finn heard Anna sigh.

"What is it?" Kai whispered. "Do you see . . . something?"

Finn turned to see Anna gesture off into the trees. "Something over there," she muttered, sounding defeated.

Iseult looked to Finn, and she nodded. Anna must have been seeing into the *gray*. To their right was something . . . magical.

Veering off their chosen course, the party all made their way toward where Anna had pointed. Before long, they heard soft giggles and masculine laughter. Finn resisted the urge to run forward, already knowing who was ahead of them. Ealasaid was the only missing female member of their party, and so, was likely responsible for the giggles.

"Well this should be interesting," she heard Kai whisper.

They continued in the direction of the giggling until Ealasaid and Maarav came into view. They were seated near a small pond, surrounded by scraggly young trees. Finn watched in horror as Maarav leaned forward and stole a kiss. Rather than being offended, Ealasaid giggled again.

Finn hurried forward and wrapped her arms around Ealasaid, pulling her to her feet. She knew a Faie spell when she saw one, and also knew that *no one* should have to kiss anyone they wouldn't under normal circumstances.

Maarav hopped to his feet just as the others reached them. "Unhand my bride!" he shouted, but Iseult cut him off before he could make a grab for Ealasaid, who struggled against Finn's grasp.

"Should we hit him?" Kai asked.

Anna snickered. "I volunteer my services." She walked right up, poked Maarav on the shoulder, then punched him as soon as he turned toward her.

He reeled back from the hit, then laughed. "My lady," he began, looking down at Anna, "while normally I'd encourage your behavior, I'm afraid I've promised myself to another." He waggled his eyebrows at her, then turned back to Ealasaid.

She had stopped struggling against Finn's grasp and instead started to cry.

Finn frowned, taking in the loving gleam in Maarav's eyes as he gazed at his *bride*. "I don't think the spell is broken," she groaned, then finally let Ealasaid go. She couldn't very well hold on to the woman all night.

Free of her grasp, Ealasaid hurried to Maarav's open arms.

Sativola stepped up to Finn's side, observing the loving couple. "This is more embarrassing than dancing in the moonlight. Agreed?" he whispered.

Finn sighed. "I believe so, at least for Ealasaid. I think she'll be quite appalled when she learns her first kiss went to Maarav."

"*First* kiss?" Anna and Kai said together.

Finn was glad the darkness hid her blush. She wasn't sure who her first kiss had gone to in her previous life, but in this one it had gone to Kai, also as the result of a Faie spell . . . at least on Kai's part.

"She told me while we were on the ship together," she explained.

"Bring them with us," Iseult ordered, putting an end to any more talk of kissing. "Hopefully the spell will break by morning."

Ealasaid and Maarav started kissing again.

"Perhaps one more slap, just to be sure?" Finn questioned, wanting to slap Maarav herself for taking advantage of the young girl, Faie spell or no. Naoki let out a low growl that Finn interpreted as her agreement.

Before anyone human could answer, a howl cut through the night, sending a chill down Finn's spine. She'd heard such a howl before.

Her canine encounter with Bedelia suddenly fresh in her mind, she turned to Iseult. "That sounded like one of the Faie wolves, the ones that bit my friend. Their bites cause illness."

"We should return to the fire," he stated. "It should serve to keep them at bay."

"What about the others?" Kai questioned.

Iseult shook his head. "I will not risk an encounter with the wolves." He glanced at Finn. "Without treatment, their bites are fatal."

Finn pawed at her hair nervously, worried about the other crewmen, though she had no desire to face the wolves again. "Perhaps they've already returned, and are wondering where we are," she suggested.

Iseult put a hand on her back and guided her to begin walking in the direction of their camp.

Maarav gallantly swooped Ealasaid up into his arms, carrying her in the same direction.

Kai moved to walk at Finn's side, opposite Iseult, with Anna beside him. "At least you weren't the one to get Faie charmed tonight," he whispered, leaning toward her shoulder.

Finn smiled sadly at him. "The night is still young,

and the Blood Forest no longer has a boundary for us to escape."

He let out a long sigh as their boots crunched over dried leaves and broken branches. "You're right. It *does* feel just like the Blood Forest. Too bad we no longer have Anders and Branwen with us to explain the Faie lore."

Finn nodded, deep in thought, highly doubting either of the twins were even still alive.

ANDERS STIFLED A GROAN. His feet were absolutely *killing* him. Niklas, the Traveler with whom he'd taken up company, never seemed to tire. His tall, spindly form, covered with a shapeless gray cloak, seemed to glide over the rocky ground. The land around them was barren and open, though given the season, it should have still boasted wild heather, and the monotonous hum of insects.

"The nights have been growing unusually cold," Niklas commented, startling Anders.

Anders looked around at the softly rolling hills, gently illuminated by moonlight, surrounding the narrow dirt road they walked. It *was* cold, almost unbearably so, but the temperature was far down on the list of his worries.

He pushed his dirty red hair out of his face, long since freed of the braids he'd worn during his time with An Fiach, *The Hunt*. "I take it the cold is somehow significant to you?"

Niklas nodded, his bald head gleaming in the light of the moon. His oddly reflective eyes flicked to Anders, then back to the road ahead of them. "Faie magic often leaves a chill in the air. It's as if the very land they tread upon hangs somewhere between reality and the in-between. It's always cold where the barriers between the worlds are thin. The changes are happening more quickly than we predicted."

Anders knew the *we* he referred to were the Cèar-daman, more commonly called the Travelers. The lore had them labeled as craftsmen, but Anders had come to learn their *craft* was prophecy, and the keeping of history. They had many gifts, most of which Anders was sure he didn't understand. Sometimes it felt as if Niklas stared into his very soul, yet the Traveler for some reason still required his aid to access his family's Archives. The Travelers could not be all-knowing if they were in need of books written by humans.

"And what changes did your people predict?" Anders asked finally.

Niklas curled his bloodless lips into a grim smile, then restated the prophecy Anders had now heard many times. "The seasons are changing. The lines are faltering, undoing the old and bringing life to the new. Trees will fall, and changed earth will be left in their place. A storm is coming."

Anders looked up at the cloud-obscured moon, just as a brilliant streak of lighting cut through the dark sky, illuminating their surroundings for a brief moment. A light drizzle of rain began to fall, but that was the second least of Anders' worries, right after the cold. The brief flash of lightning had revealed *eyes*, countless pairs of glowing eyes, watching them from the hills.

Either Niklas did not notice, or he was not overly concerned. That made *one* of them.

They walked on through the night. Anders was constantly aware of the feeling of eyes on him, but nothing ever attacked, likely because of Niklas.

By morning, Anders' new primary worries were the painful, grumbling knot of his stomach, and his feet feeling like they might be bleeding within his boots.

This was the longest they'd traveled with so few breaks, and such little food. In the beginning Niklas seemed at least a little interested in keeping Anders alive, but as time wore on, he became increasingly obsessed with their goal.

Though Anders was dreading reaching the Archive and attempting to enter with a Traveler at his side, he breathed a sigh of relief as the ornate fortress came into view in the early morning light. The golden hue of the expansive central building, domelike in shape, seemed to shimmer in the thin, cool air. Surrounding it were the lodgings, other communal buildings where many scholars spent their entire lives, and multiple long wings housing countless books and other recordings. In fact, the Archive could be considered a city unto itself, for the people within had all they needed to survive.

While the spired gates around the complex had at one

time brought Anders comfort, making him feel safe, now the sight was daunting. Positioned above and around the gates were numerous Archive Guards, supplied by the Gray City, Sormyr. Anders would only need his parents to verify his identity to pass through the gates. Niklas was another story.

Unfortunately, Anders could not simply enter and retrieve the tomes Niklas desired. The Traveler claimed he would need to be there to identify each book, and Anders would not be allowed to take them outside of the Archive.

Suddenly Niklas halted, still far enough from the Archive that the guards would not be overly concerned with their presence. "We will wait here," he explained. "Make camp and a meal if you must, but be prepared. We await the right moment."

"Is something going to happen?" Anders gasped, wondering if Niklas' people had interpreted a portion of the future involving his family's Archive.

Niklas nodded. "Yes, and you will be needed. Prepare to be important, for once in your life."

Anders sighed, surprised that the insult didn't even sting. He'd let enough people down, and had been let down in return, that his pride was a thing of the past. While he wouldn't mind regaining a measure of *importance*, he did not trust the grim cast to Niklas' features. Important men could be either heroes, or villains.

Anders wondered which one he was about to be.

# CHAPTER THREE

*F*inn sat up with a yawn. She stretched her arms over her head, reluctantly letting the cool air hit her upper body. She wanted nothing more than to retreat back into her bedroll, but after the events of the night, she knew they should not linger away from the road.

She yawned again. She and Iseult had taken first watch, while Kai, Anna, and Sativola had taken the second. Maarav and Ealasaid hadn't been allowed to participate in standing guard, since they seemed unable to pull free of the Faie spell. Sitting up fully, she searched around for the pair. She didn't see Maarav, but her eyes eventually found Ealasaid, sitting near the fire with a morose expression. Ah, it seemed the spell had broken.

Finn wiggled the rest of the way out of her bedding and stood, plucking her cloak from the pile to wrap around her shoulders. She walked toward the fire, then took a seat beside Ealasaid on a portion of tree trunk.

"I'm such a fool," Ealasaid muttered, leaning forward to bury her head in her hands.

Finn glanced around again for Maarav, but saw only Iseult and Anna tending to the horses and fixing a cold meal, respectively. Naoki circled Iseult's feet, chirping up at him, and he'd occasionally toss something down to her, likely a small scrap of meat judging by how quickly she gobbled each morsel.

Finn turned back to Ealasaid. "Where are the others?"

Meeting her questioning gaze, Ealasaid explained, "*He* went off with Kai and Sativola to search for the other men."

She smiled softly. "*He* being Maarav, I assume?"

Ealasaid nodded, then reburied her face. "He wasn't even embarrassed," she groaned. "We woke up this morning in each other's arms, and he gave me a kiss on the cheek and thanked me for the *entertaining* evening."

"You didn't-" Finn cut herself off, searching her mind for a tactful way of asking what she was thinking. "You didn't *entertain* him *too* much, did you?"

Ealasaid snorted and lifted her head. "No, thank the gods. Just kissing. Lots, and *lots* of kissing." Down her head went back into her palms.

Finn patted her back. "Try not to worry too much about it. You are not the only one in our party who's been affected by Faie tricks. Once I ran off into the woods on my own, putting all of my companions in danger, and while we were sailing, Kai nearly flung himself into the ocean to reach the Sirens."

Ealasaid groaned, but finally revealed her face and smiled. "You're right. It was a spell and not really me. I just wish Maarav had shared in my embarrassment, at least a little."

Finn returned her smile. "Come now, he's probably just feeling down that you no longer wanted to rest in his arms come morning."

Ealasaid smiled a little wider, then Anna approached and handed them each a slice of bread topped with white cheese. She looked like she wanted to say something, then Sativola came crashing out of the trees, followed by Kai, Maarav, Tavish, and Rae, the latter two with their eyes downcast and a bit of blood on their clothing.

Iseult approached the men with Naoki in tow. "Where are the others?"

Tavish and Rae both kept their eyes downcast.

Suddenly feeling wary, Finn remained on her seat next to Ealasaid, several paces away from the men. She took a bite of her bread and cheese, chewing slowly.

"They were all swept up in a Faie spell," Maarav explained for his men. "The others did not survive. We buried them as best we could."

"*What?*" Anna growled, charging up to the remorseful men like an angry wolf. "You *killed* my crew?"

Rae was the first to meet her eyes. "They would have killed us otherwise."

"And how do *we* know that," she snapped.

"You do not," Rae replied, standing his ground. "Which is why Tavish and I will take our leave of you."

"No, you will not," Maarav interrupted, his tone not welcoming arguments.

Anna turned her glare to Maarav, while Rae's expression remained impassive.

"You swore to accompany me until my mission is complete, or until I release you from service," Maarav explained, his gaze firmly on Rae and Tavish, "and you know full well what it would mean if you were to go back on that oath."

Naoki trotted over to Finn and buried her beak against the leg of her breeches, as if unsettled by the sudden tension. Finn stroked the dragon's head with her free hand, her gaze remaining on the arguing men. She had a feeling there was more meaning to Maarav's words than she was able to divine. Perhaps some secretive law pertaining to the hidden city up North?

Casting a final glare at Anna, Rae met Maarav's gaze. "I will abide by the rules."

Finn glanced at Iseult to see if he understood any more of this conversation than she did. Though his expression gave away little, he was watching his brother like a hawk. Perhaps he trusted Maarav as much as she, which was little.

"Get cleaned up," Maarav ordered the two men, then turned toward his bedroll and supplies, effectively ending the argument.

Anna gave Rae and Tavish another hard look, and

neither seemed to miss how her hands hovered near her daggers. They all stared at each other a moment more, then Anna turned away with a huff.

Finn took another bite of her hard bread and cheese, then turned to Ealasaid, silently asking her what she thought. Ealasaid shrugged, then stuffed the rest of her bread in her mouth, stood, and walked away, decidedly keeping her distance from Maarav.

Finn's small meal settled like a hard lump in her stomach. After what they'd seen in Migris, she knew the risk of death for her party was high, but she hadn't expected the first two men to go like *that*.

She lifted her gaze as Kai approached and took Ealasaid's vacated seat. "At least none of us *killed* each other in the Blood Forest," he muttered.

She nodded, then gave him a thoughtful look.

He raised his hands in surrender. "I wasn't about to tease you about running off that day, I swear."

She shook her head. "It's not that, I'm simply wondering why you were affected by the Sirens, but not the Faie of the Blood Forest, or the ones last night. And I'm wondering why Iseult is never affected at all."

Kai frowned. "Well Iseult, I suspect, has a heart made of black iron, warding the Faie away. And perhaps I was only entranced by the Siren's because. . . " he trailed off, pondering his answer.

"Because you're desperate for female attention?" Anna asked, walking up behind him. She handed him a piece of bread and cheese, just like she'd given Finn, then gazed toward where Maarav, Tavish, and Rae had moved to converse, out of hearing range. Sativola walked up beside Anna.

"I think it would be wise for us to look after each other's well being," Anna advised, her voice low. "I'll watch your backs, if you'll watch mine."

"Deal," Finn and Kai said in unison, while Sativola said, "Aye."

Finn met Iseult's gaze from where he stood by the horses. He gave her a subtle nod. They would all need to look out for each other.

Soon everyone gathered together to depart, a pall of heavy silence surrounding them. Rae and Tavish watched everyone but Maarav warily, as if realizing they were no longer entirely welcome.

Finn could only hope they would choose to leave on their own, along with Maarav, lest anyone *else* end up in a shallow grave in the woods.

ISEULT FELT little relief at being back on the Sand Road. Finn walked beside him, completely unharmed by the previous night's events, yet he couldn't help but think how easily she could have been the one on the wrong side of a Faie enchantment. If Rae and Tavish had harmed her instead of the other men . . . well, Rae and Tavish would not longer be in existence.

Maarav walked ahead with the two men in question,

while Anna, Kai, Sativola, and Ealasaid walked a few paces behind, leading the two horses. Iseult was glad Ealasaid had come to her senses, and seemed to want to be as far from Maarav as possible. At least *she* was fazed by the events of the night. Maarav couldn't seem to care less about any of it, including the deaths.

Iseult knew Maarav had been trained from a very young age to be a killer, and Rae and Tavish were likely the same. He also suspected there was some sort of hierarchy within their secret city that caused them to defer to Maarav's wishes, as the two men clearly would have branched off on their own otherwise.

Iseult would gladly encourage their departure, along with Maarav. The others, well, Finn had made Anna a promise, allowing her to accompany them on their journey, and that apparently meant Kai as well, and he knew Ealasaid had nowhere else to go, but the other crewman . . . he felt they would be better off without them, now that they were no longer in need of a ship and crew. Still, it seemed ignoble to force them off on their own after what they'd seen in Migris. There was safety in numbers, as long as you weren't betrayed by your own.

Finn sighed beside him. Iseult thought for a moment she was sharing his thoughts, until she asked, "Where do you think Àed is? Do you think he could have been in Migris when . . . " she trailed off, then bit her lip. Her eyes suddenly welled with tears.

"The old man is far too clever to have gotten caught

up in that," he comforted, believing his words. "I'm sure he's tracking us as we speak."

She looked to him hopefully. "Do you think he'll be able to find us, even if we make it all the way back to Garenoch?"

He nodded. "He was able to track you across great distances before. I would not worry."

She smiled, and seemed to relax. Naoki, trotted by her side, free of her cloak for now, though Finn kept it ready in her arms should they happen upon another caravan.

"About what happened in Migris-" she hesitated.

"You seemed to remember something at the Grogoch's mention of elementals," he observed.

She nodded. "Not a memory exactly, but a feeling. Something to do with them in my . . . previous life."

"That memory wouldn't have anything to do with how to fight them?" he asked hopefully.

She shook her head. "They cannot be fought. They are pure embodiments of elements, fire, water, wind, fueled by earth magic. I think perhaps the Dair can control them to an extent, since they control nature."

He went silent, pondering her words. He wondered if perhaps her roots were a form of elemental magic, or if the roots were elementals themselves, animate all on their own. Perhaps they chose to come to her call. He decided against speaking his speculations, not wanting to add to her list of memories to search for.

Gazing at the men walking ahead of them far out of

earshot, she whispered suddenly, "Do you think we can trust them?"

"No," he replied simply.

"But he's your brother," she argued quietly. "Do you believe he will betray us?"

"I cannot say," he sighed. "We had not seen each other since we were small children. I have no way of knowing what sort of man he's become, and I do not trust the place he and his men came from. I do not trust how he happened upon *you* in Migris, nor his reasons for standing idly by when Anna kidnapped you."

"I'm glad you said that," Finn muttered. "I feared I was the only one to feel that way."

Iseult glanced over his shoulder at those walking behind them. He supposed they might be close enough to catch a few words of their conversation, but found he was not entirely opposed to the idea. Though it would be difficult for him, it would be best for he and Finn to foster trust with Kai and Anna. He disliked Kai, but the knave would undoubtedly protect Finn. He'd proven that much, at least, but Anna was another story. Yet, while her motivations revolved entirely around herself, and hence she could not be fully trusted, if she believed she was trusted, then managing her would be easier.

Still, he preferred the pair, and even their remaining crewman, to Maarav and the others.

"You are not the only one," Iseult assured, turning his gaze back to her. "I would never have taken up company

53

with him to begin with, except I needed a ship to reach you, and he offered his."

"And why does he travel with us still?" she questioned softly. "Surely he has better things to do."

Iseult smiled softly at her. "You must remember, he is of my blood, so he is just as cursed as I. He does not seem motivated by vengeance, but there is no way to tell for sure. He recognized you when he first saw you, and could have harmed you then, but did not. He either follows out of curiosity, or his hopes are the same as mine."

"To remove the curse from your bloodline," she muttered.

"Yes," he answered, "but the place he comes from may have altered his perceptions. Perhaps he has darker motivations unbeknownst to me."

Finn sighed. "I'm just glad this will all be over soon. All we need to do is reach my meadow."

Iseult gazed at the stormy sky above them, tasting the rich scent of damp earth on the back of his tongue. He did not believe things would be anywhere near *over* once they found the Faie Queen's shroud. Finn still did not have her memories, and he believed the loss of her child in her previous life was the reason. Her devastation had caused her to lay a curse upon his people before she retreated, never to be seen again . . . until now. There was great power within her, and he could only hope her memories would not change the bond he shared with her, lest his quest end in his death.

BEDELIA SWATTED at the branches catching in her shoulder-length hair. While she was glad to be back on dry land again, she found everything a constant source of rage. Keiren didn't care if she lived or died since she had failed so horribly in her quest. No one cared.

She sighed and swatted at another branch as Rada, her black and white horse, carried her further down the trail. The animal also seemed relieved to be back on dry land after sailing all the way to that forsaken island just for her owner to spy and burn down a tree.

Thoughts of the island where the Archtree resided brought thoughts of her recent, short-term friendship with Finn. Unlike Keiren or anyone else, Finn *cared*. She'd heard Finn question Maarav about her well-being. After knowing her only a short while, Finn cared if she lived or died. How cruel that she was now set out to harm Finn even further. Keiren had already taken Àed away, and Bedelia knew just how much the old man had meant to Finn. Now she was supposed to take away even more of Finn's support.

The trees grew sparse as she neared the Sand Road, her final destination, for the time being. Keiren had informed her that Finn would cross her path within the day, though the estimate was anything but solid. Keiren still couldn't *see* Finn clearly with her arcane gifts. She'd thought it was Àed keeping the girl from her, but now he was gone, turned into a tree, and Finn still eluded Keiren's ever-watchful eye.

*Good.* For the first time in many, *many* years, she was glad Keiren was unhappy, and she almost hoped being near Finn again would block her from Keiren's sight too, not to mention Òengus. He'd been given another mission, since Finn and her companions would never be foolish enough to trust him like they hopefully would Bedelia.

Reaching the Sand Road, she crossed it, then dismounted. Soon enough she had built a small fire, and had begun roasting a rabbit she'd snared in the woods. She sat in the dry grass and propped herself up with her arms while Rada snuffled the ground for something to eat.

She sighed, looking up at the gathering clouds overhead. A cold rain would be a welcome distraction. Perhaps it would wash away her memories of the past few weeks. Still gazing upward, she resituated her once injured leg. Though the wound caused by a Faie wolf had healed over, lines of black still ran through the veins beneath the skin, currently covered by her deep green woolen breeches and light plate armor. Even with the potion that had allowed her to heal, she still might die from the aftereffects of the bite.

At times, death seemed a welcome reprieve, but she couldn't *actually* accept such a fate. After all she'd endured in her often tumultuous life, it couldn't all just end. She had loved once, but now knew her love was never truly returned. Her past years of service had been for *nothing*. She had to make the future ones count.

She shook her head and patted Rada as the animal stepped a little closer and snuffled near her lap. No, she could not allow herself to die. She would see this thing through, and see where she ended up. Keiren had made her feel worthless. Now, after all this time, she was determined to reclaim that worth, one way or another.

EVENING WAS FAST APPROACHING, and tensions were high. Maarav knew his confrontation with his men had not gone over well with anyone, especially Iseult. Unfortunately, he'd had little choice. If he would have let the men go, it would have entirely undermined his standing in the city he would always consider home, not to mention it would have been an unwise strategic move in his current situation. He knew he was the odd man out. This journey centered around Finn, and she did not trust him. He had little doubt his brother would side with her over him, and might even side with Kai and Anna too. While Iseult had expressed little love for the pair, he technically knew them better than he knew him, not to mention Finn was in favor of their presence.

Maarav knew better than to let himself become so grossly outnumbered. He had many reasons for remaining with the party, and could not risk being ostracized.

He glanced back at his brother, walking beside Finn and her little dragon. Just as his own motivations had remained hidden, so had Iseult's, though he obviously cared a great deal for Finn. The reasons for *that* were a mystery. Maarav knew the histories, and he knew just who Finn was. She had cursed their people . . . although, he didn't fully view it as a curse. He'd always been highly proficient at his job, somehow faster and more stealthy than others. Sometimes it was as if he could even hide in plain sight. Perhaps souls just served to weigh their hosts down, and he was better off without one. Better off, until he died, at least. He was not sure just what would happen to him then. If one stuck strictly to the lore, the souls of his ancestors were *stolen*. Trapped someplace in between the worlds, never able to live or die . . . or whatever actions souls actually experienced.

He and Iseult were different. They'd been born into this curse. Perhaps they were just empty shadows, never meant to truly be men. He'd always known there was something that held him apart from other people, and his mother had explained just what that was, but it was still difficult to fully comprehend.

"Someone ahead near the road," Tavish muttered beside him.

Maarav narrowed his eyes, peering into the distance to see the subtle glow of a fire. "Scout ahead," he ordered quietly.

A moment later, Tavish and Rae were off, moving silently through the growing shadows. They should have made camp before the sun finished its retreat, but it seemed everyone was reluctant to do so. He supposed he couldn't blame them.

He chuckled, thinking of the Faie spell that had so fully ensnared Ealasaid. It hadn't affected him, but he'd been glad to play along. He'd been planning on letting her know in the morning, viewing it as a grand prank, but the girl had been so utterly embarrassed, he didn't have the heart to tell her. He hadn't expected her to react so negatively.

He walked on in silence, straining to hear Finn and Iseult's hushed conversation behind him, yet they were a bit too far off. It had been that way all day, and he couldn't help but feel they kept their voices low on purpose, just to keep him from hearing.

A few moments later, Rae and Tavish returned.

"Just a lone woman with her horse," Tavish explained. "I doubt she'll give us any trouble. Perhaps she'd even care to share her fire. I'd rather not venture back into the woods tonight." He eyed the trees to their right warily.

Maarav shook his head, ashamed that his men had fallen so quickly to Faie tricks, though honestly, he suspected his curse had more to do with his immunity than anything else, as Iseult also seemed immune.

His mind made up, he continued walking, and his men followed. Soon the fire came more clearly into view.

Iseult and the others quickly closed the distance between their groups.

"Just a lone woman," Maarav explained once everyone

was within earshot. He flicked his gaze to Iseult. "Do we want to risk setting up camp in the woods again, or should we perhaps ask to share her fire?"

"We can decide once we've reached her," Iseult replied, then turned to Finn. "You should cover your dragon."

She nodded, then scooped the little dragon up into her arms, wrapping her in a cloak. The dragon purred happily, likely just as cold and tired as the rest of them.

Soon enough they reached the woman, lounging by her fire with a serene expression. Maarav thought it odd at first that the woman should be so relaxed, but then he recognized her. He quickly debated his next course of action in his head. Finn already knew that Maarav and Bedelia were acquainted, so it would not do to pretend he didn't know her, but that would of course bring about many other questions, most from his overly suspicious brother.

He was saved from further action as Bedelia acknowledged their presence, and Finn squealed and began to dart toward her, then seemed to remember the dragon in her arms. She quickly passed the creature off to Kai, then finished her approach, lunging for Bedelia, who stood as she wrapped her in a fierce hug.

Bedelia, however, didn't seem to know what to do with the sudden attention, and awkwardly patted Finn's back until the woman released her.

"I'm so glad you're alive!" Finn exclaimed while everyone else watched on. "Maarav told me he delivered the potion for your illness, but I've been so worried. I'm sorry for leaving you, it was not my choice."

"Slow down," Bedelia chuckled, glancing past Finn toward the rest of their party. "It seems you've acquired quite a few friends along your journey, or are these the ones you were looking for when we met?"

"Well you already know Maarav," Finn replied excitedly, much to Maarav's chagrin. If everyone hadn't already caught the first mention of his name, they would surely catch it now. Hopefully they would not feel compelled to ask for further explanation past Bedelia and Finn staying at his inn.

"And this is Iseult," she continued, gesturing to the tall, ominous figure at her side. She went on to introduce everyone else, including Tavish and Rae. "We're still looking for my friend Àed," she added sadly.

Was it just Maarav's imagination, or had Bedelia's expression tensed at the mention of Àed? He pursed his lips in thought. He'd have to ask Bedelia later, once he managed some privacy. There were *many* things he wanted to ask the woman, as he didn't believe for a moment her appearance was mere happenstance.

Finn continued to chatter on, and soon enough, everyone was seated around the fire. Bedelia was formally introduced to Naoki, letting Maarav know how much Finn trusted her *friend*. He found himself almost glad Finn had the ever-suspicious Iseult around to keep her from trusting every person she came across. She was obviously a poor judge of character.

It didn't take long for Ealasaid to join in the conversation, and even Anna, who seemed to slowly be forming some sort of bond with the other women, another surprise. He'd known of Anna and her reputation as a heartless smuggler for years, and she knew of him as, well, a man of many trades, though the two had rarely crossed paths. He was surprised she'd form an allegiance with women as seemingly *nice* as Finn and Ealasaid, but he supposed it was a wise move on her part. He knew he should be making allegiances of his own.

Their conversations went on late into the evening, until everyone was ready to fall asleep. Bedelia's presence seemed to have lifted a measure of tension in the group, and Maarav was grateful. Iseult and Anna took first watch for the night, while everyone dozed off, including Maarav. It was odd, resting easy around such a large group. He knew he had little to fear from any of them, save perhaps Bedelia.

It would be unfortunate if he later needed to betray them, but he'd always done what he must. The present was no different.

## CHAPTER FOUR

The next long stretch of travel went by easy enough as far as Kai was concerned. Camping near the road with a large fire seemed to keep the Faie at bay, and several times they came across traveling caravans willing to share a bit of warmth and merriment, at least for those willing to accept it. Iseult had mainly kept to himself, watching over Naoki to allow Finn the comfort of warm meals and a toasty fire when they shared camp with strangers. The last caravan had even shared a bit of brandy, bringing deeper sleep to those who'd partaken. Needing to sleep doubly well, Kai had sipped a bit more than necessary.

Still, he could hardly wait to reach Port Ainfean. According to the travelers they passed, the port town was yet unharmed by the Faie, or An Fiach, for that matter. In fact, little had been heard of the uniformed men since some massive battle up in the North. Few knew much about the battle, save Iseult, Maarav, and Ealasaid, who'd all been present. He had learned from Iseult that An Fiach had marched on a small settlement of refugees, led by a Reiver from the far North. The Reiver had been collecting magic users, and the initial battle had been bloody, but no one knew just what had happened since Iseult and the others left the battlegrounds behind.

Yet, that was not at the forefront of his mind. Lifting a hand to shield his eyes from the light drizzle of rain, he watched Bedelia, silently leading her horse while glancing warily at the rest of their party. Finn's new friend, he'd learned, was the woman she'd traveled with after she'd been kidnapped . . . if being pulled through the earth by animate roots could be considered kidnapping. He found it odd that Bedelia had been readily willing to travel with Finn to Migris back then, just as he found it odd that she'd happily joined them in their travels now, claiming she was heading south, then west all the way to Sormyr. He would have to keep an eye on her. He knew what Finn, Iseult, and Anna sought was exceedingly valuable, and he would not put it past Bedelia, Maarav, or any of the others to try and steal it. A few months prior, Kai himself would have tried to steal it. Now, he wasn't quite sure *what* he was doing, besides trying to help Anna. Yes, that was his primary goal, or so he kept telling himself. Risking life and limb to chase the gray shapes out of Anna's head.

He let out a sigh of relief when the spires of Port Ainfean came into view, illuminated by large fires in the watchtowers, even during the rainy day. Hopefully there they would all find hot meals and warm beds within the port town. In the morning, they could attempt to acquire more horses, and their journey would become much easier. It was a long way between Port Ainfean and Garenoch. Horses were nearly a necessity.

Finn and Ealasaid were walking together on the other side of the road, whispering and glancing his way every so often. He had no doubt Finn was regaling the girl with the story of their *last* visit to Ainfean, when Finn had imbibed a bit too much, only to sneak away the next morning, leaving him behind.

Ealasaid let out a loud chuckle, probably amused at what a fool Kai was.

His mood turning sour, he picked up his pace, eager to reach Malida's tavern where he would procure a nice dram of whiskey . . . or two.

Ealasaid laughed again.

Or *three.*

They eventually reached the gates and passed through unhindered, though the guards looked each of them up and down with thoroughly disapproving glares. It was well known that Port Ainfean was a den of smugglers and thieves, so the guards were more in place to keep out the Faie, or any humans who would hope to enforce the laws of the realm.

Finn surprised Kai by moving to his side as they walked down the wide dirt road, lined on either side with vendors bundled against the cold. She had her dragon once again wrapped up in her arms, covered by the cloak. She had to be rather heavy to carry that way, though at least the dragon seemed content to remain hidden, likely pleased to be so near her mother's warmth.

"Will we be seeing Malida on this visit?" Finn questioned casually, lifting one arm from her dragon to tug her hood over her hair.

Kai raised an eyebrow at her. "*I* intend to see her. I didn't know I was part of any *we*."

Finn scowled at him from the shadows of her hood. "She was very kind to me, and I'd feel wrong if I did not at least stop by to offer my thanks."

He sighed, glancing at the rest of their companions surrounding them. "I suppose that means Iseult will be coming as well."

Finn bit her bottom lip, curled into a soft smile. "Yes, he seems reluctant to let me out of his sight."

He snorted at the understatement. "Yes, I'm not sure if the man has even slept since we reached dry land."

Finn laughed and nodded, eyeing a vendor's table filled with various pies and freshly baked breads, covered with sheer cloth to keep off the road dust and occasional drizzle of rain.

"Ready for a proper meal?" he asked, not quite ready to let the semi-private conversation end.

She nodded. "Oh yes, though I'm worried about Naoki." She glanced down at the bundle in her arms. "She's doing quite well now, but I'm terrified of what might happen should she see something to excite her.

I've a feeling it will not end well if she decides to burst forth in the middle of a tavern."

"Perhaps Malida will allow us to take our meals in privacy," Kai suggested.

Finn turned her gaze to him, her dark eyes suddenly filled with hope. "Do you think so? That would be wonderful. I'm not sure if the bounty for me still exists, but I imagine it's best if I don't draw attention to myself either."

Kai's eyes widened. He'd entirely forgotten about the bounty on her head, even though he and Anna at one point had kidnapped her in an attempt to claim it. "Yes," he replied. "We should hurry to Malida's." He glanced around the street warily. "Suddenly I feel perhaps we were safer out in the wilds."

Finn smiled, seemingly not as worried as he suddenly was, but at least she was smiling at him.

FINN EXHALED in relief as they reached Malida's tavern. She had assumed they would go around to the back entrance like they had previously, but Kai led them through the heavy wooden doors of the front entrance instead. She supposed their extra party members had something to do with it, especially Anna. Malida had made it quite clear she didn't care for Anna.

Finn scanned the mostly empty room as they entered. She knew the establishment would fill up come evening, but it was still early enough in the day that few patrons filled the low chairs surrounding the round wooden tables. Her gaze moved next to the woman at the bar, not Malida, but her daughter. The girl's eyes lit up as she noticed Kai, then narrowed into a glare as she spied Finn with her draconic bundle in her arms. Unperturbed, Kai and Finn moved toward the bar with Iseult in tow, while the rest of their party took up seats around a vacant table.

Malida's daughter, whose name Finn had somehow never learned, glanced toward the occupied table, then flipped her dark brown hair over her shoulder as Kai, Iseult, and Finn approached. "My mother will not be pleased you're back in Anna's company," she said, her gaze drifting to Kai as she slowly dried a pewter mug with a cloth.

"I'm sure she'll change her mind after I explain a few things," he replied. "Now where is she?"

Finn watched as the girl's eyes narrowed once more, glancing between herself and Iseult, then back to Kai. "You know better than to ask for her whilst in the company of strangers."

"They're not strangers," Kai sighed. "Is she in the back? I'll go in alone."

Finn tapped his shoulder, quite sure he was forgetting something important. Meeting his gaze, she glanced down at the bundle in her arms. The bundle that was beginning to squirm while emitting soft growls.

His eyes widened in realization. "Ah, yes," he said,

turning back to the girl, "Finn and I will go back. The rest will remain out here, though it's likely they will want a hot meal."

The girl scowled at Finn. "I thought her name was *Breya*," she spat.

Finn's eyes widened. She'd forgotten she'd gone by a false name the last time they saw Malida.

"Where is *Malida*?" Kai asked again, ignoring the girl's comment.

The girl sighed, then gestured toward the end of the bar where there was a space to pass through. "She's filling out her ledgers in the back."

Iseult gently caught Finn's arms before she could follow Kai toward the end of the bar. He didn't need to speak to voice his concerns.

"It's alright," she assured, steadily meeting his gaze. "I trust Malida."

He seemed to think about it for a moment, then nodded, though he was clearly not pleased.

Finn gave him a final reassuring smile, then followed Kai, clamping down on Naoki to keep her from breaking free of her bundle. The few midday patrons in the establishment were beginning to look at her strangely, and she wanted to be out of sight before the dragon burst forth and caused a commotion.

She hurried to the other side of the bar, then through a door Malida's daughter had moved to unlock for them. As soon as the door shut behind them, Finn released her dragon, hoping Malida would not be too frightened when they found her.

Naoki scrambled across the wooden flooring of a long hallway, her talons clicking hollowly on the boards.

Kai watched the little dragon as she skittered up and down the hall, wanting to explore, but apparently afraid to go too far on her own. He turned, raising an eyebrow at Finn. "Now you see what I had to deal with the entire voyage to Migris?"

Finn rolled her eyes, blowing a stray lock of hair from her face. "She's not *that* bad. It was likely difficult for her to be bundled up for so long."

Kai snorted. "If you say so. Let's find Malida."

Finn nodded and followed Kai. Naoki was finally able to calm herself enough to prance by Finn's side, though she chittered and nipped at Finn's cloak as they walked, hoping for treats.

Kai reached the end of the hall, then took a right. Finn estimated they were somewhere near the main sitting room, though she'd never entered through the front side of the home. Reaching Kai's side at the end of the corridor, she saw that her estimations were right. Malida sat on an overstuffed chair, hunched over a pile of parchment in her lap. Standing, the woman would barely reach Finn's shoulder, which made her tiny, given Finn's small stature. Though she was yet to look up from her parchment, Finn remembered her muddy brown eyes and hair, and a face that boasted numerous lines from years of laughter.

Kai cleared his throat, and Malida jumped, then glanced over at them with a hand held to her chest. "You scared me out of my wits," she gasped. "Didn't anyone ever teach you to knock before entering someone's home?"

"Your daughter let us in," Kai explained, stepping forward.

Naoki was staring warily in Malida's direction, though Malida could not see her over the high-backed, padded bench blocking her view.

Malida gave Kai a final hard glare, then turned her suddenly kind gaze to Finn. "You, however, I am over-joyed to see." She stood, grinning wide enough to show-case her few remaining teeth, then walked around the padded bench toward Finn.

Naoki chirped excitedly, and Malida jumped back. She lifted her arms as if afraid the dragon might attack. "What in the ancestors is that!" she shouted.

Kai hurried to the small woman's side and gently took one of her arms. "It's alright, this is Naoki," he explained, gesturing toward the dragon with his free hand, "Breya's . . . pet."

Finn frowned at the renewal of her fake name, but she supposed it would save them some explanation . . . for now.

Naoki jumped up and down excitedly, but restrained herself at Finn's side.

"She's very friendly," Kai added, a hint of sarcasm clear in his tone.

Malida seemed unsure, but bravely took a step forward, then crouched down to Naoki's level. Taking this as some sort of signal, Naoki trotted forward and began prancing circles around Malida, clearly excited to have found a new friend.

Malida let out an uneasy chuckle, hesitantly patted the little dragon between her folded wings, then stood and approached Finn, wrapping her up in a hug.

Surprised by the sudden show of affection, Finn tensed, then relaxed into the embrace, hunching forward to put herself at Malida's level.

"I'm glad you two are back together," Malida muttered.

"Oh we're not-" Finn began, pulling away from the hug.

"We're working *things* out," Kai interrupted, cautioning Finn with his gaze from behind Malida's back.

Finn knew that Malida was touchy about who Kai brought into her home, so she just smiled and nodded. It seemed they'd be maintaining their previous ruse of husband and wife, though Finn would punch Kai right in the nose if he thought it meant he could walk in on her in the bath again.

Malida put her hands on her plump hips, narrowing her gaze. "Why do you two seem suddenly nervous?"

"We have a few extra companions this time around," Kai explained, moving to stand by Finn's side, wrapping a companionable arm around her. "Not that we would dream of asking you to extend the same hospitality to them as you have given us in the past."

Finn fought the glare she wanted to give Kai, and smiled instead. "Yes, we were only hoping for a little help with Naoki. It's difficult to keep her concealed for long, and it would likely not go over well with her running freely in the streets. We'll gladly offer you anything we can in return."

Malida glanced at the dragon, who was now inspecting the rest of the sitting room, then nodded. "I suppose she can stay back here, as long as she won't cause any trouble. The two of you will stay as well, of course, though the rest of your companions will need to find lodgings elsewhere."

"Of course," Kai agreed, before Finn could interrupt.

Though the comfortable bed and access to a nice hot bath were more than they'd likely find at any of the inns in the small port town, Finn was reluctant to accept Malida's terms. Her primary concern was the injustice of leaving the others to lesser accommodations, especially Iseult, but there was also the discomfort of staying in a room with Kai once more. Though they had developed what could amount to a tense friendship, shared lodgings had not gone over well the last time.

Finn let out a long breath. "I am grateful for your hospitality, but I would not feel comfortable leaving behind our companions. There is a young lady in the group who I feel would not be entirely comfortable sharing lodgings with some of the others. Perhaps it would be better for only Kai to stay here with Naoki."

Malida looked suddenly suspicious again, but nodded. "I will not force you to stay, as long as Kai is willing to watch over your . . . pet, but I do hope you'll reconsider." She looked Finn up and down, her eyes lingering on her breeches. "*And* I'll find you a proper dress."

"Oh that's not-" Finn began to argue, loath to lose her breeches, but Kai stopped her with a look. "Thank you," she said instead, grateful for Malida's kindness, even if it was a bit misplaced. It seemed their problems had been solved, at least for a single night, dresses not withstanding.

"Now I'd say it's time for a hot meal," Malida announced, "and some scraps for your pet? The only payment I require for my hospitality is a full account of the things you have seen during your travels. We are living in strange times, and it pays more than mere coin to be informed."

"Of course," Finn agreed, thinking to herself just how right Malida was in her assertion. Information could be more valuable than land, ships, armies, or anything else that could be purchased with mere coin. She only wished she had more of it to share.

AFTER GETTING Naoki set up in a bedroom with a large

plate of meat scraps, Finn and Kai rejoined the others in the tavern. Kai was *not* pleased it had fallen to him to once again watch over the temperamental dragon, and he was kicking himself for not arguing. He wasn't even sure *why* he hadn't argued, except that being back in Malida's home brought forth memories of their previous time there. A time when Finn had decided he was perhaps a decent man, and he had regrettably gone out of his way to scrub such an absurd notion from her mind. Perhaps he was still trying to prove himself decent, even now, though he felt he'd already done so several times over.

Malida hadn't heard much hearsay of any bounties, so they deemed it safe for Finn to return to the common room, though she'd keep her hair hidden by her cloak, just in case.

Drawing himself out of his thoughts, Kai looked up from his seat at the round wooden table as a barmaid placed a massive bowl of lamb stew in front of him. He watched while everyone else received their meals, placed next to half empty mugs of ale.

Anna sat next to him, seeming to pay as much attention to the ongoing conversations as he was, which was little. With a sigh, he lifted his bowl and mug, then stood, moving toward the bar where Malida waited. He could have told her what she wanted to know later that evening, but decided he preferred her company at that moment, as opposed to his travel companions, especially Maarav and his men.

Malida watched him cross the room, a thoughtful

expression on her round face as she wiped the perfectly clean wooden bar with a rag.

Reaching her, he set his meal down and took a seat on one of the tall stools. "Ready for my epic tale?"

She smirked. "I'm ready for you to tell me what's going on between you and Breya . . . or is her name *Finn*?"

"I see you've already spoken with your daughter," Kai sighed.

"I did," she replied, "and now I'm wondering about a great many things. Last I saw *Finn*, she was sneaking out of my home at dawn. Now you are somehow back together, but not as husband and wife. Instead, you're traveling with a large party. You *never* travel with large parties, so I assume that part is *Finn's* doing."

"Yes," he sighed, wondering if he should attempt to keep the ruse going at all, "she's a very demanding wife."

"She's not your wife," Malida stated bluntly. "Did you truly think you could deceive me? I can see that you love her, but there is no clear understanding between the two of you."

He blinked up at her, entirely dumbstruck. He knew Malida had been suspicious, but to have known all along? "Then why did you go along with it?"

She chuckled, then grabbed Kai's ale to take a swig. "Why not? After all this time, I knew I could trust your judgment, and I genuinely like her. She's a sweet lass."

Kai leaned his elbows on the bar and buried his head in his hands, letting his tangled, chestnut brown hair fall forward. "I suppose I'll start from the very beginning," he sighed, "long before we came here the first time. It's the only way I can fathom explaining it all in a way that makes sense."

Malida took a moment to refill his ale from one of the large casks behind the bar, then gestured for him to go on.

He snuck a quick glance over his shoulder at his party, then began, "It all started back in Garenoch, when we met an odd, long-haired girl, and her elderly companion . . . "

He went on to detail their entire journey, leaving out exactly who Finn was, and what she and Iseult sought. He told Malida of their long sea voyage, and detailed all that happened once they arrived back on land. He also admitted, though Malida already seemed to know, that Finn was never truly his wife, but that he really was trying to help her. He hoped in coming clean Malida would take pity on him, and would still allow him to stay in her home that evening. She was at least still speaking with him, which gave him hope she understood his reasons for lying.

As he finished his long-winded tale, Malida pursed her lips in thought. "So when you first came to me, you were simply attempting to help Finn find that man?" She nodded in Iseult's direction.

He gazed down at his uneaten stew. "Yes," he admitted after a moment. "I was only trying to help her find Iseult and her other friend, Àed, again, but I was worried someone else might try to collect the bounty on her. I still don't know the meaning behind the bounty, or who originally ordered it, but at the time it seemed the safest option to keep her hidden, and to use a false name."

He lifted his eyes to meet Malida's narrowed gaze. "So you lied to me," she began again, "to protect a young lady, even though you had nothing to gain, and in fact, stood to lose not only your partnership with Anna, but a great deal of coin."

He frowned. "When you put it like that, I sound like a fool."

"And even after she left you," she continued, ignoring his lament, "you then went on to follow her. You traveled all the way to Migris, just to make sure she was safe, then sailed to a legendary tree, just so she could find answers. Now you've followed her all the way back to this Faie infested land, and in all of this, you have absolutely *nothing* to gain."

He huffed in exasperation. "Is the point of this entire conversation just to make me feel like a blithering idiot?"

Malida smiled warmly. "I see my early speculations were correct, and yes, you're a blithering idiot, but only if you won't admit you love her."

He took a long swill of his ale, relishing in the slight feeling of numbness it brought. There was that word again. *Love.* "I'd be a blithering idiot if I thought that it mattered," he replied finally, seeing no use in denying it any longer.

Malida simply smiled, then slid his stew bowl closer to him.

He narrowed his eyes suspiciously. "What are you thinking?"

She smiled wider and shook her head. "Never you mind. Eat your food and tell me more about what you saw in Migris. We've had a few travelers make it this way from the West, but it's been difficult to believe what they've been saying."

He took a bite of his now cold stew, then replied, "Believe it. Believe everything you hear. After the things I've seen and experienced, I will never question any odd Faie tales again."

She nodded. "I trust your judgement, but I must ask, where are you off to now? Most travelers who've come into contact with the Faie are hiding in the smaller towns, or wherever else they can find shelter. Few want to brave the roads anymore."

He took another long swig of his ale, draining his mug. "Anna and Finn are both on a mission for the same, um, item," he took another swill, hoping Malida wouldn't pry into what that item was. "I'm coming along to make sure they don't kill each other," he finished, lowering his glass.

Malida smirked and glanced over at the occupied table. "If it's a fight to the death, my bet is unfortunately on Anna."

Kai shook his head, thinking back to the few incidents where Finn had been forced to protect herself.

Anna might be deadly, but she didn't stand a chance against that sort of power. "I'll not comment on who would win, but it's better for all of us if *that* fight never happens."

Malida nodded, then lifted her gaze past Kai. He turned on his stool to see Finn and Iseult approaching.

"I was hoping to check on Naoki before we search for rooms at one of the inns," Finn explained upon reaching Kai's side, her face shadowed by her hood.

He turned to see Malida narrow her eyes in thought before nodding. "No offense meant," she began, flicking her gaze up to Iseult, "but I only trust Kai and," she hesitated, "*Finn* to enter my home."

Kai watched the blush creep up Finn's face upon hearing her real name.

Malida rolled her eyes. "I know you were in trouble, I cannot blame you for giving a false name, and Finn is much prettier than Breya."

Finn smiled graciously, though her blush did not lessen.

"I understand," Iseult said in reply to Malida's initial statement. He turned to Kai. "You'll accompany her," he added, no hint of questioning in his tone.

Kai sighed and stood, shooing Finn away from where she stood beside his stool to make room.

"And the two of you can find a few things for me in the cellar while you're at it," Malida added, an impish grin on her round face.

Kai gave her a questioning glance, wondering what

she was up to, then nodded. It wasn't the first time Malida had put him to work. He gestured for Finn to lead the way behind the bar, all the while wondering what the glint in Malida's eye was about.

AFTER CHECKING ON NAOKI, Kai showed Finn the way to the cellar. She'd felt a little wary descending the dark, rickety staircase beneath a trap door within the bedroom Malida shared with her husband, but she figured she owed Malida a great deal. She'd gladly carry up whatever supplies she needed.

They'd only been down in the space for a few moments, searching the various barrels and storage crates by lantern-light, when Malida's daughter came thunking down the stairs, a piece of parchment in hand. She offered the parchment to Kai, glared at Finn, then retreated.

Holding his lantern aloft, Kai's eyes skimmed the list. He sighed. "It seems Malida thought of a few more items for us to carry up."

Finn widened her eyes, then plucked the parchment from his fingers. He held the lantern toward her so she could read what was written. She didn't even know what half of the items on the list were, let alone where to find them in the cramped, dark cellar.

"Is this punishment for lying about my name?" she questioned in disbelief.

Kai smirked, but did not answer.

Finn had a feeling he knew exactly why Malida was punishing them, but instead of explaining, he took the list to glance over it once more.

Finn crossed her arms as he stuffed the list into his breeches pocket, then set the lantern down beside a crate, crouching to examine its contents.

She watched him clearly avoiding her gaze. Why was he suddenly so uncomfortable. Malida's list obviously meant something *more* to him. She began tapping her foot impatiently.

He glared up at her. "Yes?"

She scowled, wishing he would take the hint. "What aren't you telling me?"

He observed her face for several moments, then sighed and rocked back on his heels, still crouched. "I told her *everything*," he admitted. "She knows we were never husband and wife, and she knows why we lied to her. She does not know who you truly are, or what you seek, but she knows everything else."

She blinked at him for several seconds in the dim lantern light, utterly shocked. She couldn't fathom a reason why he would have done *that*.

"Oh don't look so surprised," he muttered, turning back to the crate.

She crossed her arms. "I'm justified in being surprised. I've come to expect lies from you, and truth only when you have no other choice."

He glared at her. "That's *not* true. As far as I'm

concerned, the only lie I ever told you was who I was in the beginning, and you told the same lie yourself."

She felt her expression falter. Pursing her lips, she tried to think of the other lies he'd told her. Surely there were more. She had very good reason for being angry at him all the time, didn't she?

"Let me see the list again," she demanded.

He looked up at her, but did not offer the list.

She shifted her weight from foot to foot, suddenly feeling embarrassed.

He smirked, his eyes twinkling with sudden merriment. "I'd expected a few more insults."

Ignoring him, she bent down and plucked at the parchment sticking out of his pocket, soon tugging the list free to peruse. "You're right," she admitted. "I have no remaining reasons to be angry with you. You've more than made up for kidnapping me, and I suppose things have ended up alright . . . as alright as can be expected, at least."

He stood, looking slightly stunned. "Was that an apology?"

She glared. "Yes, and I've given them to you before, so don't look so surprised. Now please tell me why Malida would like us to spend the entire evening in her cellar."

His shoulders slumped in defeat, but he did not speak.

"Go on," she pressed. "You're already brimming with truths tonight, so you may as well continue."

He narrowed his eyes at her. "She seems to think I'm in love with you," he stated bluntly, "and I imagine this is all part of some grand scheme of hers to force us to spend time together. Time without any of the . . . others."

Suddenly she wished he was a liar. She opened her mouth to speak, to in some way make light of what he'd said, then a stack of crates crashed down in the far corner of the cellar. She met Kai's gaze for a split second, then he snatched the lantern and rushed toward the sound with Finn hot on his heels.

The cellar was like a maze, filled with rows of stacked storage receptacles. Finn tried to keep her breathing steady as she raced after Kai, telling herself that the crates had fallen on their own, and that no one had been in the cellar listening to them. Listening to what he'd just said to her.

Reaching the source of the crash, Kai came to an abrupt halt. In front of him stood a small girl with sallow skin and stringy black hair, trembling in fear. The tattered tan cloth of her shapeless clothing showed patches of her frail flesh through numerous tears. She looked up at Kai and Finn with small, muddy colored eyes.

Kai held his free arm out to herd Finn back away from the girl. "I don't think she's human," he muttered. He aimed the lantern at the girl, illuminating her gaunt face.

Finn pushed his arm aside. "She's also terrified." She lowered to one knee, bringing herself down to the girl's eye level. She couldn't have been more than seven. "What are you doing down here?" she asked softly.

The girl took a deep breath, and Finn noticed gills, like those of a fish, flexing along the underside of her jaw. Not human indeed.

"I'm hiding," the girl croaked, her voice barely audible. She lowered her eyes to the ground.

Kai moved to kneel beside Finn, bringing the lantern along with him. The girl's skin shimmered in the light. It took Finn a moment to realize it wasn't skin at all, but scales.

"Is she a Merrow?" Kai whispered, gazing at the girl in awe.

Finn nodded. "I think so. They live in rivers and ponds, don't they?"

"Yes," Kai replied, "and don't they also entrance humans, much like the Sirens?"

Finn took a moment to scowl at him, then turned back to the girl. She was only a child, not some dangerous Siren. "Where are your parents?" she asked softly.

The girl shrugged. "We came in from the river to hide from the Dair, but I think my parents were taken. I've been down here a while. There's lots of salty fish in that barrel over there." She pointed to a nearby receptacle that seemed mostly empty.

"The Dair?" Finn questioned, forcing her voice to remain even. She knew others of her kind had returned to the land along with her, but what could they possibly want with the Merrows?

The girl nodded. As if reading Finn's thoughts, she

answered, "The Dair control the earth. The Faie *are* the earth. We cannot resist them."

"What do the Dair want?" Finn pleaded. She didn't want to scare the child into going quiet, but she could sense she was close to the answers she desperately wanted.

The girl shook her head. "I don't know. No one knows where the Dair came from, why they left, or why they have returned. We know only that we must fear them."

The girl tensed at the sound of someone walking across the wooden flooring above. The footfalls stopped somewhere near the cellar stairs, then began to descend.

Finn and Kai both looked over their shoulders to see who approached, and when they looked back, the girl was gone.

"We need to leave," Iseult stated, ignoring the slightly stunned expressions on Kai and Finn's faces. His heart was threatening to leave his throat. If he had not overheard that man . . .

Finn continued to glance at the empty space behind them for some reason, but there was no time for explanations.

"An Fiach is here," he explained, hoping to get them moving. "They are looking for someone fitting your description," he looked at Finn, "and yours," he turned to Kai.

"Me?" Kai asked, slack-jawed. "I haven't even swindled anyone recently."

"It doesn't matter," he growled. "They outnumber us three to one. We cannot risk remaining in Ainfean tonight. Maarav and the others have already gone to purchase horses. They will meet us on the road."

Kai sighed. "Let's go." He put his hand at the small of Finn's back to guide her onward.

Iseult resisted the urge to part Kai's hand from his body. For now, they needed to focus on escaping unseen.

He followed the pair back toward the stairs, then grabbed Kai's arm before he could follow Finn up. "The bar mistress suggested you would guide us out the back entrance."

"Yes," he replied simply, "but we need to fetch Naoki first."

Iseult took a steadying breath, then followed Kai up the stairs. He'd forgotten about the dragon. An unfortunate complication when their objective was stealth.

He reached the landing to find Finn already in a room across the hall, trying to calm the frantic dragon down enough to bundle her in a cloak. It wasn't going well. Kai moved to help her, and got a talon across his palm.

"Try to be calm," Iseult instructed as he approached. "It will soothe her in turn." He imagined the same principles would apply to dragons as horses. They could sense their master's moods. If you wanted a calm, obedient horse, you had to be calm and in control . . . qualities with which Iseult rarely struggled.

Finn nodded frantically, clutching the writhing dragon in her arms. Naoki grunted and squirmed, but at least seemed to be aware of her mother's delicate skin. She incurred no scrapes as Kai had.

Finn's chest beneath her blouse and corset rose and fell with deep breaths. Her eyes drifted closed and the dragon began to calm. Iseult forced his own breathing to slow, though he knew they were running out of time.

Kai tip-toed further into the room and lifted a cloak off the small bed, then helped Finn gently wrap it around Naoki before guiding them both out of the room. Once they were all in the hall, Kai took the lead, stepping lightly on the wooden flooring as he guided them past the entrance Iseult had come through and down a narrow hall, ending in a door with a heavy wooden bar across it.

Together Kai and Iseult moved the bar, and the three of them, plus one dragon, hurried out into the darkening night.

Avoiding the main thoroughfare, they made their way toward the town gates where their companions would hopefully be waiting with extra horses. Iseult knew it was unlikely that Ainfean would have enough horses to suit everyone, but a few extras would do. Finn had already proven she was comfortable riding with her friend, Bedelia, and the other two women could double up as well.

A million other thoughts ran through Iseult's mind as they crept through the darkness. They had gathered enough supplies in the remains of Migris to last them roughly five days, seven at most. He would have liked to resupply more before leaving the port town, but it was not worth the risk. If An Fiach was looking specifically for Kai and Finn, everyone was in danger.

That led him to another disturbing thought. Why

would An Fiach be looking for those two in particular? It didn't make any sense. The purpose of the Hunt was to track down the Faie.

Distant shouts suddenly caught his ear, bringing his thoughts to the present.

"It's coming from the direction of the gates," Kai whispered, his eyes darting about their dark surroundings.

Iseult nodded. "More soldiers were likely waiting outside. They may have stopped the others."

"What's our plan?" Kai questioned.

"I'll scout ahead," he replied, hating the idea, but knowing it was the best one. "Do not leave Finn's side."

Finn watched the whole exchange wide-eyed, clutching her dragon like a child.

He hoped he was making the right decision.

"We'll continue on cautiously," Kai whispered, more to Finn than to Iseult.

Still, he nodded, then took off at a jog.

Nearing the riverbank, he pushed his body to move faster. A row of buildings concealed him from the main road, but occasional doors opened in the backs of homes and establishments. To his left, the River Cair thundered, too wide and violent to be used as a possible means of escape. The shouting seemed to be dying down to be replaced by the low murmur of arguing voices.

Nearing the final buildings and stables before the gates, Iseult slowed, his hand on the pommel of his short sword. He peered around the nearest building to see a dozen or so figures silhouetted in the moonlight. He recognized Maarav first, arguing with another man, though he could not tell if the man with whom his brother argued was wearing the customary dark brown uniform of An Fiach. Several more men stood in a line, near a row of horses tied to a horizontal post.

"We are but simple travelers," he heard Maarav explain, "hoping to make it to the next town before our caravan departs without us. The only way we will accomplish that is to travel through the night. We only stopped here to purchase more horses."

"No one leaves until the Captain approves it," the man said in reply.

Iseult sighed. Now that they'd drawn attention to themselves, there was no way Kai and Finn would be able to depart with everyone else. He was prepared to turn around to report his findings, when Maarav cocked back his fist and punched the soldier square in the nose. Chaos erupted, accompanied by the metallic sound of blades being drawn.

He debated going back for Kai and Finn, but adrenaline and instinct took over. He drew his blade and launched himself out of hiding and into the fray. They needed to end this before the other soldiers could rush out of the taverns and inns. Hopefully Kai and Finn would see what was happening, and would use the distraction to sneak out on their own.

Iseult's blade met with another man's, just before he could bring it down across Anna's back. He couldn't help but think, as he turned to knock another man in the head with the pommel of his sword, that he should have left Maarav and the others behind, escorting Finn to safety. A fainter, secondary thought coursed through his mind, that by the gods, it felt good to enter into battle again, for a cause that truly mattered.

~

KAI COULD HEAR the sound of blades meeting, and the thudding of footsteps as the fight broke out. Since Iseult had not returned to them, he knew he must have joined the fray, which meant the rest of their party was also involved.

"We shouldn't go any closer," he whispered, his back pressed against the wooden wall of a guard tower beside Finn's.

"They may need our help," Finn argued, moving to peer around the building. Naoki was beginning to struggle against her grasp. Finn had shown no change in attitude at his proclamation of love, and he half wondered if she'd even heard him. He truly hadn't expected her to return the sentiment, but she could have at least said *something*. Of course, he'd only said that Malida thought he was in love, not that he actually was.

He sighed, knowing now was not the time to dwell on it. Glancing down at the bundled dragon, he gently pushed Finn's shoulder back against the wall, then moved around her to assess the fight.

It was difficult to tell in the darkness, but Anna, Maarav, Iseult, and Sativola seemed to be doing most of the fighting, while Ealasaid and Tavish had snuck off to a row of horses tied near the gates. Bedelia and Rae where nowhere to be seen, though they could have just been fighting outside the gates.

Taking in the short expanse between the horses and the gates, and hearing doors slamming open and shut down the main road as others heard the fight, Kai made his decision. He turned back to Finn and motioned for her to follow.

Still struggling with her dragon, she jumped at the opportunity. Together they hurried forward, keeping to the shadows near the city gates until they reached the row of tethered horses where Tavish and Ealasaid were covertly untying reins from the post. Ealasaid glanced at them, her eyes wide and startled, then relaxed.

With a smile and a wink, Tavish handed Kai the reins of a horse he'd freed. "They're looking for the two of you," Tavish whispered. "Use the distraction to escape."

Nodding to Tavish in thanks, Kai helped Finn and Naoki onto the horse's saddle, then climbed up behind them. He would have liked to stay and aid in the fight, but Finn's safety had to be his priority at that moment, lest Iseult kill him later.

With one arm around Finn's small form, and the other gripping the reins, he jabbed his heels into the horse's side and galloped toward the gates, skirting around the fight.

They sped through the gates without interference, only to be met by three guards on horseback, barring their way. Finn screamed as Naoki escaped from her arms, tossing the cloak aside to fly past Kai's head and onto the ground.

Letting out guttural squawks, Naoki took flight, then spiraled down through the air toward the men. Their nervous horses pranced and bucked, throwing one of the men while Naoki dove in and out, pouncing to the ground, then springing erratically upward. Bedelia and Rae appeared from the darkness, drawing the soldiers' attention away from the dragon.

While Finn shouted for Naoki, Kai urged their horse forward, taking off into the dark trees away from the road.

FINN GRIPPED onto the saddle's pommel for dear life, while Kai's arms trapped her on either side. She could hear the thundering of hooves behind them, but did not know if it was their companions or some of the soldiers. She tried a few times to glance back, but it was too dark to see much of anything.

"We'll find them once we're safe!" Kai shouted, pressing the insides of his arms more firmly around her to keep her from turning.

"What about Naoki!" she shouted back. She couldn't see her little dragon anywhere.

Kai's arms did not slacken, and instead he flicked the reins to urge the horses on. "She'll find you! She can track your scent better than any wolf!"

Finn's heart shuddered. She wanted to tell him to go back, but what could she do if they did? She wasn't sure she could survive another incident of her odd powers running amuck, melting the skin from a man's bones, or swallowing them up with the earth. It was probably better for her to be far from any fight. She trusted Iseult to find her again, but of Naoki, she was unsure. What if one of the soldiers harmed her? Most men would run the other way at the sight of a Faie creature, but some would be brave enough to fight.

"We have to go back!" she shouted finally, making up her mind. Branches whipped at their cloaks, threatening to pull them from their mount, yet Kai did not allow the horse to slow.

"They are after you and I," he cautioned, his voice near her ear. "Everyone is safer without us."

Tears streamed down Finn's face, but she could not argue. This was all her fault. Everyone was attacked because An Fiach wanted *her*. And Kai, she reminded herself . . . though they likely only wanted him because of her. She was a danger to everyone.

They rode on for what seemed like ages, until their horse tired and slowed to a walk. Kai had kept them away from the road, which was likely wise if An Fiach was looking for them specifically. He now guided their horse deep into a copse of trees, near a rocky crag mostly obscured with vegetation. The deeper shadows within the foliage seemed ominous to Finn, or perhaps it was just her mood.

"We'll wait here," Kai explained as he dismounted. "I'll keep watch while you rest, then in the morning we will scout for the others."

Finn climbed down and waited as Kai tied the reins of their stolen horse loosely to a small fir tree. She wished he would glance at her so she could catch his gaze. Had he truly meant what he'd said in the storeroom? Did he love her, or was Malida mistaken? And if he did actually love her, did he mean in a romantic way, or did he love her like a sister?

She watched as he began searching the few satchels tied to the back of the saddle. Next, he moved to the bedroll strapped at the saddle's base, near the horse's gray dappled rump. She felt a little bad for the soldier that would have to do without, then corrected herself. He was probably dead. She had never seen Maarav in battle, but Iseult claimed he was just as fast as he, and she knew Anna could take care of herself, and Sativola too. They would all escape, and would find her and Kai. They *had* to. Preferably before they had time to finish their storeroom conversation. She needed time to figure things out.

Suddenly, something came crashing toward them. Kai threw himself in front of Finn, dagger drawn, but there was no need. As soon as Finn gathered her wits, she recognized the horse trotting toward them, and its riders. Finn had always thought Rada was one of the prettiest horses she'd ever seen with her black and white coat.

Heaving a sigh of relief at the sight of Kai and Finn, Bedelia climbed down from the saddle, then helped Ealasaid do the same.

"We're lucky there's a full moon tonight," Bedelia began, "else we would have never been able to track you."

"Which unfortunately means An Fiach will be able to track us," Kai added. "We should keep moving."

"We should wait for the others," Finn protested.

Ealasaid stepped forward sheepishly, pushing her frothy mess of hair away from her face. "I agree, we should wait. If An Fiach should find us first, I'll create a . . . distraction."

Bedelia smirked. "You can trust what she says. She's quite good at *distractions*."

Ealasaid looked at the ground, embarrassed.

Finn wasn't sure what was going on. Iseult had mentioned that Ealasaid had magic, so she assumed she'd used it to aid in her and Bedelia's escape.

Noticing Finn's unsure expression, Ealasaid stepped forward and took her hand. "Don't fret. I'm sure the others will be along shortly. Maarav and Iseult are excellent fighters, faster than any I've ever seen."

"That's not saying much, coming from a village girl," Kai joked as he took Rada's reins to secure her beside their stolen horse. "I still think we should move on," he continued, "but I know better than to argue with three women at once. You all should get some rest while I keep watch."

"I will keep watch as well," Bedelia offered.

Kai finished untying the bedroll from the saddle, then pushed it into Finn's arms. "Sleep with your boots on," he advised. "We must be prepared to leave quickly."

Nodding, Finn turned with the bedroll in her arms and searched for a place to lay it. She felt uneasy, like her journey was once again about to become greatly derailed. Beyond that, she could not shake what the little Merrow girl had told them. All must fear the Dair. All must fear *her*. Kai would be a fool to love such a frightening creature as herself, like a sister, or otherwise.

"I KNOW they passed through here before," Óengus stated coolly, aiming his icy glare at the diminutive, aged bar mistress. He'd tried kindness initially, but the woman had somehow seen through the act.

"And how would you know that?" she replied just as coolly. Though she was small in size, with muddy brown hair, and numerous missing teeth, a keen intelligence shone out of the woman's eyes.

Óengus knew Kai and Finn had stayed with the woman previously, and were likely hidden away somewhere in her home, along with the others. Still, he'd stationed half his men at the gates, just in case. He had no desire to chase them further down the Sand Road.

Suppressing a growl of irritation, both at the bar mistress, and at the thought of the men of An Fiach, he turned away from the bar. Though he was used to commanding others, he wasn't impressed with the soldiers in his contingent. Most of them were mere peasants who'd never held a sword until the day they enlisted.

He strode through the double doors of the establishment without a word. The icy wind played with his short silver hair, tickling the whiskers of his neat beard, but he hardly noticed the cold. He knew there was a back entrance to the establishment. He'd take the time to post several men outside of it, then would find himself a hot meal while he waited for his quarry to reveal themselves. Just because he was now an imposter Captain of An Fiach, didn't mean he wasn't allowed to enjoy himself.

Before he could walk around the building, the sound of steel on steel caught his ears. He sighed. Incompetent fools. He had no doubt the clanging steel came from his men battling those he sought. His men would lose, and their quarry would escape. Of that he had little doubt.

Taking long, confident strides, he walked past the townsfolk trickling out into the streets to observe the commotion. He resisted the urge to cut down the curious onlookers getting in his way. He would be too late to catch those he sought, and it would take time to gather all his men and give chase.

Keiren would not be pleased.

~

ANOTHER DAY HAD COME and gone while they waited outside of the Archive. Anders had expected more Travelers to join them, but none had shown themselves. Instead, he was stuck with Niklas, eating meager portions of a grouse he'd snared, along with a few foraged roots, all boiled in a pot with no seasoning. While it was no fine meal, Anders ate it with abandon. Since he'd started traveling with Niklas, his breeches had grown loose, and the occasional reflections he caught of himself in ponds and puddles showed gaunt cheeks and sallow skin. His parents would hardly recognize him, if he managed to see them at all.

He couldn't help but wonder where he'd be if he'd stayed with An Fiach. He'd never gone hungry after joining, and had even felt almost safe with Radley and the other men at his side. He'd even briefly envisioned returning home after finding his sister, a proud man in uniform, his life sworn to protecting the weak.

Unfortunately, protecting the weak wasn't what An Fiach was really about. He would never be able to clear from his mind the battle with the refugees, and Ealasaid's conviction that he had somehow been involved in destroying her village, murdering her kin. Though he'd had no involvement in what happened to Ealasaid's family, the dead of the ruined city in the North would haunt him forever.

He shook his head and glanced at Niklas, who stood immobile, staring at the distant Archive. While Anders was terrified of the Ceàrdaman, they weren't going around slaughtering entire villages or attacking refugees . . . at least, not to his knowledge.

"There," Niklas pointed.

Anders squinted past his outstretched finger. A woman dressed in fine black silks conversed with a guard at the main entrance to the Archive. Her long, fiery red hair stood out in contrast, even from a distance. "She is not one of the Archive scholars, unless someone new was appointed after I left."

"Not a scholar," Niklas replied, "but our cue to approach the Archive."

"I told you before, even if the guards know me, they will not let one of the Ceàrdaman past the gates." He turned to raise a skeptical eyebrow at Niklas, then jumped back in surprise.

Though Niklas still maintained similar facial features, his skin was now a healthy, tan hue, and his odd eyes were now a normal, deep brown. He gestured toward the archive. "Our cue is getting away from us, and your sister's life is still dangling in the balance."

Anders darted his gaze back toward the Archive to find the woman had been let inside the gates. Shaking his head in disbelief, he started forward, prepared to finally fulfill his part of their bargain. Niklas hurried along beside him, still unnaturally graceful despite his human appearance.

Anders felt lightheaded. His boots crunching over the rocky dirt road seemed impossibly loud. He would be questioned by the guards. Then he would be questioned by any scholars he met. Finally, he would be questioned by his parents. He could scarcely bear to face them. With a steadying breath, he forced his shoulders to relax. First thing first. He needed to get past the guards.

He exhaled in relief as they reached the massive gates. He knew both guards who stood there. One, an older man named Lochlan, he had known since he was a child, and the other, a youth named Barrett, was Lochlan's son.

"Anders!" Lochlan gasped after looking him up and down. "I almost didn't recognize you, lad. You look like you haven't eaten since you left!"

Anders forced a smile onto his face and ruffled his cloak to hide his thinness, as well as his uniform. He'd had no opportunity to change out of the dark brown jacket with a red wolf embroidered on the breast, but Niklas had at least given him a cloak to cover it. "My journey has been an eventful one," he explained vaguely. "I'm here to see my parents."

Lochlan blinked at him several times, as if not truly believing he was there.

Barrett moved to his father's side and cleared his throat. "Father," he whispered, "the gates?"

Lochlan startled back into awareness. He met Anders waiting gaze and shook his head. "Sorry lad, I just can't hardly believe you're real. After no one heard from you, we all assumed you were dead. Where is Branwen?"

Anders felt his face flush.

"She's up North," Niklas cut in smoothly. "We

wouldn't dream of bringing the young lady on such an arduous journey, when our visit shall be short."

Lochlan nodded, his gray mustache bristling. "And *you* are?"

"Lord Seastnàn," Niklas lied, bowing his head in greeting. "From the Gray City."

"Ah," Lochlan began, comprehension in his eyes as he turned back to Anders. "One of the emissaries?"

Gritting his teeth, Anders nodded. All in the Archive knew Anders and Branwen had departed with an emissary from the Gray City, along with a guard. Unfortunately, both were fakes. Kai and Anna were lowly thieves, nothing more.

"Now please," Niklas continued. "We've had a very long journey, and I must admit, I'm not used to *waiting*."

"Of course, of course," Lochlan muttered. He still seemed unsure, but nodded to his son, who trotted back to his post and gestured up to the gatekeepers watching from the high wall.

Seconds later, the gates swung inward.

Anders smiled in relief. Feeling slightly more at ease, he turned back to Lochlan. "By the way, who was that woman you let in just before we arrived?"

Lochlan squinted in confusion. "What woman? You're the first to approach the gates in several days."

Anders' jaw dropped. He felt Niklas tug at his sleeve, hurrying him along before he could ask any more questions. He said his goodbyes and hurried through the gates, but he still felt Lochlan and Barrett's suspicious gazes on his back.

Even once the gates closed behind them, Anders could not relax. Niklas observed the grand entrance of his home, while he stood still for a moment, suddenly close to tears. The main gates led to a wide corridor that opened out into a massive courtyard. The gardens were tended year round, filled with bright colored flowers in the warm half of the year, and waxy leafed holly and hearty snow flowers in the cold half. Right now, they were somewhere in between. The last of the bright flowers were dying, to be replaced by more muted tones.

Niklas cleared his throat, drawing Anders' attention. "Where is the main library?"

It took him a moment to respond. Shaking his head to clear his mind, he pointed. "The left wing houses the more ancient tomes in need of preservation. The right wing," he pointed in the other direction, "houses the transcribed volumes, available to all scholars no matter their station. The central dome," he pointed to the large golden structure at the far end of the courtyard, "houses the volumes belonging to the Gray City, mainly histories and local lore."

His eyes continued to dart around the courtyard, searching for his parents, though he was not sure he was ready to face them. He'd hoped to avoid the Archives all together until he had Branwen back by his side.

"The left," Niklas said simply, then eyed Anders not-so-patiently to lead the way.

He took a steadying breath, then cut across the courtyard toward the first entrance into the left wing. He'd had access to the wing previously, but would have to speak with one of the watchers before he could enter. Niklas would likely not be allowed inside, but he decided against voicing his concerns. Niklas would not listen anyway.

Reaching the door, he held it open for Niklas to walk inside. He followed him, glancing each way down the hall, half-expecting to spot the red haired woman they'd seen at the gates.

Instead, they saw a brown-haired woman, peeking her head out one of the many book-filled rooms. "Anders!"

He sighed in relief. "Lissandra," he greeted, approaching her. "Could you perhaps give me access to the High Wing?"

Her smile faltered as she moved fully into the hall. "Anders, where have you been? We expected at least the occasional messenger. Everyone thinks you're dead."

He chuckled, attempting to give off an air of calm, though he'd never been a skilled liar. "It was a long journey, and I was given few opportunities to send word. I'll explain everything once I've seen my parents. I simply wanted to look over a certain tome to compare it to the information I have to share."

"Information worth recording?" she asked slyly, her attitude quickly transitioning. "I will be your chosen scribe, won't I?"

"Of course," Anders replied.

"Well if that's the case," Lissandra replied, "I suppose I can wait to hear of your adventures until later." Grinning, she scurried back into the room and began riffling through the drawers of a parchment scattered desk. Candles littered the desk's surface, dripping wax onto papers yellowed with age. Anders bit his tongue before he could insult her. Lissandra had always been careless.

"Aha!" she chuckled, turning around with a golden key in her hand.

She walked past Anders into the hall, then finally took the time to observe Niklas. Her eyes narrowed. "Greetings, do I know you?"

"An emissary from the Gray City," Anders explained.

"Ah," she replied, nodding. She continued past them further down the hall, her shapeless burgundy scholar's robe trailing behind her

They followed her as she chattered about what had been happening in the Archive since Anders' departure, though he could scarcely gather his thoughts enough to listen to her. The corridor curved at the end, leading to a set of ornate wooden doors with heavy gold locks. A guard was stationed at either side of the doorway.

"Greetings," Lissandra muttered, barely even looking at the guards as she unlocked the doors. As one of the Archive's head scholars, her access to the secured room was a normal affair.

She led Anders and Niklas inside, then froze. The

fiery-haired woman stood by one of the massive shelves, running her fingers along leather-bound book spines.

Lissandra gasped, then stepped inside the room. "You're not supposed to be in here."

The woman turned around casually, piercing Lissandra with her sparkling blue eyes. "*You're* not supposed to be here," the woman purred, then muttered some words under her breath.

Lissandra dropped to the ornately pattered rug.

Anders rushed to her and knelt, then exhaled in relief to find her still breathing. She just seemed to be in a heavy sleep. He looked over his shoulder toward the guards, but they both faced forward outside the door, still as statues. What in the Horned One's name was going on?

Niklas stepped fully into the room as the woman muttered a few more words. The doors slammed shut behind him, seemingly of their own volition.

"One of the Ceàrdaman," the woman observed, curling the corner of her rouged lips. "How . . . interesting."

Anders stood, glancing at Niklas in confusion. He still had his tanned skin and normal eyes. How had she distinguished his true identity? He would have asked her, if he didn't feel frozen as that piercing blue gaze turned to him.

"And *you*," she added. Using only her eyes, she looked him up and down, seeming to recognize him.

"D-do I know you?" he stammered, straightening his cloak to make sure his uniform was covered.

She rolled her eyes. "No, but *I* know *you*. Not that you're special. I know most everyone." She moved her gaze back to Niklas. "Perhaps you can offer me aid. I'm looking for a particular volume."

"Ar Marbhdhraíocht?" he questioned.

The woman widened her eyes in surprise. "Why yes."

Humming to himself, Niklas glided across the room to a shelf far from where the woman had been looking. He pulled out a massive, black volume, then walked back to the woman, thunking it into her waiting palms.

She looked down at the book like a noblewoman examining a fine jewel. Her eyes flicked to Niklas, then to Anders, then she clutched the book against her chest protectively. "I suppose I'll be off."

Niklas stepped forward and placed a hand on her arm, still hugging the black book. "Not quite, my dear. You have bargained for information from one of the Ceàrdaman. Now you must grant me a boon."

She scowled at his hand. "I'll grant you your death if you don't remove your *paw*."

Niklas *tsked* at her. "You may be powerful, girl, but you do not want to incur the wrath of the Ceàrdaman. We are . . . many."

She glared at him, stepping back out of his reach. "What do you want?"

"I want to *help* you," he explained, letting his hand

drop to his side. "When I come to you next, I expect to be welcomed with open arms."

The woman sneered. "I'll open the *door*. How about that?"

Niklas nodded. "Acceptable."

With a final scowl for both of them, she marched past Niklas and muttered words at the doors. They both swung inward. She muttered more words under her breath at the guards, and they remained perfectly still, never once looking at her.

"They won't remember her," Niklas explained, moving to Anders' side. "And we should escape this room while the spell still lasts." He glanced at Lissandra, still on the plush rug covering most of the floor. "She's not likely to remember either. I recommend we leave her where she lay."

Anders glanced at Lissandra, still confused. "I thought you were searching for a certain tome."

"Yes," Niklas sighed. "To give to *her*." He gestured in the direction the woman had gone. "Now let us find your family. I'm sure they'll offer you a fine meal."

Anders' stomach dropped, his thoughts torn away from the red-haired woman. Ceàrdaman and strange, magic-wielding women he could handle. His mother's disapproving eye was another matter entirely. Swallowing the lump in his throat, he followed Niklas forward, resigned to his frightening fate.

# CHAPTER SIX

Finn woke up cold and alone. At one point during the night, she'd woken to relieve Bedelia from her watch duties, then later Bedelia had gotten back up to stand watch with Ealasaid, while Kai got some rest. Now the extra bedroll beside her was empty, but she could hear voices not far off.

She sat up and watched her breath fog the air. By the gods it was *cold*. Steeling herself against the forthcoming discomfort, she wiggled out of her bedroll and stood, straightening her breeches and corset. As Kai had suggested, she'd slept with her boots on, leaving her feet sweaty and sore. All for nothing, obviously, since they'd needed no quick escape.

Catching the sound of voices again, she hurried toward the noise, soon spotting the source. What she found filled her with joy. Perhaps her journey would not be derailed after all.

Seeing her, Iseult ended his conversation with Kai and approached. He smiled down at her warmly. A smile that, she was beginning to realize, was reserved only for her. "We thought we'd let you rest awhile," he explained.

Maarav and his men stood several paces back, tending their horses. She spotted Iseult and Maarav's large warhorses, along with four new ones.

"Naoki?" she asked hopefully, searching around for the dragon.

Iseult shook his head. "Kai explained what happened, but we did not see her."

She held a hand against her stomach, and the sudden knot that blossomed there. Had she been killed?

Iseult placed a comforting hand on her bicep, and she allowed herself a shuddering exhale.

"I was worried you wouldn't be able to find us," she muttered finally, then glanced at the nearby horses, "but I see you've not only done that, but have gone far beyond."

Iseult frowned and withdrew his hand from her arm. "The soldiers we fought were undertrained. It was not difficult to escape with the horses. We led them on a chase for much of the night, then circled back around to find you."

Anna approached from the nearby trees, looking tired and irritable. "You're welcome for that," she said snidely. "It's fortunate you're so . . . shiny, else we might not have found you so quickly."

Finn sighed, knowing Anna was talking about seeing her magic. It suddenly dawned on her that if Anna could see it, others likely could too. Was that how the Ceàr-daman had found her in Migris? And the Cavari who'd stolen her away through the earth? She stifled a shiver. She should probably learn how to hide her . . . shine, but the only person she knew to ask how was Àed.

Iseult softly cleared his throat, startling her back into awareness. Reading her worries, he comforted, "Perhaps Naoki will still find you. She should be able to follow your scent from quite a distance."

She nodded, but wasn't hopeful. "Let's go," she muttered, glancing at Anna as she walked away toward the horses. She'd need to ask Anna more about her *shini-ness*, but in that moment, she didn't have the heart. Later.

Nodding to herself, she walked with Iseult as everyone congregated around the horses. She ended up riding with Bedelia, while Ealasaid and Anna rode together. Anna had complained that it wasn't fair that only the men should get their own horses, but she really couldn't argue against the fact that she and Ealasaid weighed less than any of the men, except maybe Tavish, who had already *graciously* offered to share a horse with any of the women.

Finn, however, had not complained about riding with Bedelia. They had ridden together all the way to Migris once, and she took comfort in riding together once again. She'd formed more of a bond with Bedelia than she'd managed with either Ealasaid or Anna, and knew she could trust her. Soon enough Bedelia had managed to unsour Finn's mood, though her heart still ached for

Naoki. Still, they chatted happily as they rode through the woods, avoiding the Sand Road for fear of running across An Fiach.

It was clear that the threat of the Faie was heavy on everyone's minds. It was not wise to travel through the woods, but they had little choice. Hopefully the next Faie they came across would be friendly, like the tree-like Trow. They seemed to like her, and could perhaps elaborate upon what the young Merrow girl had said, which she had yet to tell Iseult.

She glanced in his direction, but he was intent on watching their surroundings. Yes, she still needed to tell him what the Merrow girl had said, even though he knew better than most that all must fear the Dair.

MAARAV TIGHTENED the bandage on his arm as they rode, annoyed that the young soldier had gotten through his defenses enough to cause minor damage. Still, he was glad he'd judged the situation well. The extra horses had everyone in high spirits, chattering amongst themselves rather than eyeing him suspiciously. Banding together against the soldiers had also taken some of the attention off Tavish and Rae for what happened to Anna's men. They were all comrades in arms now.

He glanced around at his party as they rode on. Silvery clouds were forming in the sky, casting occasional shadows across the group. It almost seemed cold enough to snow, though given the season, the sun should have been beating down on their backs. He doubted it was *just* the Faie's presence affecting the weather. There was no mention of unseasonable cold in the accounts of the Faie war. Something else was going on. It was as if the earth itself had taken notice, and was trying to freeze its inhabitants into submission. Hopefully it would freeze An Fiach first.

He hadn't expected *that* additional complication. There were already too many complications. First, the Faie were highly unpredictable. It was difficult to tell if they had a leader, or just acted upon impulse. The attack on Migris had definitely been organized, but was it an isolated event, or a hint of what was to come? Then there were the Reivers. They'd heard no word of them so far, but he knew they would pop up again as the land fell further into chaos. An Fiach seemed to be the largest local faction, but the great cities had their own militaries.

At the center of it all were Finn's people, the Cavari. Iseult had not divulged much, but if Finn was back, the others likely were too.

Maarav was yet to choose his side in it all. He knew Slàine, the woman who had cared for him like she was her own son, would want him to be on the side of the highest bidder, but he'd never been overly motivated by coin, nor was he motivated by power. While he had made a few allegiances over his lifetime, they did not drive his day to day life. What drove him was the only game he'd ever known, to come out on top of any situation thrown his way. The game had occupied most every moment of his life, a life that was nothing more than waiting to see what happened when a soulless man died.

He shook his head. It was better not to think about *that*. For now, he needed to focus on the most imminent threat of An Fiach, and why they now wanted Finn. *Someone* must have reported just who she was, else so many men would never be sent after a single girl. Kai was likely but an extra token, wanted for his associations with her.

Something wet hit his cheek. He looked up to see a gentle white flurry descending upon them. It was *actually* snowing in the middle of the warm season. Maarav couldn't help but feel that perhaps even he was out of his depth. The snowfall began to thicken, making it difficult to see through the already dense trees surrounding them.

Iseult rode up by his side, looking grim as snowflakes gathered in his dark hair. "Keep your eyes open for shelter," he advised. "We're not outfitted for this type of weather." He peered around at the falling snow like it was an enemy that had suddenly ambushed them. A fitting analogy, really, since most only had light cloaks to ward away the cold.

They rode on in silence as the others oohed and aahed about the snow. Maarav did not ooh, nor did he ahh. It was a pretty sight, but it could quickly turn deadly. At least An Fiach would have trouble tracking them as the snow slowly covered up their passing.

The trees thinned as they continued onward, leaving

the riders fully unguarded from the icy flurry. The complaints of it being too cold began. Maarav scanned the land, freshly painted a crisp white.

"Over there," he stated to Iseult, catching sight of a large structure.

Iseult narrowed his gaze in the direction Maarav pointed, then nodded. "I will ride ahead."

He took off without further explanation, though Maarav knew he was likely scouting for dangers. Glad to let his brother handle the risky work, he turned to halt the other riders.

Finn and Bedelia reached him first. The hoods of their cloaks were pulled up over their heads, Finn's a forest green, and Bedelia's a dark brown that would easily blend in with most surroundings.

"Iseult has gone to scout our shelter," he explained as the others reached them.

Anna seemed to have gotten over her irritation at sharing a horse, and now huddled close to Ealasaid for warmth. "I assumed we would ride on through the weather," she commented around her chattering teeth.

"Unwise," Tavish replied before Maarav could. "This is no natural storm."

"Obviously," Anna snapped. "Which is why we should continue riding until we're out of it."

"Too dangerous," Rae chimed in. "We would be fools to risk the horses."

Anna snorted. "You two sure picked the perfect time to begin offering input."

Neither of the men replied, but they were right. The snow was beginning to pile above the horses' fetlocks. There was no predicting the duration of the downfall, nor how far the storm spanned.

A hazy shape appeared from the direction Iseult had gone, soon revealing itself to be the man in question. He wordlessly gestured for all to follow him.

Maarav turned his horse, taking a final look at the suddenly unrecognizable, empty expanses around them. While he was grateful they'd found shelter, he had the odd feeling that once they slept, they might not find their way back again.

BEDELIA TOSSED and turned in her bedroll. The shelter Iseult had scouted was the remains of a castle, long since fallen to disrepair. Fortunately, most chambers had a roof, granting the horses and riders a reprieve from the snow.

The fire still blazed in the center of the expansive room where they had all congregated, their bedrolls circling the warm flames. One bedroll was notably empty. Iseult was prowling around in the snow outside, keeping an eye out for anyone who might attack them in the middle of a blizzard.

Bedelia's hand flexed around her dagger, concealed within her bedding. Was now the time? Her mission was to eliminate Finn's protectors, namely Iseult. Would she be able to sneak up on him in the blizzard?

Cold sweat beaded on her brow as she slowly sat up. Everyone in the room was motionless, and judging by the gentle sounds of snoring, fast asleep after the exhausting ride through the snow. If she killed him now, what would she do? Try to run off in the blizzard? Pretend he was murdered by bandits?

No, it was likely best to wait, but she could at least check outside to see if an opportunity presented itself. Her stomach in knots, she slid the rest of the way out of her bedroll, silently sheathing her dagger at her side. She crept around the fire and her sleeping companions toward the place she'd hung her cloak on the wall to dry, above her damp boots.

She tugged on her boots, lacing them haphazardly before wrapping the thick fabric of her cloak around her shoulders. With a final glance back in the direction of her sleeping companions, she ventured onward, stepping lightly down the stone corridor that would lead her outside. Cool moonlight filtered through the missing top portion of the door at the end of the hall, though the rest of the ancient wooden door stood fast against the elements.

Reaching the entrance, Bedelia wrapped her gloved hand around the rusted iron bar holding the door shut. She slid it back, then pulled the door open. The air that streamed in was so cold it hurt to breathe. Beyond the doorway was a dazzling display of white. The snow had continued to fall while they rested, enough to nearly reach Bedelia's knees. There was no sign of Iseult's footprints on top of the snowbank, but he'd gone outside sometime ago, so they had likely been covered. Fortunately, the snowfall had ceased, else she might have turned back around to resume her warm spot in her bedroll by the fire.

She took a deep breath, then let it out slowly, fogging the air in front of her face. Steeling herself, she stepped out into the night, not sure what she intended. Perhaps Iseult could be reasoned with, and convinced to leave Finn's side for a time so she wouldn't have to kill him . . . and perhaps the sky was really green and horses could fly.

She gently pulled the door shut behind her, then made her way through the snow. Her boots crunched down through the ice, making it near impossible to walk without stumbling. Eventually she reached level ground where the snow had not piled quite so high. Stopping to steady herself, she scanned the glittering darkness. Everything was still.

She started walking in a randomly chosen direction, staying near enough to the castle perimeter to not lose sight of it. Truly, she hoped she would not find Iseult at all, and she could return to her bed like nothing had ever happened.

She wrapped her cloak more tightly around herself. Keiren had the *sight*, so Bedelia knew it was a possibility she was watching her at that very moment, but she also knew it was difficult for Keiren to see those surrounding Finn, so perhaps not. Would she know if Bedelia simply gave up on her orders, choosing instead to remain by Finn's side where she could not be seen?

She shook her head at her cowardly thoughts. It was not in her nature to hide, but it was against her better senses to fight a battle she could not win. Keiren would crush her like an insect beneath her boot.

Perhaps if she told Finn the truth, they could figure out a solution together. She wasn't sure exactly what Keiren wanted with Finn, but she knew it wasn't good. Perhaps together, she and Finn could both survive.

She continued walking, so absorbed in her thoughts that she forgot to search for Iseult. Instead she watched the glittering snow beneath her boots. The transformed landscape was stunning, really, especially in the cool moonlight, though it was hard to enjoy since it was so cold.

She froze mid-step as a shiver ran up her spine, and not from the cold. She sensed a presence at her back seconds before a low growl met her ears. Thoughts of Faie wolves raced through her mind, and her old leg wound seemed to throb with the memory.

Her breath caught in her throat. She turned slowly and drew her dagger, wishing desperately she hadn't left her bow inside with her other belongings.

She saw not Faie wolves, but three normal ones. Their eyes glistened in the moonlight as their paws crunched forward through the snow. She drew her blade, knowing the odds were against her. Her hands were nearly numb with the cold, and the wolves looked emaciated, desperate for a meal. If there were only two of them, perhaps she could have fended them off, but with three, they would easily be able to flank her. All it would take was a bite to a leg tendon and she would go down.

She took a hesitant step back, and the wolves darted forward. She held up her blade to fend off the first attack, blinded as a flash of fiery light cut across her vision. Someone stepped between her and the wolves, pushing her back while waving a burning torch toward the feral creatures.

The animals backed away, frightened more by the fire than they ever would be of a blade.

"Stay near me," the man with the torch said, and Bedelia realized with a start that it was Iseult.

He herded her behind him, keeping the wolves at bay with his fire as they backed toward the castle where their friends slept. The wolves snapped at the flames, urged on by their hunger. Bedelia's breath hissed in and out through gritted teeth. She had just come so close to death. After all she'd endured in life, it almost seemed oddly poetic that it could have ended that way, with her nothing more than a meal in a wolf's belly.

When they reached the snowbank in front of the door, she stepped back and her foot sank. She lost her balance and began to fall, but Iseult's free hand darted back and caught her wrist, holding her steady. Her breath caught in her throat as she noted the wolves' hungry expressions, made menacing with shadows from the firelight. If she would have gone down, they would have pounced, fire or no.

"Keep moving," Iseult ordered.

Nodding to herself, Bedelia trudged backward through the deeper snow until her icy hands hit solid wood. Keeping her gaze on the wolves and Iseult, she pushed the door open and stepped into the hall. Iseult followed her, keeping the torch between himself and the wolves until he was inside, then quickly pushed the door shut and slid the iron bar into place.

Scratching, whining, and a few thuds could be heard as the wolves tested the door, then all was silent.

Iseult turned toward her, torch still in hand, lighting his face and the hall around them. The snowflakes that had gathered in his black hair and on his shoulders began to melt, leaving dark stains of moisture in their place.

"Always have a source of fire at hand when wandering the wilds at night. It will do more for you than a blade," he explained.

Bedelia nodded as she slowly relearned how to breathe. She tried to keep her thoughts out of her expression, especially the guilt. Did he know she'd only gone outside to stalk *him*? She would have killed him had she been given the chance . . . and he'd *saved* her. Perhaps she did deserve to be eaten by wolves.

He stared at her, and she had the feeling he was somehow reading every single thought in her mind.

"I-" she began, then cut herself off, unsure of how she could ever explain.

"Go back to sleep," he ordered. "I'll watch the door."

Bedelia looked down at her feet and nodded, then shuffled away. Halfway down the hall she turned to find Iseult still watching her. "Thank you," she muttered.

He did not reply. He was clearly suspicious of her now, or perhaps he had been from the start. She would have to step much more carefully from this point on. She didn't look back again until she had reached her bedroll. She curiously noted that two other bedrolls seemed empty, but did not take time to investigate who was missing. Instead, she noted that Finn was still peacefully sleeping, then quickly climbed back into her bedding. Still half-sitting, she gazed at the illumination of Iseult's torch at the end of the hall. A moment later, the light went out, leaving her in darkness.

She was beginning to realize that darkness was a place where Iseult was far more comfortable than she. Sure, she'd tasted darkness at Keiren's side, but it was not where she would choose to live.

Perhaps once, but not now.

## CHAPTER SEVEN

$\mathcal{I}$seult watched the lumps that were his companions bundled up in their bedrolls, secretly hoping the lump that was Finn would wake first. He hadn't missed the two empty bedrolls at the other end of the room. They'd belonged to Tavish and Rae. Either they'd gone out while he was escorting Bedelia back to safety, or they'd somehow snuck by him while he was in the hall, which he doubted.

He'd slept little during the night, and what rest he did allow was spent leaning against the wall near the door. He'd never needed much rest. He'd always thought perhaps it was due to his curse, but Maarav seemed to sleep just fine. Or perhaps he simply pretended in order to feign ignorance about his missing men.

His gaze moved to the lump that was Bedelia, near Finn. What had she been doing wandering out in the snow? Had she entered into a plot to distract him from the other men? If she'd only needed to relieve herself, she could have stayed much closer to the door. He'd been watching her since she walked out, noting the way she moved, how she favored her right leg, and had seen the wolves stalking her. He'd almost debated stepping in.

He knew it was too great a coincidence that they would happen upon her on the Sand Road after she and Finn were separated in Migris. His suspicion was only increased by the fact that she knew Maarav, and that he had been the one to deliver the potion to cure her ailment after Finn was kidnapped by Anna. Was she somehow affiliated with the secret city, or did she simply know Maarav as in innkeeper in Migris?

One of the lumps stirred, drawing his attention. A clump of fluffy blonde hair came into view. Only Ealasaid.

He shook his head. What an odd group they had gathered. He at least trusted Ealasaid, and her magic was useful.

Next rose Finn, then Kai. Slowly the others awoke and sat up. Last was Bedelia, likely tired from her late night exploits.

"Has the snow stopped?" Finn asked of the room in general as they all struggled out of their bedrolls.

"Yes," Iseult replied, stepping toward her to offer her a hand up.

She took it, smiling up at him, melting his icy heart . . . just a bit.

"Though riding will be treacherous for a time," he

continued. "The snow will disguise the lower areas and holes in the ground, so we'll need to be cautious of where we ride. We'll make for Badenmar, and hope it has not been . . . affected."

Iseult watched as Finn glanced across the fire at Kai, meeting his gaze. The three of them remembered well what happened the *last* time they were in Badenmar. That was the night Kai and Anna had first kidnapped Finn. No such thing would happen *this* time.

Ealasaid and Bedelia left the group, heading toward where the horses were tethered. A few minutes later they returned with hard bread and dried fruits, passing them out to everyone in the group. Bedelia did not meet Iseult's eyes when she handed him his portion.

Anna peered at the two empty bedrolls, confused.

"I did not see them depart," he explained, stepping up beside her, "but I doubt it was long after everyone went to sleep. I do not believe they will return."

Maarav stepped up on his other side. "Those blighted, worthless midges," Maarav hissed, staring at the space his men should have occupied. "They could have at least challenged me, rather than running away in the night like cowards."

Iseult simply looked at him, attempting to divine whether or not he was just playing at being surprised, then turned away. It did not matter if he acted. Iseult was watching him regardless. Perhaps they'd go outside and find the men eaten by wolves, and the riddle would be solved.

After everyone had eaten their small meals and attended to their morning duties, they prepared the horses and set out. Finn had attempted to climb onto Bedelia's horse, but Iseult stopped her, requesting that she ride with him instead. Kai commented on the human and wolf prints near the door, though neither Iseult nor Bedelia offered to explain.

The castle grew small behind them as they rode across the frozen landscape, glittering fiercely in the early morning sun.

"It's beautiful," Finn muttered softly near his ear. Her arms were wrapped loosely around his waist, keeping herself steady as his horse trudged through the deep snow.

While he'd requested she ride with him in part to keep her away from Bedelia, he also trusted his horse more than the others to not lose its footing in the snow. Her added warmth at his back was merely a bonus.

"Do you have any memories of the snow?" he asked, knowing that she returned to the human world after the snows had passed for the season.

She sighed. "I remember the snow when I was a tree, but not before. Though, sometimes I see it in my dreams. I see it just like this," she removed one arm from his waist to gesture at the glittering landscape, then quickly resumed her hold as their mount lurched forward into a hidden dip.

"What do you think it means?" he asked gently. While he didn't necessarily mind the crisp air biting into his skin, they should have been feeling comforting rays of warmth, given the season. He'd seen Faie magic before, but he was not sure even the Faie were capable of covering the land in ice.

"I wish I knew," she replied. "I wish I knew a lot of things. If only I could speak once more with my-" she cut herself off, as if only then realizing she'd been speaking her thoughts out loud.

"Your mother," he finished for her. She'd told him about her encounter with her mother. She wasn't sure if it had been a dream, or some alternate reality, but her mother had warned her of great danger, and had advised her to stay near Iseult's side. Her mother had also implied she had been hiding Finn from their tribe, the Cavari.

Finn was silent for several seconds before replying, "Yes. I just wish she could explain things to me. I wish *anyone* could. For some reason, this snow makes me feel like a child again, but I do not understand why. I don't even remember anything about being a child. I just . . . I feel like it means . . . something."

"It will come to you in time," he offered, hoping to comfort her.

"Will it?" she questioned, sounding almost hostile. "It feels like it's been ages since I was a tree, and yet I'm still in the same place I was before. Searching for answers that seem to get farther away the more I look."

He could understand her discouragement, but he also suspected she didn't truly want the answers she sought.

He suspected her missing memories were her own doing, a way to deal with the pain of losing her child in her previous life. She would never be able to unlock them if she could not accept that loss.

"I apologize," she said in reply to his silence. "I should not complain. At least I now know who I am, though my people are strangers to me."

He placed a hand on her arm and gave it a squeeze. Though he was unused to displaying any sort of affection, he felt she needed it. "Knowing who you are is the most important part."

"Yes, you've taught me that," she replied playfully. "And after that, I suppose it's knowing who your friends are?"

He chuckled, another rare event. "Yes, *you* have taught me that."

They rode on in companionable silence after that, while their party members occasionally complained about the snow. There were no complaints on Iseult's mind though, for the snow suddenly seemed a little less cold, or perhaps it was just the effect of the warm presence at his back.

OF ALL THE things they could have encountered, snow was the last thing Maarav would have guessed. The second to last, were the black shapes he occasionally noticed watching them from the trees. He knew Iseult had noticed them too, judging by the way he gripped the pommel of his sword, and the way his eyes darted about. He also knew it was no coincidence that Tavish and Rae had disappeared the night before.

He sighed, refocusing his attention on their present predicament. They'd ridden out of the denser snow to find a small path with only a light dusting. Hopefully soon they would ride out of the snow altogether, and things could go back to normal . . . at least, as normal as they could be in a land plagued by the Faie. Perhaps the stealthy black shapes were only observing them, and upon seeing him, would leave them alone.

He sighed as several black clad figures stepped onto the path ahead of them. Things wouldn't be going back to normal after all.

He drew his horse to a halt, recognizing those who stood before them, though they wore black cowls over their heads, with additional fabric covering the lower parts of their faces. One in particular he would know anywhere.

"I'm surprised to see you this far south, Slàine," he called out as his companions stopped their horses a few paces behind him.

"I have a job to do," called back the woman who'd raised him like he was her own son.

Iseult trotted his horse up to Maarav's side, cool rage in his expression. It was clear he thought he'd been betrayed. "What is the meaning of this?" he demanded of Maarav.

Maarav paused to analyze the situation. Finn did not look at him, but instead glanced around from her seat behind Iseult. Several more black clad shapes had closed in around them, and he knew there were likely more still hidden in the snowy trees. He thought he noticed the shapes of Tavish and Rae. It was difficult to tell with the hoods, but a strand of bright red hair stuck out near the eyes of one of the men. He'd had nothing to do with this, but Iseult knew Slàine, and would likely deduce the black clad figures were Maarav's people. In this, Iseult would never believe him innocent.

"I honestly do not know," Maarav replied in vain. He was unsure what *job* would draw Slàine this far south. Usually she and the others worked only as assassins, but if that was their aim, they would already be dead.

Slàine glanced at the men and women to either side of her. "Take the girl," she demanded. "The one riding with the man."

*Ah*, thought Maarav, now it all made sense. This must have something to do with Finn's bounty. "She must be worth a great deal of coin to catch your interest," Maarav replied, hoping to halt the assassins' progress.

"She is worth more than coin," Slàine explained. "I have an old debt to settle. A *very* old debt."

"Call them off," Iseult interrupted, "unless you care to sustain great casualties."

Slàine laughed, then gestured for her people to attack. There was a moment of utter stillness, then they swarmed forward as one, focusing on Iseult and Finn. As fluid as water, Iseult jumped down from his horse and met the nearest attacker with his blade, skewering the young man. Another black clad man leapt toward him, and fell just the same.

Seconds later, the rest of their party joined the fight, surprising Maarav as he stepped back out of the way. Sure, he'd expected Iseult and Kai to fight for Finn, but not the others. An arrow struck a woman who'd taken hold of Finn's leg, and Maarav followed its path to see Bedelia, still mounted on her horse with her bow raised. Anna and Kai fought back to back with smaller blades, no less deadly than Iseult's. Even Sativola swung a small ax, warding away those trying to reach Finn. None of the assassins attacked Maarav, likely believing he was on their side. Truth be told, he wasn't sure which side he was on, though at the moment, the assassins, many of whom he'd grown up with, were interfering with his plans. Across the chaos, he spotted the black clad figure with the tuft of red hair showing. Meeting each other's eyes, they both shrugged and joined the fight.

Maarav unsheathed his sword and blocked the path of an assassin heading toward Iseult. He didn't recognize the eyes above the black fabric, but it was clear whomever it was recognized him. The man hesitated, then lifted his blade. Their weapons rang out as they clashed, and Maarav began to fight against his own people with all his might. His loyalties lay with himself, just as they always had, and he wanted to see this adventure through. He slashed the man he fought across the chest, watching him topple to the ground. Slàine leapt in front of him. He met her blade for blade. Her eyes widened in shock for a split second, then she attacked with a ferocious growl. He sensed someone at his back, then his hair stood on end as lightning struck directly behind him. *Ealasaid.* A man cried out in pain, distracted from sticking a blade in Maarav's back.

"Thank you!" he called before dodging another one of Slaine's attacks. He turned just in time to witness Kai sustaining a wound to his side, though he could not look long enough to tell if it was fatal. He heard Finn scream at the sight, then more assassins swarmed in from the surrounding woods. He moved to parry another of Slàine's attacks.

"You do not understand!" she growled, evading his next attack.

"Then explain yourself!" he panted.

Even with his and Iseult's sword skills, and Ealasaid's lightning, Maarav knew they would soon be overwhelmed. Perhaps he'd chosen the wrong side of the battle after all. At least he'd die with a sword in his hand —an arrow struck another of the assassins charging him —and *friends* at his side.

Slàine glanced at the man felled by the arrow, then struck again.

"Stop!" Finn cried out, still atop Iseult's dancing steed.

Maarav wasn't sure if she was ordering someone specifically, or just shouting in vain at everyone. Either way, her pleas were ignored, and his attention was once again drawn away as Slàine landed a slice across his bicep. He'd never hoped to fight the one who had taught him everything he knew. She seemed able to predict his movements with ease.

"Stop!" Finn called again. This time, the ground rumbled beneath Maarav's feet.

The fighting ceased for a split second. Everyone glanced around for the source of the rumble, but the earth had stilled. Nearly as one, they resumed motion.

"Just stop fighting," Slàine hissed, crouching back into a defensive stance.

"Stop this now!" Finn echoed, her screams competing with the sound of clashing of blades.

The earth began to rumble again, but this time did not quiet. The ground erupted where they stood, sending many of the assassins flying. Maarav and Slàine both dove aside as the soil beneath them exploded, but they were not fast enough.

Their bodies were flung aside in different directions. Maarav lost sight of both Finn on her horse and Slàine as he landed with a thud. Massive roots, dripping soil and flinging snow, coiled toward the cloud obscured sun above him. Regaining his senses, he pushed himself away from the quaking earth toward the still tree line, watching the roots in awe as he stumbled to his feet. They struck like vipers, coiling around the suddenly frightened assassins, ensnaring their limbs before hauling them upward. Slàine grunted frantically as she fought against the root that sought to imprison her, but her blades were no match for the thick appendage. Soon, Slàine and her assassins were all held immobile, their feet dangling off the ground.

Maarav had a moment to feel relief, then another root darted up, quick as a speeding arrow, and ensnared him like the others. Suddenly dangling in the air from a root around his torso and arms, he craned his neck to see Finn still atop her prancing mount, red-faced and looking close to tears.

Iseult and the others slowly climbed to their feet on the turned earth, avoiding the vines dangling black forms all around them. Kai clutched at the wound in his side, and would have fallen had Anna not darted in to hold him steady.

Sativola muttered curses under his breath, glancing between Finn and the silent, dangling assassins. His left leg slowly saturated itself with blood from a gash on his thigh. He also seemed to have an injured hand. His wide-eyes finally settled solely on Finn, seeming to have deduced the roots were her doing, though it was clear he'd never seen such a scene before. Ealasaid wore a similar expression, her gaze lingering on Tavish and Rae, somewhat distinguishable through their hoods, caught up in the roots side by side. Maarav wished he had noted which side they had fought for, though he knew they'd likely turned on him.

He twisted against the roots to watch as Finn finally broke down and started weeping, though he was unsure why she was upset. She'd just bested an entire swarm of assassins. She should be beaming with pride. The captured awaited her next move with bated breath, likely terrified to even speak, lest she order the vines to crush the life from them.

Bedelia, who'd managed to keep her mount like Finn, trotted her horse toward the remaining startled horses hiding in the nearby trees. She obviously wanted no part of the dealings soon to come.

Maarav wished he could join her.

Iseult, uninjured as far as he could tell, moved to stand beside Finn atop his mount. He stroked his hand across the horse's neck to calm the nervous beast, then scanned the clusters of assassins until his eyes found Maarav.

Their gazes locked. "You were part of this," he stated.

Maarav struggled against the coarse root, but its spindles had wrapped around him multiple times, suspending him above its base, as thick as a tree trunk. "I know them yes, but I had no part in setting up this ambush," he replied. "I had no knowledge that Slàine hoped to collect Finn's bounty."

Slàine cast him an evil glare. He knew that glare all too well. She'd tried to explain herself, but he hadn't listened. Now she was about to take him down with her. "He knew," she lied. "He's been secretly communicating with us, planning the perfect time for an ambush."

"She's lying," Maarav argued, but his heart wasn't in it. He had already seen the suspicious glances of his party members days before Slàine attacked. Those same suspicious gazes were aimed at him now. All they needed was an excuse. The roots flexed around his midsection, threatening to crush him. They might as well. If Iseult left him with Slàine and the others, he was as good as dead.

Iseult turned his attention from Maarav to Slàine. "Now that you have been bested, will you call off your hunt, or do we have to kill you?"

Slàine glared at him. Her cowl had fallen to reveal the grim line of her mouth. Finally, she nodded. "I suppose I have no choice."

Iseult took one last look at his brother and those dangling around him, then took his horse's reins. "Let's go," he ordered, then began to lead the horse, and Finn by default, away. Bedelia had gathered the rest of the horses, and now led them toward where Anna and Sativola waited with Kai.

Looking between Finn and Iseult, Kai's group, and Maarav, Ealasaid scurried around the roots in her way to catch up and block Iseult's path. "We can't just leave him here!" she argued, glancing once more at Maarav. "He'll freeze to death come nightfall."

Iseult silently stepped around her and continued walking, leading Finn atop his horse behind him. Kai, Anna, Sativola, and Bedelia, now each leading their horses, seemed content to do the same, though Kai seemed to be having difficulty walking as he clutched his side, his face as white as the remaining snow.

"Iseult," Finn said softly, finally halting his progress.

He turned and looked up at her. "Perhaps we should at least let them go." She glanced back at the assassins.

"They just attempted to kill us," he stated blandly.

"Not Maarav," she reminded him. "He fought them along with us."

Iseult turned his gaze from Finn to peer further back to Maarav. "We cannot risk the possibility that it was just an act, I apologize."

Maarav wasn't sure if Iseult was apologizing to him or Finn, and it didn't really matter. He could tell by the look in Iseult's eyes that his fate was sealed.

"I'm staying then," Ealasaid cut in. She had taken hold of Maarav's horse as if deciding he was now hers.

Finn turned sad eyes down to her. "I think the roots will go away on their own eventually. They're not likely to freeze."

Ealasaid glared at her. "I'm staying."

Finn leaned back in the saddle as if Ealasaid's glare had physically struck her. She looked like she wanted to cry again, and Ealasaid looked teary herself. Yet, both women steeled their expressions and turned away from each other.

"Do not follow us," Iseult said to the group in general. "Next time, mercy will not be shown." He continued leading his horse away as Anna and the others paused to climb atop their mounts. Anna helped both Kai and Sativola into their respective saddles, though Sativola seemed far better off than Kai.

As they all began to ride away, Ealasaid gave them a

final glance, then hurried toward Maarav, trailing his horse behind her.

"You should go with them," he urged. He knew the girl had no home, and no family. It would not be right to part her from those who would stand the best chance of protecting her.

She shook her head stubbornly, tossing her curly blonde hair from side to side. "You are an intolerable man, but I do not believe you betrayed us. You do not deserve to be left here." She removed the dagger from her belt and stepped toward him.

"They were right to leave," he replied. "My company is not worth the risk."

The assassins watched on silently, clearly hoping Ealasaid might free them next.

Ignoring their company, she reached up and began sawing at the roots restraining him. "I do not agree," she muttered.

He sighed, then waited for her to finish freeing him, which took what seemed like ages given the size of her blade versus the size of the roots. By the time his feet hit the turned earth below him, his limbs were sore from hanging in the awkward position.

Wordlessly, Ealasaid climbed atop his horse and waited for him to join her.

"What about the rest of us?" Slàine finally snapped.

Maarav smirked. "I know you well, Slàine. Son or no, you would not allow me to live after fighting against you."

She glared daggers at him. "Your chances are better now than they will be if you leave me here to freeze. Perhaps if you let me down, I might be inclined to explain things to you."

"You heard the girl," he replied, gesturing in the direction the others had ridden. "The roots will loosen their hold eventually." He knew better than to take Slàine at her word, as badly as he wanted to know why she'd attacked, she'd stick a dagger in him long before she'd breathe a word.

"And I will find you," she growled.

"Then I hope they do not loosen their hold too soon," he answered, then climbed up in the saddle behind Ealasaid.

"Do we follow the others?" Ealasaid whispered as they rode away.

"Not yet," he whispered, glancing at the dangling people as they rode past. "Let's worry about our own hides first."

Together they continued off into the melting snow. Maarav knew the next few stops Iseult had planned, so he would have no issue picking up their trail later. For now, he would worry about getting far away from Slàine. Deep down, he knew he should have killed her, but he found he didn't have it in his heart, as black as it was, to do so.

~

NOT LONG AFTER leaving Maarav and Ealasaid behind, Kai was forced to stop and bandage his wound, and Anna pushed the same treatment on Sativola. While Sativola's wounds were mainly surface injuries, and would likely heal within the next few days, Kai's were serious. He'd lost a large amount of blood, soaking his shirt, breeches, and even his cloak. He hoped nothing vital had been damaged within him, but feared the worst. He felt . . . wrong, and it wasn't just the blood loss. He'd lost plenty of blood before.

Finn had started crying again while Anna bandaged Kai's wounds, though he didn't think the tears were for him. Well, perhaps a few, but most seemed to be for Ealasaid.

"I cannot believe we left her behind," Finn muttered, still sitting in the saddle behind Iseult.

Kai noted the edge of her green cloak was speckled with blood, though she was the cleanest out of their small group. It was fortunate Anna and Iseult had chosen to wear all black. The blood on Kai's and Sativola's clothing, some theirs, some belonging to their attackers, was readily apparent.

Kai lifted himself back into his saddle, gritting his teeth against the pain.

"It was her choice," Iseult replied.

Kai suspected Iseult was secretly glad the girl had stayed behind to cut his brother free. While he agreed with the decision to leave Maarav behind, he still felt a little guilty. What if Maarav had been telling the truth?

He'd traveled all this way with Iseult, and now he'd been cast off like they shared no blood, nor bond of kinship.

Secretly Kai worried the same fate might befall *him*.

He watched as a freshly bandaged Sativola gingerly pulled himself up into his saddle. He felt eyes on his back, and turned to see Finn staring at him as they began to ride.

"Are you alright?" she questioned, as if suddenly noticing his poor state.

He nodded, pressing his heels against his horse to urge it onward. "Just a scratch."

She stared at him like she didn't quite believe him. He noticed how her hair formed a tangled nest around her head, and how thin she'd grown from their long travels, yet her concern was for everyone else.

"If only my powers were meant for healing instead of violence and destruction, perhaps I'd be more useful," she lamented.

Iseult patted her arm where it rested around his waist. "You just saved our lives. There would be no one to heal if we were all dead."

Kai nearly laughed. He'd never expected such comforting words to grace Iseult's lips. Although, Iseult's cold expression did not invite further comment.

Finn nodded at Iseult's comment, but continued to watch Kai with a worried expression, bobbing gently from the horse's relaxed gait.

"Let's put more distance between ourselves and those assassins before we worry about anything else," Kai advised, wanting her attention off him. If he was going to die, then that was his fate. There was no need to worry everyone when there was nothing more to be done.

She nodded, though she continued looking back over her shoulder at him before gazing further down the path, presumably hoping Ealasaid would come riding up at any moment. Each time she glanced at him, he tried to give a reassuring smile, but suspected it came out as more of a cringe. It was all he could do to remain in his saddle.

Eventually they rode far enough to reach the end of the snow. Kai's wound had stopped bleeding beneath the makeshift bandage, but he felt dizzy and ill. Hopefully a good night's rest would help him recover, though the worried glances of Anna and Finn begged to differ. They watched him like he might topple from his horse any moment. They might not be wrong.

Hoping to reach civilization by nightfall, the party ate their meals while riding. Kai found himself wishing they'd procured some whiskey from the ruins of Migris. The pain in his wound had faded to a dull throb, but his mind was beginning to tire of dealing with it.

The sky was black by the time the scent of cookfires reached Kai's nose. A moment later he exhaled with relief as the gentle glow of illuminated windows came into view.

"Badenmar," Iseult said simply, then gave Kai a stern look over his shoulder, the harsh moonlight accentuating his expression.

Ah yes, it was quite clear that Iseult also remembered what happened the last time they were in Badenmar. For some time afterward, Kai suspected Iseult had plans to kill him, but that suspicion had slowly passed. Though they would never be friends, a peculiar form of trust had grown between them. A trust that might soon be for naught if he keeled over and died.

Iseult pulled the hood of his cloak up to shadow his face before continuing onward, as did Finn. Kai should really have done the same given An Fiach was looking for him too, but the people of Badenmar would likely grow suspicious if their entire group refused to show their faces. Fortunately, Kai had no overly distinguishable features. He was of average height, with average, chestnut colored hair. Iseult, however, stood out with his height and black hair. It was likely fortunate they'd parted ways with Maarav, because the two of them together tended to draw attention.

They continued on toward the lights and scented air. Sativola rode between Kai and Anna, looking glum but determined. "One of the two of ye better be buying me a dram," he grumbled, sitting stiff on his horse to avoid extra pressure on his leg wound.

"You should be *thanking* me," Anna replied. "If I hadn't hired you in Migris, you might have been there during the attack. The few scrapes you've suffered are nothing compared to what those people experienced."

Sativola sighed. "I suppose yer right on that. Still, I wish I'd had the time to hire on with a crew in Ainfean.

No offense meant, but trouble seems to follow ye all around. Who knows what might happen next?"

"Quiet," Iseult ordered as they approached the small town. "I don't want to hear anyone muttering their true names, where we've come from, or where we're going. More soldiers of An Fiach could already be waiting here."

"Plus, you're likely still wanted for murder," Kai added.

Iseult sighed. "I imagine the townsfolk barely remember that, after all that's happened in the countryside."

Sativola leaned toward Kai and whispered, "Murder?" but Kai simply shook his head in reply. Everyone fell silent and moved their horses close together to fit on the narrow road leading into the burgh. On their last visit, the burgh had been in the midst of festivities. Now, the small cluster of farms and homes was near silent, though many torches still burned throughout the square, as if to ward away the night.

They rode toward the inn where they'd previously stayed in a storeroom. Kai had a feeling there would be plenty of proper rooms available that night. There didn't seem to be an overabundance of inhabitants in the village.

Reaching the tall wooden walls of the inn, all but Kai dismounted. There was no stableboy out waiting to take the horses to the stalls mounted on the side of the inn, so instead all reins were handed to Bedelia.

"We should probably take turns guarding the horses

throughout the night," Anna suggested. "We wouldn't want them stolen away by village folk hoping to escape to one of the larger cities."

"Yes," was Iseult's only reply.

Kai looked down at the ground, which seemed exceedingly far away given how he was currently feeling. He would have liked to avoid falling once he attempted to dismount, but it felt like a likely possibility.

As if sensing his predicament, Sativola moved to stand beside his horse, and offered his meaty arm. Frowning at the hit his pride was about to take, he allowed Sativola to brace him while he climbed down from the saddle, flexing his wound uncomfortably. The movement brought on a wave of pain, and darkness ate at his vision.

A second pair of hands took hold of his other arm, keeping him upright, then the world went black.

# CHAPTER EIGHT

*A*nna glared down at Kai's sweaty face, his features slack with unconsciousness. If only the fool had expressed how badly his wound was affecting him, they could have better tended him sooner. She could just kill him . . . if he wasn't already dying.

Finn sat on the other side of the bed on which he rested, in one of the cozy, warm rooms they'd purchased from the innkeep. Her long hair was a snarled mess, and deep bags marred the skin beneath her dark hazel eyes, occasionally flickering with reflected firelight. Anna imagined her own features showed the same strain as Finn's. Yet, neither of them looked as bad as Kai.

"Do you think he'll be alright?" Finn questioned softly, her eyes intent on the man between them.

Anna stood and removed the damp cloth from Kai's forehead, replacing it with another from a nearby wash-basin. Once they'd dragged him inside the inn, she'd realized his skin was burning with fever. Not a good sign when accompanied by severe injuries. Rough blankets were pulled only halfway up his body. Anna had raised and lowered them several times, unsure if it was best to keep his body warm, or try to cool him down. Occasionally he mumbled with fever dreams.

She resumed her seat in the same type of wooden chair Finn rested in. "There's no saying. If he makes it through morning he may be fine, as long as infection doesn't set in."

Finn looked about ready to cry, and Anna sincerely wished she wouldn't. She'd never been good around tears, and Kai was the one who needed her care right now, not Finn. She widened her eyes to deny their own sudden watering, then had an idea.

Thinking of *care*, she looked up to catch Finn's gaze. "Are you sure you don't have any healing magic?" she asked, not even sure if healing magic existed, or if all magic was simply meant for destruction. If the woman could summon massive roots from the ground, surely she could do other things? Her heart fluttered with hope.

Not seeming to sense the way Anna's heart was attempting to escape her chest, Finn shook her head sadly and lifted her gaze. "I do not believe so."

"Pity," Anna muttered, barely able to force out the words. She debated whether or not to press the topic. Even if Finn thought she had no healing magic, she could at least *try*.

She opened her mouth to say more, then a knock

sounded on the door. A moment later it opened to reveal Bedelia with a tray of food. Sativola, his wounds freshly tended, trailed in after her.

Bedelia set the tray down on a table near the fire. There were three steaming bowls of stew and a loaf of fresh baked bread that Anna imagined would remain untouched. Kai wouldn't be eating, and Finn seemed as disinterested in the food as she, having not spared Bedelia even a glance.

Anna's stomach churned uncomfortably. Having your oldest friend in mortal peril was a bit of an appetite killer.

"Iseult is watching the horses," Bedelia explained, her eyes on Finn's back, "but he'd like to speak with you after you've eaten."

Finn finally turned toward her, her eyes wide and jaw slack with questioning.

Anna watched the exchange suspiciously, wondering what Iseult might need to say in private. At times she suspected a romance between the two, but neither seemed the type for late-night clandestine meetings. Perhaps he simply wanted to discuss their separation from Maarav and Ealasaid, as Finn had seemed rather hurt by the occurrence.

After glancing at the food tray, Finn nodded and stood. "I'll go to him now."

Bedelia inclined her head. Wiping her hands on her breeches, she led Finn out of the room, leaving Sativola behind. He took Finn's vacated seat and stared down at

Kai. The door shut behind the departing women, the gentle hush of its closure sounding like a thunder clap, further jolting Anna's frayed nerves.

She nervously fiddled with one of the daggers at her hip, wishing she had something or someone to fight. All that was left to do was wait, something Anna had never been good at.

WRAPPING her tattered green cloak around herself, Finn hurried across the empty common room. She had an extra cloak since Naoki had run off, but she refused to wear it, both because she was determined her little friend would find her once more, and because the old cloak reminded her of Àed. It had once belonged to his daughter, and he had gifted it to her when they first set out on their journey.

She pushed one side of the heavy double doors open and walked out into the night, quickly spotting Iseult leaning against the front of the building, his tall frame seemingly at ease. Though his breath fogged the air, he did not have his cloak tightly wrapped around himself like she did, leaving the sword pommel at his hip to glint in the moonlight.

He turned his expressionless gaze to her as she approached. "How is he?"

"I'm not sure," she muttered. She leaned against the building beside him, wincing at the knot in her stomach.

"Anna seems to think if he makes it through morning he'll survive, but she seems unsure."

He nodded, but did not comment further.

"Bedelia said you wanted to speak with me?" she pressed, wishing they could have their conversation by a warm fire instead of outside near the stabled horses.

He nodded again, but seemed hesitant to speak. She turned her gaze up toward the sky, hoping a lack of eye contact might make him feel more comfortable with whatever he needed to say.

Unfortunately, the silence drew on for several long moments.

As she watched, sparse clouds drifted in to cover the moon. There was a crispness to the air that hinted at more snow, though she'd been told repeatedly it was the wrong time of year for it. Perhaps the strange weather was following them, just like the assassins and An Fiach. One of the horses whinnied behind them, drawing Finn back to the present.

"Do you think we made the correct decision?" Iseult asked finally.

"To come here?" she asked, confused. Iseult wasn't normally one to ask for opinions.

"To leave the others," he clarified.

She turned her head to search his face. Was he regretting leaving his brother behind? He hadn't seemed overly concerned with Maarav's welfare when they left him, but she knew better than most that Iseult had many hidden depths.

Finding no further clues in his expression, she turned her gaze back to the moon. "I'm not sure, really. I do not believe he was responsible for the ambush, but I cannot necessarily say the same for Rae and Tavish. They did not fight against us, but did not help us like Maarav. Still, I have not trusted Maarav from the start."

Iseult nodded. "His motives have remained unclear to me. I do not think it happenstance that he found me in Migris, nor do I think Bedelia just happened to be traveling the Sand Road at the same time as our party."

"Bedelia?" she questioned, startled by the abrupt subject change.

He nodded. "I would like you to tell me more about the time you spent with her. How you met, and how you parted."

"I told you already," she replied, feeling slightly defensive about the subject. "After I was stolen away by the Cavari's Faie creatures, I escaped and ended up lost in the woods. I saw a campfire in the distance and hurried toward it to find Bedelia. She fed me and accompanied me to Migris."

"And you were far from the Sand Road when you met her?" he pressed.

"Well yes," Finn began.

"And she did not tell you what she was doing by herself, so far from the road?"

"Well no," she replied, starting to see his point.

He sighed. "I caught her wandering around outside the castle ruins while everyone slept," he admitted. "I

154

believe she was looking for me. Once I had safely escorted her back, I sensed guilt in her expression."

Finn felt like a fist was slowly clenching around her heart. "What are you saying?"

His expression softened as he looked at her. "My apologies, I did not mean to upset you, and perhaps I have misjudged her. I would simply like you to be careful what you say to her."

"And you would like me to consider leaving her behind, like we did to Maarav and Ealasaid?" she accused. "You would like me to leave yet another friend behind?"

He opened his mouth to say more, but the inn door opened to their right. Bedelia peeked her head out. "Kai is awake," she explained.

Finn's heart thundered in her ears. She turned back to Iseult.

He nodded for her to go. "Be careful," he advised.

She nodded, then followed Bedelia inside. There was much to discuss with Iseult, but her priority at that moment was Kai. She'd already lost Àed and Naoki. Though she hadn't been as close to Ealasaid, her loss stung as well. Now she might possibly lose Kai.

Perhaps she should be suspicious of Bedelia, but she could not bring herself to question her friendship. She'd lost enough friends already. She wasn't about to chase away the few that remained.

~

ANNA BIT her lip hard enough to make it bleed. She would *not* cry. Kai had awoken, and it was clear by his unfocused, sad eyes that he believed he was going to die. She believed it too. His face was horribly pale, coated in a sickly sweat, his breathing ragged and weak. She thought it likely his internal organs had been damaged, and were now beginning to fail him. She could think of no other explanation.

Even more disturbing than the readily visible signs, was the fading of the color surrounding him. Since developing her curse of seeing the in between, she had started seeing soft colors surrounding people. Kai's was usually a calm, deep forest green. Now it seemed that it was fading to a bleak gray.

The door creaked open across the room and Finn poked her head in. Anna gestured for her to come inside. Though he was just feverishly mumbling to himself now, Kai had asked for her.

Shutting the door gently behind her, Finn hurried across the room, then sat on the bed beside Kai. She listened to his mutterings for a moment, then looked to Anna, confused.

"He was coherent for a short time," she explained. "He asked to see you."

Finn furrowed her brow, then turned her gaze back to Kai.

"I don't think he's going to make it," Anna softly explained, the truth behind her words stabbing her like a spear through her heart.

Finn took Kai's hand in hers and stared down at him intently. "I refuse to accept that."

Anna's heart gave a nervous skip. "I thought you said you do not possess the power to heal," she said evenly, determined to keep her turbulent emotions out of her voice. Kai *couldn't* die. He was her only friend, the only person on this terrible earth who cared about her.

"I don't," Finn said softly, still staring down at Kai, "but there has to be something," she took a shaky breath, "*something* we can do."

Anna felt like her heart was going to stop beating at any moment, right along with Kai's. Damn Finn for being such a destructive creature. She had so much magic in her, but she couldn't use any of it to help someone she cared about.

Hot rage washed over her. She was a willing recipient of the scalding emotion, much more comforting than sadness and defeat. She stared at Finn and willed her to do something, *anything*, to help Kai.

The lighting in the room suddenly shifted. Part of Anna's mind registered that the candles illuminating the room had begun to flicker, as if a breeze was circulating, yet the curtains over the window did not flutter.

"Are you doing that?" she asked, suddenly nervous. The incident with the assassins was the first time she'd seen Finn's magic, though Kai had explained it to her previously. She didn't think roots shooting up through the floor of the inn would help Kai any.

Finn turned wide eyes to her, though she maintained

her grip on Kai's limp hand. "I'm not doing anything," she breathed.

The candles flickered again, and the fire began to sputter. Suddenly the room went dark. No, not just the room, Anna realized. She seemed unable to move, and at some point her eyes had closed. Part of her sensed she was still sitting in her chair, but her body felt like it was being pulled under water. She was sinking into an endless sea of darkness.

Suddenly the feeling of drowning stopped. She took a gasping breath, then stumbled to her feet. She nearly fell to her knees, but managed to regain her balance as her vision slowly returned. She was looking at a solid stone wall.

Stone? The walls of the inn had been made of wood. Where was she?

"Where did you come from?" a woman's voice asked, echoing from somewhere down the wide, winding corridor in which Anna stood.

"I'm not sure," Finn's voice answered, muffled the same as the first woman's voice. She sounded confused, and maybe a little groggy.

Anna turned and hurried toward the sound of the voices, her boots echoing along the stone floor and off the stone walls encasing her in a narrow hallway. Torches lit the way periodically, but there were long gaps of darkness in between.

She let out a huge sigh of relief as Finn came into view. She was sitting on the floor, and Kai was with her.

She still clutched his hand as he lay unconscious, sprawled out just like he'd been in the bed. A woman was standing at their backs.

Finn blinked up at Anna's approach, but she seemed unable to focus, so Anna turned her attention to the extra woman, suddenly recognizing her long red hair and pinkish, freckled skin.

"Branwen?" she questioned, utterly shocked to see the woman alive.

Branwen didn't seem at all surprised. "It's good to see you again," she said, her gaze on Anna. Her tawny hair hung limp and matted around her gaunt face, and she wore a white, shapeless gown, but she otherwise seemed just like the naive girl Anna and Kai had tricked into funding their travels.

Branwen turned her gaze away from Anna and down to Finn, who finally seemed to be regaining her senses. "I never expected to see you here," she said happily.

Finn stared over her shoulder at Branwen in awe, but she seemed reluctant to stand and let go of Kai's hand. "Where are we?" she asked instead.

Anna observed the wide, stony corridor around them, and suddenly it dawned on her. They were in the gray place. She'd traveled these halls when the Ceàrdaman had put her in a trance to find the Archtree. Yet, she'd only walked these corridors in her mind. This time, she felt like she was fully there, not walking through a hazy dream.

"We're in the in between," Anna explained. "The gray."

Branwen pursed her lips in thought. "Yes, I suppose that's a fitting name for it." She turned her body to fully face Anna, revealing a large crimson stain on the side of her dress, near her abdomen.

"You're injured!" Finn exclaimed, seeing the stain at the same time as Anna.

Branwen shrugged. "I've been this way for quite some time now."

Finn finally released Kai's hand and stood, then went to Branwen. "I don't understand," she gasped, holding out her hands as if she could somehow help her.

Anna moved to take Finn's place beside Kai. His chest still rose and fell with breath, but his hand was icy cold. "This is the place I see in my dreams," Anna explained, her gaze remaining on Kai. "I don't know how to explain it, other than to call it the in between. It's the place between reality and fantasy, the living and the dead. How we arrived here is anyone's guess."

"*You* brought us," Finn accused. "The Travelers told me you're the Gray Lady of Clan Liath. This place is in your blood."

Anna craned her neck to roll her eyes at Finn. "Don't be absurd. I simply see things that should not be seen. I don't have true magic."

Kai started muttering again in his sleep, and Finn hurried to his other side, taking his free hand as she knelt. "How are we supposed to help him now? We can't even give him water if he needs it!"

Anna bit back her tears. Had she really somehow

transported them all to this place? It didn't seem possible. It had to be Finn. It was Finn's fault Kai would lose his life in this place.

Kai's breathing became ragged and all of Anna's thoughts rushed away. Her best friend was about to die. She felt like she couldn't breathe. The air she sucked into her lungs was dense and moist . . . wait, was that fog? Her eyes searched the expansive corridor, now slowly filling up with moist, white, bog-like mist

Finn and Branwen seemed to notice the mist too as it thickened. Anna felt compelled to keep silent, and it seemed her conscious companions did as well. Something about this mist was oddly familiar, and all she could think was, *danger*.

Movement caught her eye further down the corridor, a cloaked shape. It moved toward them, gliding smoothly as if its feet didn't touch the ground, but as it neared, Anna could see that it actually walked, just gracefully. Feminine hips outlined beneath the thin black fabric of the cloak swayed with every step.

Anna watched awestruck, unable to move, until the cloaked figure reached them. The figure removed its hood, revealing a face startlingly similar to Finn's, except her hair was dark, her eyes blue, and her features perhaps a touch more angular. Anna also had a sense of great age. She knew Finn was technically centuries old, but this woman before them somehow felt *ancient*.

"Did you bring us here?" Finn squeaked, her words seeming to pull Anna out of her trance.

She moved her gaze to Finn, who seemed frightened, but at the same time, angry.

The woman, Finn's mother Anna assumed, chuckled. "The Gray Lady brought you here. I saw an opportunity to speak with you, and I took it."

Finn's face crumbled into confused lines, then she slowly seemed to grasp what the woman was saying. "I've been to the in between before, haven't I? That's how we were able to speak on the island."

Finn's mother nodded. "The Archtree's presence made the barriers between the worlds thin. It allowed me to make contact without physically being in the same place as you."

"I think I understand," replied Finn, though Anna couldn't say she agreed. Finn's mother claimed Anna had brought them all to this place. It couldn't be possible, could it?

As if reading her thoughts, Finn's mother turned her cool gaze to Anna. "The seasons are changing," she explained. "The barriers grow thin all across the land. The old bloods are returning. The Cavari, the Faie, and the elder clans, one of which is Clan Liath. Their blood runs strong through your veins. Magic is returning to the earth. It is returning to *you*."

"It cannot return if I never had it to begin with," she snapped, suddenly defensive.

Finn's mother chuckled. "You'll see in time. You are not the only one reconnecting with the power that should have been your birthright."

Birthright? Anna wanted to ask her more, but Kai's hand spasmed around hers, drawing her attention away.

"His blood has been poisoned," Finn's mother explained. "He will die."

"No," Finn argued, shaking her head over and over. "He cannot, I will not allow it. I will not lose another friend."

"You wish to save him?" her mother asked.

"She does!" Anna interrupted. "Can you help us?"

Finn's mother smirked, then turned her gaze back to Finn. "You truly have forgotten much, much I am loath to remind you of, but I will tell you this. Immortal blood runs through your veins. Share it with him, and he will be changed. He will not live forever, but he will be stronger than he once was, able to fight the poison within him."

"How do I do it?" Finn asked frantically, staring down at Kai's sickly face.

Something like hope blossomed in Anna's chest.

"There are consequences to changing the natural order," her mother warned.

"I do not care," Finn replied. "How do I do it?"

"Cut your hand and his, place the wounds together," she explained, taking a step forward. "This can only be done if you are entirely willing to share a portion of your immortality. If you do not truly mean what you say, it will not work."

Anna searched her belt and found that both her daggers still rested there. She had not noticed them until then. She withdrew one, and hurriedly offered it to Finn, but Finn presented her palm instead. "Help me," she urged. "We will save him together."

Anna had never felt any love for Finn, but she would have kissed her right in that moment if Kai wasn't slowly fading away between them. So instead of kissing her with her lips, she did it with her dagger, slowly drawing it across Finn's open palm. She then took Kai's hand that she'd been holding and spread it out, then sliced his palm in the same direction.

Finn leaned across his body and intertwined her bloody fingers with his. Deeply concentrating, her eyes drifted shut.

"It may take some time," Finn's mother warned, but Finn seemed unable to hear her. She laid down beside Kai with her mouth near his shoulder, maintaining a tight grip on his hand.

Anna watched them for several moments, willing whatever Finn was doing to work, then turned her gaze back to Finn's mother. "Can you tell me how to take us back? Saving him will do little good if we are trapped in this place."

"Give it time," she explained. "You are not meant to be here, and you will eventually be pulled back. Falling asleep might help."

It was difficult for Anna to remember she was talking to Finn's mother, and not Finn, they looked so similar, but she had to remember she didn't know this woman. She needed to be cautious.

"Why did you come here?" she asked finally.

Finn's mother tilted her head. "My daughter is on a dangerous path, and there are many things she does not know. Many things she *refuses* to know. They will come to her eventually, and I would like to make amends with her before they do."

"You make it sound like she'd cause you harm," Anna observed.

"My dear," she replied, "she's quite capable of harming us *all*. It is why my clan has acted with caution. Why *all* have acted with caution. You would be well advised to do the same, Gray Lady."

With that, the mist began to gather once more, and she turned to walk away. She had almost faded from sight, when she turned to face Anna. "The exchange of life will take a large toll on her," she explained, gesturing with a nod toward Finn. "Make sure she remembers I was the one to help her. You would do well to remind her of your part as well." She turned and slowly faded from sight.

Anna's shoulders slumped in relief. She peered down at Finn and Kai. Kai's breathing had gone back to normal, and his expression was peaceful, as was Finn's. They appeared to be softly sleeping lovers, not an immortal being giving away part of her life force to a dying man.

Branwen stepped forward out of the dissipating mist, and Anna nearly screamed. She had completely forgotten the woman was even there.

She moved around Kai and Finn, then took a seat on the stone floor next to where Anna knelt. Sensing they might be there for a while yet, Anna leaned back and swooped her legs around into a more comfortable position.

"Will you be able to come with us when we leave this place?" she asked, still wondering at Branwen's presence.

Branwen shook her head, tossing her matted hair about. "No. The three of you have simply stepped between the realities, but you belong in the one you left. I am trapped between the living and the dead. I'm here, but I'm not really here. I think-" she cut herself off, as if deciding just what to say. "I think if someone were to save my body, I would go back. Or if I were to finally die in full, I would move on to somewhere else."

"I apologize," Anna replied with a sigh. "I can't help but feel I'm the reason you're in this state. I'm the reason you first entered the Blood Forest, and ended up here."

Branwen smiled softly. "Do not apologize. I can sometimes catch glimpses of the world where my body is. The entire land is the Blood Forest now. I do not entirely envy your return to it. And," she hesitated, "and I feel it is somehow my fate to be here. I've seen you when you visit in your dreams sometimes, and I felt compelled to be in this very place when you arrived. Perhaps I have a purpose to serve."

Never one to believe in the guidance of the old gods, Anna frowned. She could not think it fate that her life seemed to be interwoven with Finn's, and even Kai's and

Branwen's. It was merely bad luck, or good luck, however you chose to look at it.

Anna stared down at Kai and Finn. It seemed they all might live, but for how long? And at what cost? Finn's blood was now running through Kai's veins, at least in part. That alone couldn't be good.

"I still apologize," Anna said finally, looking to Branwen. "I'd much rather be around to fight, even if the odds are not in my favor. I'd rather live, than wait around to die."

"Well I hope you do," Branwen replied. She glanced down at Kai and Finn. "I hope you *all* do, and I hope that if you see my brother, you will tell him to do the same. He always was a bit lost without me."

Anna nodded, letting Branwen's words slowly sink in. She'd always been a loner, depending on no one, while no one depended on her, but perhaps Anders was not the only one who was lost without the person most important to him. Perhaps she had depended on Kai from the start, even if she had never been willing to admit it.

At some point she drifted off to sleep, and when she woke, she was back in her chair at the inn. The curtained window was still dark, and the candles and fire in the room all burned as if they'd never gone out. Finn sat across from her, asleep in her chair, and Kai rested peacefully in the bed.

For a moment Anna thought perhaps it had all been a dream, so she stood and did the only thing she could think to do. She checked both Kai and Finn's hands. Each held a shiny new scar, the only remaining remnant of the strangest night of Anna's life.

~

BEDELIA TOSSED and turned in her bed, reliving the events of the previous night at the abandoned castle. Oddly, it had affected her more than the battle with the assassins, mainly because she thought it might soon put an end to her friendship with Finn. She'd aroused Iseult's suspicions. It was the beginning of the end.

She wasn't dense enough to believe that Iseult and Finn had been discussing anything but her when she'd found them outside, whispering in the dark. The whispers had abruptly ceased at her appearance, and Iseult had given her a look that said, *I know what you're up to, and soon everyone else will too.*

She turned on her side and pressed a lumpy pillow over her head. Perhaps she was worrying for nothing. Sure, he was suspicious, but there was no way for him to know she worked for Keiren, and he likely didn't even know Keiren still lived, if he even knew of her existence at all.

Bedelia didn't know why she cared. She did work for Keiren, and she'd have to do her bidding one way or another. Her friendship with Finn would most definitely end at that point. Previously, she would have been fine with the idea of being cast back into Keiren's waiting arms, but she truly believed those arms no longer waited for her. Keiren had stopped loving her for some reason, or perhaps she never really did to begin with. Perhaps she had been Keiren's puppet all along.

"Of course I loved you," a voice cut through her mind.

"K-keiren?" Bedelia stammered. Had she been listening to her thoughts all this time?

"Do not speak out loud," Keiren's voice snapped. "You know I am not truly there. Something still prevents me from seeing your *friend*."

Bedelia took a shaky breath and sealed her eyes tightly shut. *You can read my mind?* she thought.

"Of course I can," Keiren's voice echoed back. "You swore a blood oath to me. You are *mine*."

"Then you-" she cut herself off, realizing she was speaking out loud again, but it seemed she had said enough.

"Of course I knew," Keiren replied. "I know how you have questioned me. How you have wondered if you could *save* your friend from me. I didn't stop loving you. *You* stopped loving *me*."

*I did not*, Bedelia thought. *I have always obeyed you. Even when I felt morally opposed to my tasks.*

"You simply didn't want to be alone," Keiren accused. "And now you think the girl can replace me. Just like my father thought she could replace me. It doesn't matter now. You have betrayed me."

Bedelia's heart plummeted, but for the first time, the sinking feeling was answered not with despair, but with anger. She had devoted so much of her life to Keiren, only to be spurned for wanting a friend.

"Ah," Keiren's voice mused. "So you still have teeth after all?"

*I do,* Bedelia thought. *So what will you do now? Turn me into a tree like you did your own father? Then do it. I do not care anymore.*

Keiren chuckled in her mind. "Foolish girl. You will come back to me yet. When you once again wander the earth alone, you will come back to me. I'm the only person who could ever love a woman like you."

"I will never come back," Bedelia whispered out loud, though her voice cracked as she said it. "I would sooner die."

"So be it," was the only reply she received before Keiren's voice left her mind.

Bedelia knew what she needed to do. Come morning, she would tell Finn *everything*. If she was truly her friend, she would understand, and as long as she remained near Finn, Keiren could not touch her.

# CHAPTER NINE

*K*ai sat up in bed and rubbed his tired eyes. Weak daylight streamed in around the edges of the curtained window, providing enough light to see by. He flexed his right hand, the skin feeling oddly tight. He lifted his palm up in front of his face and traced a large, fresh scar with his free hand. Where on earth had that come from? He gently patted his abdomen, searching for his bandages to check on the state of his wound, but the bandages were gone. He jerked his shirt up and was met with more fresh scar tissue. How had the wound already healed? Had he been lying in that bed an entire month?

Suddenly frantic, he hopped to his feet. He'd expected to be sore, or stiff, or . . . something. Somehow he felt wonderful, as if he'd gotten a good night's rest after a hearty meal. Nearly bouncing with energy, he searched for his boots, finding them near the foot of the bed. After quickly tugging them on and straightening his clothing, he opened the door and hurried out into the hall in search of his companions. Perhaps they'd be able to explain just what had happened to him . . . though even if they couldn't, he wasn't about to complain.

His boots echoed down the narrow wooden hall, then he took the stairs two by two, leading down into the common room. His traveling companions all waited below around a large round table, eating their morning meal. Few other patrons graced the establishment, and the innkeep hunched behind the bar, looking glum.

Kai paused at the foot of the stairs as Finn lifted her gaze to him across the table. Her eyes widened in surprise, then she quickly looked down at the table, her face blushing furiously.

Narrowing his eyes in suspicion, he approached the group, gaining everyone's attention. No one spoke.

Agitated, he raked his fingers through his hair. "Can someone please assure me that I wasn't in that bed for an entire month?"

Anna craned her neck to smile up at him, though it didn't quite reach her tired, dark eyes. "Just a night," she assured, gesturing to an empty chair beside her. As he sat, she asked, "How do you feel?"

He looked down at the boiled eggs and pottage already waiting on the table for him. "I feel good, if painfully hungry." He reached for one of the peeled eggs and plopped it into his mouth.

His chewing slowed as he realized everyone was still

staring at him, especially Iseult, who was practically boring a hole through him with his gray-green eyes.

Kai swallowed, then met the angry gaze with one of his own. "Have I done something to offend you?"

Iseult stared for a moment more, shook his head, then returned his attention to his meal. Everyone else followed his example, but continued to glance at Kai warily.

He lifted the spoon from his pottage in an attempt to ignore them, then put it back down with a huff. "Could someone please explain to me what in the Horned One's name is going on? Judging by your speculative glances, you all have some notion of why I woke up fully healed from a near fatal injury."

Finn's blush burned even brighter at his words. Why was she blushing? Had they done something horrible to him in his sleep? Was there some massive price to pay for the seemingly magic healing? And what about the scar on his hand?

Finn placed her hands flat on the table, then pushed herself to standing. "Perhaps we should speak in private," she advised sheepishly.

He sighed, grabbed another egg, then stood. Finn slunk around the table, then led the way back across the common room, her back rigid. Casting a final questioning glance at Anna, he followed. His eyes remained on the stained shoulders of Finn's shirt, and her recently combed, waist-length hair as she led the way up the interior stairs. Soon they were back in the room where he had awoken, and the silence once again ensued.

Gently shutting the door behind him, he placed his hands on Finn's shoulders, then gently directed her to sit on the bed.

She obeyed, then studiously stared at her lap.

"Spit it out," he ordered, staring down at her.

She raised her eyes, her brow furrowed in sudden confusion. "Spit what out?"

"Whatever everyone is avoiding telling me," he explained, "which I'm assuming has something to do with me waking up with my wound healed, and a fresh scar on my palm."

"There is much to explain," Finn began, her gaze returning to her lap, "but to put it quite simply, I mixed my immortal blood with your mortal blood, thus giving you a fraction of my life force." She met his eyes briefly, then quickly added, "I had little choice, you were about to die."

Stunned, he sat down on the bed beside her, holding his palm open to stare at the new scar. Finn held out her own hand, revealing a matching mark.

He stared at their hands side by side. "I'm afraid I cannot quite comprehend what you're telling me."

"Does it matter?" she asked, her expression pleading. "You are alive and well now."

He closed his hand and rested it in his lap, then turned to fully meet her worried gaze. "I'm not sure what

I should say, or what I should *ask*, but I suppose I should start with thanking you."

Her shoulders slumped in relief. He had a feeling there was much she wasn't telling him, but he'd get it out of her once she was ready. For the time being, he could only think of two important questions.

"Will this change anything for me?" he asked, "Having a bit of your . . . *immortal* blood?" It was odd to even think of Finn as an immortal being. Rationally he knew she was hundreds of years old, but just being with her, he simply couldn't fathom it.

"I do not know," she breathed, gazing distantly at the cold fireplace. "I apologize."

He nodded, not as worried about that answer as he was about the next one.

He took a deep breath. "Will this change anything for *you*?"

Her shoulders gave a slight jump, as if he'd surprised her. She turned wide eyes to him, her jaw slightly agape. He had the urge to lift his hand to gently close it, but resisted.

She blinked several times, considering her answer. "I feel the same as I always have, but I'm not sure, really. I believe," she hesitated, "I believe there will be consequences, but only time will tell what those consequences might be."

He nodded again, then decided not to resist his next urge. He took her scarred hand in his and gently traced the mark she'd incurred for him. She had resumed looking at her lap, and he finally had to use his free hand to turn her face to him. She still seemed to think he was going to react badly.

He smiled to reassure her. "My thanks, dear lady."

She shook her head. "Don't thank me. You may still curse me yet."

He laughed. "I have cursed you several times already. It doesn't seem to have worked."

Finally she smiled. "And I you. Perhaps I'm to blame for your poor luck."

"Whatever do you mean?" he joked. "It's not every day a man gets to fight assassins and live."

She laughed as he stood, then pulled her up off the bed with their joined hands. "We should probably pack up and move on before said assassins come and stab me all over again. I don't want to push my luck with requiring your blood a second time."

She grinned mischievously. "A wise choice, as I'd be loath to give it to you again."

He playfully glared at her, and she tugged her hand free to shove his shoulder.

Together they left the room and went back downstairs to join the others. He was still horribly confused, but there was one thing he now knew for sure. Finn cared whether he lived or died, and that was worth all of the *consequences* in the world.

~

WHILE KAI and Finn discussed things *privately,* Iseult left the common room to tend the horses. He'd watched over them most of the night, only briefly relieved by Sativola, who seemed to not have suffered any of the negative reactions to his wounds as Kai.

It had been nearly morning by the time Sativola relieved him, and he'd gone upstairs to find Finn asleep in a chair in Kai's room. He'd carried her to her own room, at which time she'd woken and detailed all she had experienced.

He trusted none of it. Finn believed the woman she'd encountered was her mother, but without her memories, there was no way to know for sure. The woman had previously admitted she traveled with the Cavari, and the Cavari were after Finn.

He stroked his horse's soft muzzle as it shifted its hooves, clearly ready to get back on the road. So was he. He'd never remained in one place for long. As long as he kept moving, he felt like the ghosts of the past would never find him. A chill crept up his spine.

Now they had more reasons to keep moving than ghosts. Though Finn had easily bested the assassins, he suspected they might still follow and try again. Slàine did not seem the type to give up, and neither did Maarav.

He frowned, realizing he half-wished Maarav *would* follow. Here he had been ready to be rid of his brother, and now he found he almost missed him. *Almost.*

It made sense, he supposed. The idea of family had always appealed to him, but it was something he'd hardly known. He didn't know what to do with the emotions it elicited.

He was saved from his own thoughts by Bedelia, the companion he questioned even more than Maarav. Her muddy brown hair, styled unusually short for a woman, framed the grim line of her mouth and her determined eyes.

He turned to face her, noting that her bow was nowhere in sight, and her hands were relaxed at her sides, not poised near the pommel of her blade.

"I have something I must tell you," she said upon reaching him, brushing her pin-straight hair behind her ear. She wore her lightweight armor, and had her belongings slung across her shoulder, as if preparing to leave . . . though that did not make sense without her bow. Perhaps she wanted to project an air of harmlessness. He knew better.

Leaning back against the wooden poles of the stable, he gestured for her to continue.

She sighed. "This would be easier if you wouldn't eye me so coolly."

He crossed his arms. "It is the only way I know how to . . . *eye.*"

Her shoulders slumped as she looked down at her feet, then seemed to force herself to meet his gaze. She eyed him defiantly. "I wanted to say this to Finn, but I fear I am not brave enough. I know you and she are close, so I hoped you could be the judge. Tell me whether I should tell *her*, or tell me to leave."

He nodded for her to go on, hiding his surprise. He knew she was hiding something, but had never suspected she'd so easily divulge her secrets.

She opened her mouth to speak, then turned her gaze as the inn door opened. Anna and Sativola hurried toward them.

"An Fiach is near," Anna huffed. "We must depart immediately."

"How do you know?" Bedelia gasped.

Anna glared at her, then turned her gaze to Iseult. "I just *know*," she hissed. Her eyes urged him to comprehend what was unsaid. She must have experienced one of her visions. "We must leave," she pressed. "Please trust me."

Iseult found that against his better judgement, he did trust her. He knew she could see things others could not, and her goals were currently aligned with his. If Anna said they needed to depart, then it was wise to listen.

"Ready the horses," he ordered, his gaze on Anna and Sativola.

"But-" Bedelia began to interrupt, but he cut her off with the raise of his hand.

"You come with me," he instructed. "We'll help the others gather our supplies, then we will depart."

Bedelia's shoulders hunched, but she nodded and followed him toward the inn, while Anna and Sativola branched off toward the horses. Iseult would get everyone moving, then he'd aid them with the saddling.

Like an angry storm, he burst through the inn's

double doors to find Finn and Kai frantically speaking with the innkeep. Anna had obviously already alerted them. Good.

He turned toward Bedelia. "Gather your weapons and check the rooms. Then return to aid Anna and Sativola with the horses."

She nodded and rushed off toward the interior stairs. While it was against his better judgement to let her out of his sight, time was short, and he'd just keep Finn in his sights instead.

He approached the pair arguing with the innkeep, just as the stout, round-bellied man waved them off.

Finn turned to him first, while Kai watched the man walk off with a scowl.

"He won't allow us to purchase any extra supplies," Finn huffed.

"We'll make do," Iseult replied. "Anna and Sativola are readying the horses. Gather your belongings."

Finally turning to join the conversation, Kai gestured at a few satchels and bundled cloaks piled against the lower portion of the bar. "Already done. Anna seemed to think we don't have much time."

Iseult's shoulders relaxed. It was . . . *pleasant* to travel with competent companions. "Let us depart then."

Thundering footsteps above them announced Bedelia a moment before she appeared on the stairs, her cloak flowing behind her shoulders. Her satchels were still slung across one shoulder, along with her bow and quiver. Her sword hilt poked up over her opposite shoulder, the silver knob on its pommel matching the dagger at her waist.

She really was a dangerous creature, one Iseult could stand to be more wary of. Looking at her brimming with weapons, he desperately wanted to know whatever she had nearly divulged to him, but it would have to wait. Nodding in her direction, he turned and ushered Kai and Finn toward the door.

To evade An Fiach, they would need to ride away from the main road, near the area where the Blood Forest had initially resided. He had no idea what they might find there, but hopefully it was something less deadly than a meeting with An Fiach.

KAI'S HORSE danced beneath him. He kept a firm hold on his reins, else the creature was likely to bolt. Everything had happened so quickly. From Anna announcing An Fiach was on its way, to the thundering of approaching horses, to their narrow escape down a back street of the small burgh. They could only hope the remaining townsfolk would not give them away too quickly, and it would take An Fiach time to pick up their trail. If they kept moving, and perhaps found a few streams to cross, they might just escape.

Finn glanced warily around at their expansive, rocky surroundings from her perch behind Iseult in the saddle. Kai knew if they continued on in the same direction, they would reach a more densely forested region, cut in half by a wide river. Following that river upstream would eventually lead to the old border of the Blood Forest. Fortunately, they would turn south well before they reached that point, as long as An Fiach didn't follow them too far into the wilds.

He sighed and scanned their surroundings, giving his horse's reins another tug. The yellow grass swayed in the breeze, growing sparse around black, scraggly trees and large clusters of rocks. The rocky terrain would likely make tracking them almost as difficult as a large stream bed would, but he still could not help his nerves.

He patted his heels against his horse's sides, urging it forward. Continuing in that direction, they'd reach a large valley. If they instead moved south, there was no saying what they might find. The area was densely forested.

Anna, Sativola, and Bedelia followed his lead. He glanced back toward Iseult and Finn, just as Iseult hissed, "Halt!"

Trusting Iseult's judgement, Kai instantly obeyed. A moment later, he realized what had caused the alarm. They were approaching the entrance to a wide canyon, bordered by rolling hills on either side. In the distance was a rocky escarpment, dotted along its top edge with the silhouettes of riders. He hadn't noticed them at first with the odd angle of the sun. It was only as the clouds shifted that the riders became visible. They'd chosen their position wisely. Any looking toward them would have been staring straight into the bright sun, while the riders had it at their back.

It was clear by the riders' stances they had not yet seen his party. They all peered outward across the ravine, as if expecting someone from the North, while their party approached from the West.

Silently, Kai followed Anna's example and turned his horse around, slowly retreating to where the hills of the valley would conceal them. Once being sighted was no longer a danger, they trotted their horses toward the distant tree line. Once there, they gathered in a small circle.

"Not An Fiach," Iseult muttered.

"Nor assassins dressed in black," Anna added.

"Their armor seemed strange, didn't it?" Finn cut in. "It was difficult to see, but their helmets appeared oddly shaped."

Kai nodded. "I can't help but wonder . . . " he trailed off, allowing his gaze to linger on Finn.

"The alleged Faie Queen?" she gasped, suddenly catching on to his meaning.

The Merrow girl in Ainfean had said someone claiming to be the Faie Queen was forcing the Faie to rally toward her cause. Could the riders they'd just seen have been something less than human? Indeed, they had seemed otherworldly, standing perfectly still in a straight line, elongated helmets glinting dully in the sun.

Everyone turned their gazes to Anna.

"I can't see everything!" she snapped. "My thoughts

feel . . . jumbled. Like there's too much energy around for me to decipher."

Sativola nodded thoughtfully, though he knew very little of Anna's visions..

Anna turned her glare to him. "Don't pretend to know what's going on," she growled.

Sativola frowned. "Finn can melt men's flesh and call the earth up to do her bidding, and either ye or she brought Kai back from the dead. I don't need to know just what's going on to accept that I'm out of my depth, and to accept that ye can somehow see the future, or something like it."

Anna's glare was softened by shock, then the barest hint of a smile. "I knew there was a reason I hired you," she mused.

"We should move on," Iseult interrupted. "It does not matter who the riders are, we already know of many who pursue us. We'll keep to the trees and make for Garenoch."

They moved on, but the conversation continued.

"What's this about a Faie Queen?" Sativola whispered, leaning toward Kai as they rode. "Didn't the death of the last queen happen centuries ago?"

Kai nodded. "It may just be a rumor, and if it's not, it's just another concern on the long list of many. Perhaps this new *queen* is responsible for what happened in Migris. Anna believes someone powerful was controlling the Faie who attacked there."

"Well then I'd say this Faie Queen is *everyone's* concern," Sativola countered. "And a primary one at that."

Kai nodded, deep in thought. Iseult and Bedelia both rode silently ahead, ignoring them, though Finn was glancing over her shoulder from her perch behind Iseult, observing his and Sativola's conversation.

"I believe the Faie Queen is a concern of ours as well," she said finally. "She may not know of us, or have her sights set on our demise, but she likely seeks what we seek."

Iseult lowered his arm and subtly squeezed near Finn's elbow. Kai only caught the movement because he was looking right at her, but he would have done it himself had he been closer. Neither Bedelia nor Sativola knew exactly where they were going, and what they hoped to find there, and it was best to keep it that way.

As far as Kai knew, none of them knew just what mystical powers the Faie Queen's shroud held, but it was rumored to be a uniting factor amongst the Faie. If the rumors were true, the simple piece of cloth could make its owner the most powerful ruler in the land. Powerful enough to wipe out entire cities with a thought. Powerful enough to defeat not only the armies of the great cities, but the Ceàrdaman, the Reivers, and even Finn's people, the Dair . . . unless the Faie Queen herself was of the Dair.

Kai shook his head. Perhaps if all remaining factions banded together, they might stand a chance, but old hatreds and fears lived on, ready to conquer any shreds of bravery or common sense that might stand in the way. If this Faie Queen truly existed, and managed to obtain the shroud, they were quite likely doomed.

ÓENGUS TUGGED at the leather cord in his gloved hand. The creature at the other end fought him, but eventually lost ground and was yanked back into submission. He looped the cord around the pommel of his horse's saddle, then scowled down at the beast, which had once again pressed its sharp beak, held shut with another leather cord, to the ground. It went half mad when it caught certain scents, ruffling its sparse white feathers while trying to spread its wings, also tied down with cords. Its talons scratched at the rocky ground as it once again tried to pull itself forward.

Óengus' men eyed the creature warily, occasionally shifting their gazes to *him*, then quickly looking away. They would have killed the creature, had he not intervened. He would have killed it himself, had he not been informed that it belonged to a woman with long, dirty blonde hair, riding with a man who fit Kai's description. He had little doubt the scent the creature so dutifully followed belonged to Finn. Though the reports had claimed she was on horseback, the creature seemed quite intent to follow a certain path.

Óengus knew an opportunity when it bit him on the nose, much like the creature would likely do if he unbound its beak. For now, he would allow it to lead them to Finn. Perhaps upon finding her, the creature would then prove a useful bargaining tool.

His horse danced beneath him, and he turned as the rest of his men approached, finished scouring the small burgh for signs of their quarry. Óengus knew in his gut they had already escaped, but it would not do to leave any evidence ungathered.

Over their shoulders the men carried sacks of supplies, and led a few new horses, likely stolen and not paid for. Military men always seemed to think lowly townsfolk *owed* them something.

Óengus sneered, then gave the creature another tug. He would be glad to be rid of them all soon.

Giving his men the signal that it was time to move on, he slackened the tension on the creature's restraints. With a squeal, muffled by its closed beak, it took off at a scurrying run. His horse galloped after it, followed by the thundering hoofbeats of his men.

He knew he was close to locating Finn, and not Iseult, nor the Faie, would stand in the way of his success. There was too much at stake.

AN ENTIRE ARMY of Faie would have been less frightening than the past three days for Anders. Finally, Niklas had declared it time to depart, after he'd had his fill of fine food and vintage wine.

Now, Anders' mother eyed him sternly. She looked just how he imagined Branwen would if she ever made it to her mother's current age. Her tawny hair had strands of gray at the temples, but her honey brown eyes were just as clear and alert as ever.

"And you'll be bringing your sister back next time you come home?" she asked for the hundredth time.

"Yes mother," he sighed. "I assure you, I will not come home again without her."

"You shouldn't have come home without her at all," she said, also for the hundredth time. "I cannot believe you'd leave her alone in some unprotected burgh to the North."

"She's *fine*," he lied. As far as he knew, her wounded body *was* somewhere up North. Whether or not she was in a burgh, he did not know.

His father had already gone about his work, leaving only Anders' mother to see him off. It was just as well. He was once again facing the idea of never seeing either of them again. It was easier just to say goodbye to one. The *meaner* one.

He gave his mother a light kiss on the cheek, then turned to go with Niklas at his side. The gates were opened for them, and soon enough they were back on the road. He was glad to at least have fresh supplies. Niklas would not be able to starve him like he had before. Though, judging by how much the Traveler could eat in one sitting, he would not be surprised if their supplies did not last long.

"So where is Branwen?" Anders asked as they walked back in the same direction they'd come. "I've fulfilled my end of the bargain, now it's time to fulfill yours."

"In time," was all Niklas said in reply.

Anders frowned, thinking of the red-haired woman they'd met in the high wing of the Archive. Niklas had planned a meeting with her, but surely he didn't expect Anders to come.

He glanced at his companion, noting his eerie smile on skin suddenly returned to ghostly pale. He knew the Travelers always kept their deals, but often not in the way one might hope. He was a fool to trust Niklas at all, but what else could he have done?

Sighing, he turned his gaze to the long road ahead. He was a victim of circumstance, caught up in a game he could not escape. He had never really believed in fate, but only an overpowering force like destiny could put a man's life in such horrible shambles. His father had always told him destiny was a cruel mistress. His father was a wise man.

CHAPTER TEN

*B*edelia chewed her lip, unable to deny her body the small expression of anxiety. She had been prepared to divulge *everything* to Iseult. To let him be her judge, and perhaps her executioner. Then they'd had to leave Badenmar so quickly she hadn't the chance to explain herself.

Now he eyed her warily, clearly desiring a moment to speak alone. While she was grateful he hadn't forced her to speak in front of their entire group, the prolonged tension was making her ill. She was more frightened of telling Finn the truth than she was of Keiren, Óengus, and all of the Faie combined, but she refused to cower from her punishment. If Iseult did not kill her, Keiren would. She knew her fate. The least she could do was die with honor.

She glanced at Iseult and Finn. Finn was slumped forward against Iseult's back, fast asleep. She must have been exhausted from whatever she'd done to heal Kai. Those details, however, would likely never be explained once they'd discovered her dastardly truth.

"I believe it's safe to stop now," Anna groaned. "Surely An Fiach will not be able to track us all this way over such rocky terrain."

Bedelia was not sure about that, but stopping sounded nice. It was only late midday, but they'd been traveling since morning. Her legs felt stiff, her back was sore, and she knew the others must have been feeling the same, especially Sativola, who hadn't undergone any miraculous healing like Kai.

Without a word, Iseult drew his horse to a halt and dismounted, then helped a sleepy Finn down from the saddle behind him, taking her effortlessly in his arms before walking a few paces and setting her down on the stump of a massive felled tree. She rubbed at her eyes, then hunched forward, encasing her knees in the drape of her cloak.

Everyone else dismounted, but kept their horses near should a quick escape be needed. Small rations of cured lamb and dried fruit were passed around, then everyone settled in on the rocky ground to rest their weary bones.

Bedelia avoided eye contact with Iseult, hoping he would not choose this moment to pull her aside. All she wanted in that moment was to be *still*, to rest her arms and legs, and fill her belly. Setting her remaining portion of fruit on the leg of her breeches, she lifted her arms over her head to stretch, keeping the end of Rada's reins in one palm, though the animal was not likely to run off.

With a sigh, she began to lower her arms, then searing pain shot through her shoulder. Finn screamed and jumped up from her stump to rush toward her, but Iseult intercepted her and shielded her with his body.

Feeling dumbstruck as everyone drew their weapons, Bedelia looked down at her shoulder to see the shiny tip of an arrow protruding through the cloth of her tunic, which slowly became saturated with blood.

FINN SCREAMED as another arrow cut through the air, narrowly missing her chest as Iseult spun her aside. Had An Fiach found them so soon? She caught brief glimpses of figures surrounding them, bows and weapons raised. She clung to Iseult's arm around her waist, half wanting to fight against him to aid Bedelia, and half wanting to remain near him where she felt safe.

She whipped her head from side to side, trying to keep all of their attackers within sight. Their foe slowly closed in around them, revealing themselves to be not An Fiach, but the oddly armored riders they'd seen near the valley.

Their helmets were made of dull silver metal, curving upward artfully like symmetrical ocean waves away from delicate-boned faces. Their body armor was composed of plates of the same type of metal, with overlapping points like the scales of a spined lizard. One stepped forward from the rest, his narrow eyes intent on Finn. He lifted his odd helmet from his head, revealing large, pointed ears, and black hair like spider silk. His skin was as pale and smooth as a freshly made snowbank.

He knelt and bowed his head, obscuring his face with his silken hair. "Forgive me. I did not realize we were attacking one of the Dair until it was too late."

Finn pulled away from Iseult, her hand raised to her mouth in surprise. Bedelia hobbled to Finn's other side, arrow still protruding from her shoulder.

"Who are you?" Finn asked, hoping her ignorance would not incite further attack. They'd only fired a few arrows so far, but had ceased as soon as they'd gotten close.

The man before her stood, bracing his helmet beneath one armored arm. His eyes were a deep blue, reminding Finn of the sea right before a storm hit. "I am Eywen, and we are the Aos Sí," he explained. "You have trespassed on our lands, a penalty punishable by death, but we did not realize one of the Dair would travel with," he hesitated, glancing around at the rest of her party, "*humans*."

"Who is your leader?" Iseult asked, but the Aos Sí simply glanced at him, then turned his gaze back to Finn.

"The Faie Queen demands that any Dair who cross our lands be brought before her," he continued. "Forgive me, the Aos Sí know better than to anger your people, but we must insist."

She did her best not to balk at him. Just like the Merrow girl in Ainfean, this man had known she was one of the Dair on sight. And now he wanted to bring her to the Faie Queen? Was she one of the Dair as well, as the Merrow girl had suggested?

She shook her thoughts away. "And what of my companions?" she asked, glancing warily around at the rest of the Aos Sí surrounding them. She supposed they were some sort of Faie, though they looked far more human than most, except perhaps the Merrows. Though she wanted to know more about them, firstly she had to keep her companions safe. Bedelia was barely standing and would need treatment soon.

Eywen's deep blue eyes flicked to Iseult, looking him up and down as if assessing the threat he might pose. "They may accompany you, of course," he agreed with a small bow. "We have made a grave mistake in injuring one of your companions. Please, allow us to tend her wounds."

Bedelia gave Finn a terrified look, but when two more of the Aos Sí stepped forward, she allowed them to examine the arrow.

Finn was startled as she glanced behind her. At some point, without drawing her notice, Kai, Anna, and Sativola had stepped up close behind her and Iseult.

"Call me mad," Kai whispered, "but perhaps we *shouldn't* so willingly visit the Faie Queen."

Eywen shifted his gaze past Finn to Kai. His nostrils

flared, then his eyes widened in surprise. "Two of the Dair," he observed, "our offense is even greater."

Finn glanced back at Kai in confusion, then realization dawned on her. She didn't look any different from a human, so it had to be her blood or magic that made her stand apart, and she'd given a bit of both to Kai.

"Can you sense the Dair?" she asked Eywen hesitantly.

He shook his head. "I can," he cleared his throat nervously, "*smell* you, my lady. The blood of the Dair is unique indeed."

She pursed her lips in thought. So it was the blood she gave Kai that made the Aos Sí think him Dair, though perhaps the Faie Queen would see the truth.

"While I appreciate you making amends," she said politely, "we really must continue on our journey. I fear we do not have much time."

Eywen frowned. "My lady, attending the Queen is not a choice, it is a necessity, and before you inflict your wrath upon us, please be aware the Aos Sí are great in number. Kill us all, and there will simply be more to replace us."

Finn opened her mouth to argue, but no words came to her.

"We should probably just go with them," Kai whispered, glancing around at the armed soldiers.

Bedelia made a grunt of pain as one of the Aos Sí broke the arrow, then another worked it out of her flesh, pushing the point forward until the broken end came free. Her clothing and armor had been pulled away to reveal her bare skin, which the two Aos Sí began to bandage.

Eywen glanced at Bedelia, then turned his gaze back to Finn. The other Aos Sí had taken possession of their frightened horses, and now led them forward.

"The Queen is not far," he explained, offering Finn his arm. "I will escort you. Your horses will be well tended."

Finn nodded nervously, then slipped her hand through his arm. His armor was cold beneath her touch. He began to lead her away, with her friends following close behind.

As they walked the air grew increasingly cold, and eventually, snowflakes began to fall. Her arm still resting in Eywen's, Finn looked up at the soft, fuzzy flakes drifting down. She had a feeling they would soon learn of their source. Perhaps she was not the only one who could control the natural aspects of her environment.

Faie Queen, indeed.

KAI TRIED to avoid the gazes of the Aos Sí surrounding them. One of the strange warriors supported Bedelia's weight with an arm beneath her shoulders, but the rest of them were allowed to walk unhindered . . . unless you counted Finn's arm intertwined with Eywen's.

It had started snowing not long into their walk. Though the flurries had died down, they now walked through slush made by the many sets of footprints that had gone before them. It seemed the snow in this area was not recent, and more of a permanent draping.

The icy landscape ahead was dotted with wooden barricades and more Aos Sí warriors standing at attention.

Anna had pulled her cloak over her head, and now peered at Kai from within its deep shadows. "Where could they all have come from?" she whispered softly.

His gaze flicked to their escort, quickly catching her meaning. After the Faie War, most of the creatures of myth had disappeared. All except the Ceàrdaman, who debatably weren't even of Faie blood. They were obviously back now, but where had they all been hiding? Trow he could understand, blending in with the forests, and the smaller Faie who had a tendency to fade from sight at their leisure, but the Aos Sí? They seemed close to human, just like the Ceàrdaman. Surely they could not have simply faded away like the other Faie.

Finally, Kai shook his head. "Perhaps we'll soon find out."

Anna turned her gaze down to the mucky snow beneath her boots. Sativola had remained silent at her other side, though he appeared to be seriously questioning his continued association with any of them.

They reached the first of the barricades, but did not slow. Instead, Eywen gave an elaborate hand gesture to one of his men, then continued onward down the main path. After passing several more barricades, the Aos Sí's lodgings came into view. Dotting the landscape in large clusters were small, circular wooden huts, the snow covered rooftops emitting woodsmoke through vents. Upon closer view, the entrances were draped with animal hides to keep out the cold, though some had been pulled back, revealing modest sleeping spaces and not much else.

Continuing on, some buildings were larger, but similar in structure, until at last they reached the settlement's hub. Looming there was a massive oval stone edifice with a heavy wooden door mounted in the center, and multiple guards posted on either side.

Standing before the entrance, Eywen made another hand gesture, and one of the guards turned to open the door, revealing a wide arched entrance. Eywen led Finn inside, closely followed by Iseult, then everyone else. Two more of the armored Aos Sí followed them inside, then shut the door.

Remaining alert to any signs of danger, Kai peered around their surroundings in awe. The interior of the building was deceivingly spacious, with several closed doors leading to other unknown areas. Narrow slits in the stone wall served as windows, their sparse light accompanied by countless white candles, burning in sconces on the walls and on the surface of large shelves and a massive central table.

At the table sat a woman with pure white skin and hair. Her lustrous tresses blended in with her white gown which shimmered as if encrusted with tiny clear jewels. Her features resembled those of the male and female Aos Sí at her sides, though they both had more color to them, with long, black hair like Eywen's. In fact, most of the Aos Sí they'd seen so far had dark hair, though not always pure black.

The woman blinked lilac colored eyes at them, then gestured with one white-clad arm for them to sit. "I did not expect to find any of the Dair so easily, though I see there are humans among you as well."

Kai watched as Eywen led Finn forward, then pulled out a seat for her, opposite the woman he could only assume was the Faie Queen. Then Eywen surprised him by pulling out another seat, gesturing for him to take it.

After Kai was seated, those without Dair blood were allowed to sit. Bedelia, pale and sickly looking from her wound, was assisted by one of the Aos Sí.

Moving to stand behind his seated queen, Eywen cleared his throat. "Allow me to present Oighear the White, Queen of the Faie."

Oighear smiled graciously with lips almost as white as her skin, save the barest hint of pink to distinguish them from the white teeth she subtly revealed. "I will jump straight to the heart of the matter," she explained. "Since our return, I have besought my people to search out the Dair so that we might negotiate. You are the first I have found." She gestured to both Kai and Finn.

Kai wanted to argue that he wasn't one of the Dair, but decided against it. The Aos Sí seemed to respect the

Dair, while showing mild distaste for the humans, and he preferred to remain arrow-free.

"Negotiate?" Finn asked, eyeing Oighear intently.

Oighear inclined her head. Her pure white hair slithered forward like water over her shoulders. "I would like my shroud returned to me. I am the rightful ruler of the Faie, not the Dair."

Kai watched as Finn's mouth formed an *oh* of understanding. "I fear I know little of the Dair's politics," she replied smoothly, surprising him with her tact. "As you can see, I do not travel with my clan." She gestured at her companions seated on either side of her.

Oighear frowned. "Then I must ask you to point me in the direction of your clan."

"I do not know them," Finn answered simply.

Oighear's pleasant mask fell away as if it had never existed. Underneath her calm exterior, waited a wrathful queen. "You will facilitate negotiations, or you will die," she growled. "To what clan do you belong?"

Finn seemed to think about it, then answered honestly. "The Cavari."

Oighear's eyes widened in surprise, then narrowed. "The Cavari?" she intoned. "The very clan who stole the shroud from my sleeping form?"

"Sleeping?" Finn asked. "The legend says the Faie Queen died, and the shroud was stolen from her corpse."

A chill wind swept through the room. At first Kai thought perhaps the door behind them had opened, then he realized the cold was coming from the other direction. It was coming from Oighear.

"You know very well that we fell into a long slumber when magic fled from the land," Oighear growled. "The Dair survived it longer than most and took my shroud, but just because we were resting, does not mean we were unaware."

Finn seemed to be deep in thought, not outwardly showing any of the worry Kai was acutely experiencing in that moment. "I remember something of this . . . " she muttered, her words gently trailing off.

Oighear eyed her suspiciously. "What is your name?"

Finn didn't seem to hear her.

"Her name is not important," Iseult answered.

"Do not speak to the Queen, human," Eywen warned.

Finn gasped, then refocused on the situation at hand. "I remember you," she marveled. "Oighear the Snow Queen. Had you not been laid to rest, you would have brought eternal winter to the land."

Oighear slammed a bare, white palm against the table. "I would have brought greatness to my people," she snapped. "Unlike the Dair, who sullied themselves with the silly affairs of humans. The Dair are not fit to lead the Faie."

Finn's chair screeched across the wooden floor as she stood abruptly. "You were not a kind queen," she accused. "I would sooner burn the shroud than give it to you!"

Kai looked back and forth between the two women, completely lost as to where the conversation was going.

Finn had obviously remembered something of her previous life, and now she was going to get them all killed because of it. The Aos Sí in the room flexed their hands near their weapons, ready to defend their ruler. Kai stood and moved near Finn, ready to protect her, though Iseult had already reached her opposite side. Even Bedelia had staggered to her feet, though she seemed to be having trouble keeping them.

"Lock them away," the Queen ordered, and the Aos Sí surrounding her stepped forward. "Perhaps we'll find use for them later."

Finn raised her arms, as if to summon her magic, then her face crumbled into confused lines.

Oighear smiled wickedly. "This dwelling is warded against outside magic, my dear. I have no intention of falling prey to the Dair a second time."

The doors behind them opened, and armored Aos Sí spilled into the room, surrounding them.

"Do we fight?" Sativola whispered, standing with his back toward the queen, facing the door.

Kai felt a blast of ice against his back, and turned to see snowflakes streaming in through the doorway. He began to shiver, overwhelmed with cold. He tried to reach for his blade, but seemed unable to move his limbs. The Aos Sí circled them, somehow impervious to the cold. They aimed swords and spears inward, ready to skewer any with the power to run.

Oighear moved around the table and stood next to

her Aos Sí warriors. Laughter sparkled in her lilac eyes as they fell on Sativola's massive, shivering form.

"My dear," she purred, "*no one* fights a queen."

"WHAT A DISASTER," Maarav muttered, leaning against the wooden wall of the inn. He and Ealasaid had made it to Badenmar, hoping to perhaps plead their case to Iseult, or at the very least, to start following their party in secret, but what they'd found instead was An Fiach.

Fortunately, they'd seen signs of the large group well before they reached the small burgh, and so, had been cautious in their approach. They'd made it just in time to see the last few men depart, leaving sorrow in their wake.

Not sorrow at their passing, but sorrow at what they took. Badenmar had been robbed of its few horses, and most of its supplies. With the odd weather stunting the crops, they'd have a poor harvest as it was, and now they had few stores to last them through hard times.

While Maarav didn't make a habit out of caring about small burghs, Ealasaid was another matter.

"Sheep licking, soft bellied fiends," she hissed, kicking the dirt in front of her.

They'd just finished speaking with the innkeep to find there were no supplies left to purchase. Many of the villagers would be moving on toward Garenoch within the day in hopes of salvation, but Maarav knew their chances were grim.

Ealasaid obviously knew it too, but was not nearly as accepting of the fact.

"We have to *do* something," she grumbled, gazing across the square at the morose villagers adding up what they had left, and debating their chances of surviving through winter.

"Like what?" he asked, hoping she would soon realize how silly it was to worry. The villagers fates were all but sealed.

A grim look of determination took over her delicate face. "Like track down An Fiach and reclaim the horses and supplies."

Maarav burst out laughing, and that grim look was suddenly directed at him. Unfortunately for her, he was not one to quaver at the wrong end of any threatening look, especially not one from a lovely young lady.

"Forgive me," he continued to laugh. "While your lightning is highly impressive, I do not believe you are a match for fifty soldiers."

She lifted her freckled nose in the air. "So we're to just turn a blind eye to injustice?"

He smirked, but his expression slowly fell as he realized the source of her venom. "You know," he began soberly, "the men who raided this village are likely not the ones who destroyed yours."

She scowled at him. "You're right, since the villagers here were left alive. It still doesn't mean that *these* men should not pay for their crimes."

Maarav patted her shoulder. "Justice is best left to the

gods, lass. Let us focus on staying alive, for now."

Her ire-filled expression faltered. "Do you truly believe Slàine will come after us?"

He chuckled and leaned his back against the inn's exterior wall. "Oh I have little doubt. We will need to stay one step ahead for quite some time, and getting back into Finn's good graces couldn't hurt. I'd be a fool to believe that Slàine won't try for her again, but Finn has at least proven she can best an entire flock of assassins."

Ealasaid sighed. "You're an assassin too, aren't you," she muttered without the inclination of a question. Before he could answer, she turned and walked toward the stable where they'd left their horse tied outside of the pens.

He pushed away from the wall to catch up with her. "I was," he answered honestly. "And perhaps some day I will be again, if my coin purse grows light."

She stopped walking and narrowed her eyes at him. "How could you do something like that? Kill an innocent person?"

He laughed and continued walking, reaching their horse to untie its reins. "No one is innocent, lass. Not even you."

Ealasaid was silent for a long time after that, even as they mounted their horse and left the burgh. While Maarav had only spoken the truth, he sincerely hoped he hadn't gone too far. He'd do well to not alienate the last living person willing to stand by his side . . . though he didn't quite understand why she still did so at all.

# CHAPTER ELEVEN

*L*eaning her back against the cold stone wall, Finn reached out and stroked her fingers across the iron bars of her prison. Her magic, had she the ability to control it, would do her no good here. She remembered Oighear now, though she wished she could forget.

In the memory, she felt small, merely a child new to the world of man. She could recall a meeting.

*Many gathered around a long wooden table, darkened with age. It glistened in the candlelight, casting an eerie glow on the faces of those seated. At the table's head sat Oighear in a glittering white gown, with two of the Aos Sí standing at her back. On her spider silk tresses rested a delicate crown, bedecked with jewels as clear as rain.*

*Oighear, terrifying and beautiful, huddled in the corner,*

while several members of Finn's tribe looked over a treaty being passed around the table. All of the Cavari wore hoods to cover their features, as did some others around the table that were strangers to Finn.

The treaty reached Oighear. Instead of touching it herself, one of the Aos Sí pressed the parchment firmly against the table in front of her. She dipped a quill in ink to sign the treaty, but hesitated. "We will remain within the new borders, as promised," she began, "but I want assurances that our magic will remain unhindered. Though the earthen powers may be dwindling, there is still enough to share."

There were murmurs around the table, then a figure opposite Oighear nodded.

Oighear took a deep breath. "For the safety of my people in this war, I will do as you ask, but let me be clear. We will not remain trapped forever." She leveled her glare at each of the figures seated around the table in turn, then with a heavy sigh, signed the parchment.

The cloaked figures stood. One branched away from the group and approached Finn. She caught a glimpse of her mother's face in the shadowy depths of the hood, smiling at her. "Come Finnur," she whispered, taking Finn's small hand. "It's time to go."

FINN SIGHED, returning to the present, and the dreary confines of her cell. She felt an odd pang of heartache at the memory of her mother's touch. She ran her fingers up and down the cold bar again. She supposed she couldn't blame Oighear for imprisoning her. The Dair had betrayed her people. The treaty had been meant to bind the Faie to the land beyond the Blood Forest, but Oighear did not understand the full terms. The seasons were changing, and magic was leaving the land. She'd unintentionally cut her people off from too much, and they had faded away. Once she'd been weakened, her shroud had been stolen. The funeral shroud not of Oighear, but of her mother, the true Faie Queen.

Finn curled up in the corner of her cell, experiencing just what Oighear had felt when she was cut off from her power. Every inch of the compound seemed to be warded against her magic. She hadn't known just how much she felt her connection to the earth at all times, until it wasn't there.

Hushed voices nearing her cell drew her attention. She sat up, but remained in the shadows near the wall. A lantern came into view first, then Eywen's face. Had he come to torment her? To punish her for what her people had done to the Aos Sí?

Finn nearly jumped out of her skin as Iseult's face appeared behind Eywen. Several other forms lurked behind them in the dimly lit room.

Eywen lifted a heavy keyring, then unlocked the barred door of her cell. She looked up at him, confused, and he held a finger to his lips, then gestured for her to stand.

She did as she was bade, then hurried to Iseult's side. Now that she was close enough, she could see Kai, Anna,

Sativola, and Bedelia. She opened her mouth to ask Iseult what was happening, but like Eywen, he held a finger to his lips.

Eywen turned and led them back out of the room, shielding his lantern with his free arm. They moved single file down a narrow corridor. If it weren't for her death-grip on the back of Iseult's arm, she likely would have stumbled in the near-darkness several times.

They reached the end of the corridor and Finn tensed in alarm, then relaxed. Eywen's lantern allowed just enough light to illuminate several armored guards waiting for them, but they had all slumped to the floor. At first Finn thought they were dead, then one twitched, scaring her out of her wits. They were merely in a deep, unnatural slumber.

Finn continued down the corridor with Iseult in front of her, and Kai behind. Kai's hand remained on her shoulder, using her as his guide, much like she used Iseult. She caught dull flashes of silver armor as they passed a multitude of sleeping guards, until finally they reached an iron-barred exit. Ewyen produced an ornate key and employed it near-silently on the lock, then they emerged into the freezing night air. The moonlight was a relief, allowing Finn a broader field of vision than she'd had in the corridor. It seemed a fresh layer of snow had fallen while they were imprisoned, blanketing the night in eerie stillness.

They walked through the snow in silence. Only the sound of their boots crunching on the ice, and the occasional hoots of owls assured Finn she could still hear. She noted the lack of guards as they walked, and knew it must have been planned, along with the sleeping guards in the corridor. Did Eywen have allies, or had he managed to drug them all? She supposed it didn't matter, as long as they were awarded their freedom.

Eywen reached the stables first. He nodded in greeting to two conscious Aos Sí. Finn tensed again, but they did not attack, nor did they cart them back to their cells. Instead, they handed them the reins of fresh horses, with supplies strapped to their backs.

"Why are you letting us go?" Finn finally whispered, stepping close to Eywen. "I do not understand."

His breath fogged the air near her face as he met her questioning gaze, then pressed the reins of a white horse into her hands. "Oighear believes she can force the Dair into submission, but her pride blinds her. Many of us know better than to incur the wrath of the Cavari. I hope that when the time comes, you will show mercy to the Aos Sí, though I will not be alive to see it."

Behind him, one of the Aos Sí handed Iseult a sword, then turned to help Anna onto her nervous horse's back.

Finn began to ask why Eywen would not be alive, then realized her foolishness. Oighear would surely kill him when she realized he'd drugged her guards and released her prisoners.

"You should come with us," she whispered without thinking.

Eywen and the other two Aos Sí shook their heads.

"We have accepted our fates," Eywen explained. "All that I ask is that our deaths not be in vain. Please, show mercy for our people."

Finn nodded, fighting back tears. She clutched the horse's reins tightly in her shaking hands. "I swear to you, I will do all that I can."

A sudden breeze lifted Finn's hair from her face, stinging her cheeks with ice.

Eywen gave her hands a squeeze around the reins, then moved to help her mount. She looked hesitantly up at the graceful white horse, its mane reminding her of Oighear's hair. It wasn't the horse she and Iseult had ridden previously, but she supposed any horse was better than none.

"You must go," Eywen urged.

Without warning, he put his hands on Finn's waist and nearly threw her into the saddle. She managed to swing her leg up at the last moment, then gripped the pommel for dear life as Eywen thwapped the horse on its rump. It shot through the snow like an arrow, carrying Finn away from the stables.

Moments later, her friends caught up, their horses galloping on either side of her. The icy wind picked up, and she abruptly realized their hurry. Oighear had awakened.

A rage-filled shriek cut through the night, and suddenly she was blinded by snow, pelleting her face to the point where she could hardly breathe. She ducked low against her saddle, pressing her face near the base of her horse's neck. She had no idea if she was going in the right direction. She simply had to trust that her horse's lithe legs would carry her away from danger.

Something sliced into her arm, nearly toppling her from her mount as she cried out in agony. Hot blood welled to pour down her limb.

Tears covered her face, still pressed near her horse's mane. She couldn't lift her gaze enough to see her surroundings, but she heard no hoofbeats around her. She was alone, in a world gone entirely white.

Iseult rolled through the snow, righting himself just in time to deflect the blade of his attacker with his borrowed sword. He was fortunate that only one of the Aos Sí had managed to cut him off. The ancient warriors were highly skilled, and just as fast as he, if not faster.

He dodged another swipe of his attacker's blade, darting his eyes about for his new horse. If he'd had his own horse, it would have stuck by no matter the commotion, but this new creature clearly wasn't properly trained.

He lifted his sword against another attack, the force of which sent a painful jolt up his arm. Their blades slid across each other with a metallic *shwing*, then both opponents stepped back and squared off. Iseult steeled himself for another attack, but it somehow came from behind. Sharp pain radiated up from his lower back, bringing him to his knees. He slumped to his side in the snow and looked up at his attacker, another of the Aos Sí. The warrior had been utterly silent in his approach, catching him off guard like no man ever had.

Iseult's hot blood melted the snow beneath him, and his vision began to fade to gray. He had failed. He would never free the souls of his ancestors. He would never make amends to Finn. He had failed them all. As his life slowly left him, he thought he saw Finn's face, but the specter slowly faded, a last punishment to show him what he'd lost.

SEATED on a rock with her horse's reins looped around her arm, Anna buried her head in her hands. They'd made it out of the snow with three fresh mounts, and three less companions.

"We should wait for them," Kai growled, but Anna just shook her head. She knew there was little they could do. The sun had finally risen above them, bathing the party in bleak light through the canopy of tree branches. Though she welcomed the sun after their escape through the freezing blizzard, she was worried the rest of their companions were still trapped in Oighear's icy embrace.

"And allow the Aos Sí to find us first?" she argued tiredly, lifting her head from her hands. "Or perhaps An Fiach?"

Kai glared down at her. "You're the one who *needs*

Finn. You need her to take away your magic with the shroud."

"It won't matter if we're dead," she hissed. "We should make our way to Garenoch and await them there." Kai was right, but she feared Oighear more than she did her own curse. She wouldn't venture back into the snowy forest for all the coin in the land.

Sativola watched the scene nervously, seemingly as anxious to put distance between themselves and Oighear as Anna.

"What if they're in trouble?" Kai countered. "What if the Aos Sí recaptured them, and they're back in their cells? Eywen is likely dead now. There will be no second rescue."

Anna wasn't sure at what point they'd lost Finn, Iseult, and Bedelia, but she hoped the three had at least escaped and remained together. With Iseult by her side, Finn would make it to Garenoch. When she was close enough, Anna would be able to sense her . . . she hoped. At that moment, she saw no hint of the shine that usually emanated from Finn, often visible to her across small distances. She hoped it didn't mean she was dead.

She stood. "If they were recaptured by the Aos Sí, there is absolutely nothing we can do for them, except to be recaptured ourselves."

Kai sealed his lips in a grim line, then looked down at the scar on his palm. She knew what he was thinking, that there had to be *some* way he could rescue Finn, but Anna had always been realistic. Either Finn would meet them in Garenoch, and Anna would be saved from her visions, or she would not, and she'd be sentenced to eventual insanity.

"We should get movin'," Sativola muttered. "I'd rather not wait for those *things* to find us again."

"Yes," Anna agreed. She led her horse away from the rocks where she'd been seated, then climbed into the saddle, feeling unsure of the creature. None of them had regained their original mounts, perhaps because the new ones were more readily accessible. She'd only had her previous horse since Ainfean, but this new one, even though it seemed a normal brown horse, had her wary. Anything concerning the Aos Sí and their psychotic queen had her wary.

Kai continued to curse under his breath, but he and Sativola both mounted their horses and followed as she led the way. She had a keen sense of direction, but could only hope she was leading them back to the road after how turned around they'd gotten riding away through the snow.

While, for selfish reasons, she regretted the loss of Finn, she couldn't help taking a measure of comfort in traveling without her. Perhaps now they could travel unnoticed and unhindered by Faie, An Fiach, or anyone else.

FINN FELT ENTIRELY numb by the time her horse slowed

its frantic pace. She'd made her way out of the snow, deep into a forest. Though the sun now shone overhead with early morning light, she had no idea if she was near the Sand Road, or had traveled in the complete opposite direction. Now, she wasn't even sure of the direction of Oighear's compound. All she was sure of, was that she was alone.

She looked down at her mount's white neck as the creature calmly ambled onward. Its fur was stained with her blood. She gingerly pushed her cloak aside and rolled up her sleeve to take a look at the gash. It had stopped bleeding, but the skin gaped like an extra mouth. Knowing little about wound care, she did the only thing she could think to do, and pulled a strip of fabric from the edge of her tattered cloak. Clenching her jaw, she did her best to one-handedly wrap it around her wound, securing it in a knot with her free hand and her teeth. That task finished, she pushed her bloody sleeve back down and focused on her surroundings.

Though she'd left the snow behind, the air was almost unbearably cold. There was a bedroll tied to the back of her saddle, fortunately, but she'd yet to check its accompanying satchels for other supplies, and she had little motivation to do so. All she could think about was what might have happened to the others. If they'd been recaptured by Oighear . . .

She sighed. Even if that were the case, she had no idea how to find her way back to rescue them. *If* she was even capable of rescuing them at all. She patted her horse's neck, then stroked her fingers through its long white mane, grateful for the horse's company.

She worked her fingers further up its mane, marveling at the impossibly soft texture. Seeming to appreciate the touch, the horse stopped walking and turned its head back to look at her. Her gaze moved to the horse's forehead, and she nearly lost her seat. Right in the middle, its base covered by white strands of mane, was a glistening white horn. The creature looked at her askance with a crystalline blue eye, as if daring her to question its existence.

Finn stared back at the unicorn in shock. Her scant, previous memories let her know unicorns were exceedingly rare. They had been hunted to near extinction, and the remaining few creatures had faded along with the Aos Sí and other Faie. Why would the Aos Sí give up such a precious creature?

Eywen's plea rang through her mind, to have mercy when the time came. Was the gift of the unicorn an effort to gain the Dair's favor? She felt oddly guilty, since she had little to do with the Dair, and knew she would not likely sway any judgement passed upon the Aos Sí, unicorn or no.

"We should probably keep moving," she instructed, not expecting the creature to understand her, but at the same time, feeling odd about nudging such a majestic beast with her heels like she would a common horse.

The unicorn turned its head forward and started walking again without further prodding.

"Can you understand me?" Finn gasped.

The unicorn did not reply, and simply kept walking, so Finn passed off its obedience as a coincidence. Her injured arm was throbbing and she didn't know whether her friends were living or dead. It didn't matter whether or not a unicorn could understand her.

The unicorn carried her onward as the sun slowly made its progress across the clear sky. She allowed the creature full rein, hoping it would not lead her back to Oighear, while secretly wishing it would, if only to make sure her friends were not recaptured.

Eventually Finn sorted through the satchels secured on either side of the bedroll to find several day's worth of food, a fire striker, two full waterskins, and a dagger. When she pulled out her first portion of food, a crumbly bannock wrapped in thin cloth, a small coin purse was revealed. Stuffing the bannock greedily into her mouth, she withdrew the purse to examine it. Inside were several coins, and a small blue stone. She held the stone up to the waning sunlight, marveling at its clarity, then quickly stuffed it back in the purse just as the unicorn halted.

She glanced around through the trees. In the distance was a yellow meadow, just visible through the needles bedecking the heavy boughs. She turned her gaze back to the unicorn. "Are we done traveling for the day then?"

The unicorn did not reply.

With a heavy sigh, Finn climbed down from the saddle, then nearly lost her footing on the damp soil below. Her legs felt like the bones within had turned to mush, and could not properly support her. She hobbled to a nearby tree and leaned against it.

To her surprise, the unicorn followed her, then gently nuzzled against her chest. Its horn hovered perilously close to her face, but she somehow trusted the creature not to harm her. She lifted her uninjured arm to stroke its cheek, once again taking comfort in the unicorns's presence.

"What do you say we build a fire so we don't freeze?" Finn asked.

The unicorn simply stared at her, then turned so she could reach the satchels on its rump.

"*Can* you understand me?" she asked as she searched the satchel for the fire striker.

The unicorn did not reply, and instead began inspecting the sparse tufts of grass covering the ground. Feeling sorry for the creature, she removed its saddle and bridle, though as she let the heavy saddle drop to the ground, she realized she'd have a hard time getting it back on. Her wound had rendered her right arm nearly useless.

With a weak body and heavy soul, she removed the satchels and bedroll from the saddle, then set to gathering wood for a fire. She knew if she were traveling with Iseult, he would not allow the comfort for fear they might draw attention, but Iseult was not there, and part of her *wanted* to draw attention. Perhaps her friends were wandering the same woods as she, and her fire would lure them in.

It took her longer than she would ever admit to any of her human companions to coax a flame from the dried grass and branches she'd gathered. Once the flames no longer needed her gentle fanning to feed them, she slumped back in relief. Her entire upper arm felt like it had been bashed with a rock, letting her know the wound was deep, and needed proper care.

The unicorn continued to occupy itself as she moved her clothing aside to reveal the hastily bandaged wound. She unwound its covering and groaned as the fabric tugged at her sticky blood. Gritting her teeth against the pain, she retrieved one of the water skins and splashed cool liquid against the injury.

Its attention caught by her hisses and groans, the unicorn ambled over to where she sat. Its breath fogged near her face as it lowered its muzzle to examine her. It took a few steps behind her, then lowered to the ground.

Feeling unbearably weary, Finn unfurled her bedroll and covered herself, then leaned back against the unicorn's soft belly. She instantly began to doze off. As she rested, she thought she could hear soft whispers around her. Her subconscious convinced her that the whispers were part of her fervent dreams, and she slipped into oblivion, sandwiched between the warmth of the unicorn and the fire.

ANDERS COULDN'T BREATHE. He was sure his lungs would

pop at any moment. He thrust his arm upward, flailing for the next handhold. His palm scraped against rough basalt, setting his already raw skin on fire. With a final burst of effort, he pulled himself upward. He rolled across the edge to fully plant his body on top of the cliff face.

He stared upward as a flock of sparrows flew across the cheery blue sky, then a white, bald head hovered into his vision.

"It's about time," Niklas teased, not out of breath, nor scraped nor bruised in the slightest.

Anders coughed, bumping the back of his head against the rocky earth, his lungs still burning from the long climb. "How did you get up here so quickly?" he rasped.

Niklas shrugged, his shapeless robes minimizing the gesture. "My people are well suited to traveling great distances."

Anders huffed, then forced himself to a seated position. Standing would have to wait a few moments more.

"Are we at least almost there?" he groaned.

"Take a look behind you, my lad."

Though Anders didn't appreciate the condescending tone Niklas added to the word *lad*, he craned his neck to look over his shoulder. In the distance behind him was a massive castle, or perhaps the better term was *fortress*. This was not the fancy home of a lord or lady in the Gray City, this was the dwelling of someone expecting war at any moment. The high walls were topped with ballistas and massive metal pots ready to be filled with hot oil. Anders squinted, trying to make out the men positioned every ten paces, but he could not see if they wore uniforms, nor could he see any banners flying above the spires.

"Is this where that angry woman lives?" he questioned, still staring at the fortress.

"Now you can see why I wanted her guarantee of a warm welcome," Niklas explained.

Anders staggered to his feet. "To what lord does she belong? Surely none of the great cities would allow such a fortress to stand without its mistress declaring fealty."

Niklas snickered. "How little you know of politics. This woman has no allegiances . . . although she did spend some time as the Lady of Migris."

Anders shook his head in disbelief. As the Lady of Migris? He supposed it was possible. No one had seen the Lady in years. There were rumors that she was actually a man, a Reiver, or perhaps one of the Faie.

"Let's get this over with," he muttered.

Nodding, Niklas started forward. Anders staggered after him, hoping this would be his final task. Surely he'd earned his sister back after all he'd endured? He eyed the fortress ahead warily. Perhaps inside, he'd soon be joining his sister on the other side.

# CHAPTER TWELVE

*B*edelia woke with a start, then leaned forward to rub her sore back. She'd been leaning against a cold stone wall, somewhere dark, though her internal clock sensed that it was daytime. She jolted as she tried to move her shoulder, quickly remembering the bandaged arrow wound. Soon the rest of her memories returned, and she realized she was back in a cell within Oighear's compound.

She remembered taking off on horseback with the others, then the blizzard hit, blinding her. She was attacked and knocked from her mount. Her head slammed into something hard on the ground, and she'd been carried back to the compound as she drifted in and out of consciousness.

She lifted the hand of her uninjured arm to the back of her head, finding her hair snarled with congealed blood. Lovely. She'd expected Keiren to kill her, or perhaps Iseult. It seemed wrong that she'd now die in a dungeon alone, her conscience uncleared of her secrets.

"Did you see what happened to the others?" a male voice asked from across the cell she was in.

She strained her eyes in the darkness, but could not make out the man's form. "Iseult?" she questioned.

"Yes. Did you see what happened to the others?"

Bedelia shook her head, then cringed in pain. Realizing he probably couldn't see her regardless, she explained, "I lost sight of everyone in the blizzard. I have not seen them since."

He did not reply.

She resituated herself, gasping at the pain in her shoulder. Cursed injuries. "You're the last person I expected to be captured," she commented, then instantly regretted it. She could make such a comment to Kai or Anna, but saying such things to Iseult might prove dangerous.

He was silent for several moments in which she imagined him creeping closer to kill her, then he sighed, "I actually thought I was dead at first, until you arrived. Death would have been preferable to this entrapment."

Bedelia agreed, given the horrible fate that likely awaited them both. "So what do we do now?"

"We wait," he replied. "Our wounds were tended for a reason. Likely so the Aos Sí can torture information out of us." He was silent for a moment. "If you tell them anything about Finn, I will kill you myself."

So he'd been wounded, then bandaged? Hopefully

that meant her head wound wasn't severe, since it had been left unattended. "I wouldn't do that," she assured, thinking of Finn and where she might be. "I'm quite sure she's the only friend I've ever had."

"And yet, you have not been honest with her." There was no hint of accusation in his tone, he was simply stating a fact.

"I had my reasons," she sighed. "Though at this point, they do not seem important."

The silence stretched out until Iseult said, "Tell me. You should express them at least once before you die."

She snorted. "Then you'll tell me yours?"

"No."

Her soft chuckle hurt her chest. Perhaps she took a rock to the ribs during her fall, not that another injury mattered among the others. "I suppose I should start from the beginning." She took a steadying breath. "I had been traveling with a mercenary group, longing for freedom, when I met the most beautiful woman I had ever seen. I gave her my heart. Little did I know, she had no heart to give me in return . . ."

FINN WOKE to the sound of hushed whispers. Her unicorn was a solid, warm weight behind her head and upper shoulders. Tired and confused, she slowly opened her eyes. Countless brightly colored shapes flitted around her face. They seemed to glow with a gentle light that would have likely been much stronger had it still been dark outside.

She blinked several times, focusing on the shapes. The glitter of wings, beating impossibly fast, became apparent. She tried to jump back, but instead just thunked the back of her head against the unicorn as one of the shapes darted in to hover right before her nose. A tiny woman, draped in purple gauze that perfectly matched her wings and hair, hovered before her.

"G-greetings," Finn stammered, curiosity and caution warring within her.

"Greetings, my lady," the little woman buzzed back, her voice a lovely high pitch like tinkling bells. "We did not mean to wake you. We simply hoped to learn what one of the Aonbheannach was doing this close to the lands of man."

"Ah-von-ash?" Finn questioned, slowly sounding out the word.

"The horned creature you are so rudely lying upon," the little woman explained. Her fellow winged friends continued to flit about, glittering in the sunlight.

Finn sat up with a start, forcing the little woman to dart out of the way. She looked back at the unicorn, horrified that she'd somehow offended the rare creature.

The unicorn stared back at her with glittering blue eyes, not seeming to mind.

"Her name is Loinnir," the little woman buzzed next to Finn's ear. "You have been granted a great gift by her presence. She once belonged to the Snow Queen."

Finn gasped. Did she mean Oighear? So not only had Finn escaped imprisonment, she'd stolen Oighear's personal unicorn?

She turned wide eyes to the tiny woman. "And who are you, that knows so much about ah-vooh-nash?"

"Aonbheannach," the woman corrected. "I am Corcra, den mother to my pixie clan."

"Corcra," Finn began hesitantly as Loinnir rose up behind her, "could you please tell me where I am?"

Corcra sighed, though it sounded more like a high-pitched whine. "How in the tattered wings should I know? We're in the middle of nothing. I'm leading my clan on our migration, somewhere far from the Snow Queen's ice. We die in that sort of cold."

Finn stood, kicking away the bedroll still tangled around her boots. "Could you perhaps point me in the direction of the nearest road?" she asked distantly, her attention once again caught by the dazzling, colorful display of pixies.

"Aye," Corcra replied, dipping down to once again hover in front of Finn's face. "We'll have to cross it on our way to the coast. In return, perhaps you could provide a distraction for us. It is in our best interest to stay out of sight from the world of men, and the world of the Snow Queen alike."

Another of the pixies, a tiny man with pale green wings and hair, flitted near Finn's injured arm. "I smell blood," he buzzed, his voice only a few octaves lower than Corcra's.

"You have already eaten today," Corcra hissed.

Finn's pulse raised a few notches as she took a deliberate step away from Corcra and her kin.

Not seeming to notice, Corcra flew in Loinnir's direction, then turned to face Finn. "Let us depart. She says you may ride her again."

Finn scowled at the heavy saddle, still on the ground where she'd left it with the bridle. She would have trouble lifting the saddle onto the tall unicorn any day, let alone with an injured arm. Dismissing the idea, she instead rolled up her bedroll, tied the two satchels from the saddle around it, and carried the bundle toward Loinnir.

Once again, she looked at the tall unicorn doubtfully.

As if understanding the issue, Loinnir knelt on her front legs, allowing Finn to drape her bundle across her shoulders, before climbing up behind it. Having respectfully forgone the bridle in favor of allowing the unicorn to lead the way, she intertwined her fingers with Loinnir's silky mane, then Loinnir raised herself.

A fluttering sound announced Corcra, seconds before she landed on Finn's should.

She shivered. "Don't think for a moment that I've forgotten that *blood* comment."

Corcra chuckled. "Do not fear, we are mostly carrion eaters. We're not likely to taste your blood until you're dead."

Her shoulder's stiffened. "That's not terribly comforting."

"It wasn't meant to be," Corcra replied. "Still, our small hands are more than capable of stitching your wound, and Loinnir will carry you as far as she can, though I doubt she will remain in the land of men with you. I'm not sure why you would want to travel one of *their* roads."

"How do you know I'm not one of them?" Finn inquired, beginning to relax. She still needed to find her friends, but for the moment, it was nice to have conversation, and an offer to tend her wound.

Corcra chuckled. "Loinnir once carried the Queen of the Aos Sí. She would only willingly leave her mistress for a more fitting queen, and not a simple human one."

Finn chewed on her lip, wondering how much she should divulge to Corcra. "I am no queen," she said simply. "I am no one at all."

"Many women have said such a thing," Corcra replied, "only to later move entire nations."

Finn smiled softly, though she knew Corcra was wrong about her. She was tangled in a web with spiders approaching on all sides, not the queen, but the prey. Queens might be capable of moving mountains, but her only business was staying out of their way.

"WHAT DO THE DAIR PLAN?" the female Aos Sí demanded.

Iseult barely even noted her graceful features, her black hair, or the black tunic and breeches she wore.

They did not matter. If he could not escape, at the very least, he would not speak. He would die with honor. It didn't matter that he had no idea what the Dair were planning. He would give the Aos Sí nothing.

The Aos Sí woman growled, and Iseult braced himself for the pain of a hot poker, or perhaps a blade, but the pain never came. The woman stalked past him until her footsteps faded out of hearing range, only to be replaced by new footsteps heading toward him.

He tried to keep the surprise off his face as Oighear moved around his chair to peer down at him. She blinked intelligent, lilac eyes, as if she were reading his thoughts.

"You are very loyal," she said finally.

She began to pace, the long train of her glittering white gown hissing across the stone floor.

"Normally, loyalty is a trait which I highly reward," she continued. She laced her pure white hands together and turned toward him. "Unfortunately, yours seems to be misguided. The Dair stole my magic once, and I will not allow it to happen again. Lead me to my shroud, and we shall defeat them together."

Iseult was almost tempted by her offer. If they could defeat the other Dair, perhaps Finn would be safe, but he had a feeling Oighear would lump her in with the others.

She waited for his reply, but received none.

She quirked an eyebrow at him, the fine white hairs barely visible against her matching skin. "I know of your people," she stated casually. "So few left now," she mused. "I wonder, what happens when you die without a soul?"

Iseult once again schooled his expression to show nothing, though it was difficult. Few knew of his people's curse. In fact, with the disappearance of the Cavari, and his lack of kin, for many years he believed himself the *only* one with the information.

She began to pace again. "I can break your curse with the help of my shroud. It removes the barrier to the in between, where the souls of your people are trapped. Join me, and you will have everything you could ever hope for."

"If your deal were truly so sweet," he replied, "you would have offered it from the start, instead of imprisoning us."

Ire flashed through her lilac eyes. "The girl is Cavari. She would see me returned to my eternal slumber. I learned my lesson centuries ago. One does not make treaties with enemies."

"Yet you seek out the Dair?" he questioned, hoping to keep her talking, though he wasn't sure why. Any information he learned would do him little good once he was dead.

She smirked. "Not all Dair are Cavari. The Cavari are twisted and evil, far from where their people originated. I had hoped to find the other Dair to band against the Cavari, along with the other Faie. Together, we would be unstoppable."

"And let me guess," he taunted, "you would be the queen of all?"

She tilted her head, cascading her silken hair over her bony shoulder. "Naturally."

"And if I join you," he pressed, "declare you my new queen. What then?"

"We find the shroud, kill the Cavari, and rule the earth."

Iseult shook his head and laughed. "That is the problem with queens. It's never about saving your people, or bringing justice to wrong-doers. Your sole concern is power. You surely are no queen of mine."

"You have just as much reason to hate the Cavari as I," she snapped.

He shrugged. "Perhaps."

She frowned, then looked past him toward someone entering the room.

"A large contingent of men has been spotted in the Western Woods," the visitor explained.

Oighear's frown deepened. "Humans?"

"Yes, my lady."

"And why are they still alive?" she inquired.

The informant stepped further into the room, revealing himself to be one of the many armored Aos Sí. "They skirt the boundaries, my lady. A large force would need to be deployed, leaving those who remain vulnerable."

Oighear let out a throaty laugh. Iseult did not miss the way the Aos Sí warrior jumped. Perhaps Eywen and his associates were not the only ones who feared their queen.

"Let us see if these men can withstand the wrath of Oighear the White," she growled.

Without another look at Iseult, Oighear swept out of the room with the Aos Sí. The door slammed shut behind them, then a lock slid into place, even though Iseult was already restrained in his chair.

Ignoring the throbbing of his near-fatal wound, and the aching of his cold bones, he began to formulate his plan. Oighear might have been an ancient, magical being, but she was shortsighted, blinded by her own power and authority. Perhaps there was a way out of this situation yet, a way back to Finn. He wouldn't get his hopes up, but if an opportunity presented itself, he'd be ready.

ÓENGUS DREW his horse to a halt. Something felt odd. Even the winged creature at the end of his tether had lifted its head to scent the air, its spherical eyes intent on something in the distance. His men all came to a halt behind him, muttering to each other, but not daring to ask their Captain what was wrong.

He inhaled deeply, tasting crisp moisture on the back of his tongue, yet the sky was clear. Then the first snowflake came drifting in, like a lazy fly fluttering up and down through the air. It landed on Óengus' cheek.

Before it could melt, more snow began to fall. The sky suddenly grew dark.

Óengus stared upward. He'd seen sorcery many times, and knew this was no natural snowfall. A mighty gust came in, pelleting him and his men with snow. The creature tugged at its tether, making a nervous chittering sound in its throat.

"Ride!" Óengus shouted, right before the sky closed in on them. He kicked his horse forward, suddenly blinded by the stinging white snow. Judging by the initial flakes it was coming from the southeast. To ride north would be backtracking, so that meant they must ride west. He veered his horse to the right and hunched over close to his saddle.

One of his men screamed not far behind him. He turned, and could barely see enough through the snow to notice an oddly armored rider as he wielded a long sword against another of his men.

Óengus turned forward again and kicked his horse. If these riders were somehow causing the snowfall, now was not the time to fight. He nearly toppled from his horse as something struck his shoulder. The creature's tether tugged free from his half frozen hand, and she disappeared into the blizzard. Unable to chase after her, he lifted his blade to fend off the armored rider's next attack. It did not seem that there were many of them, but the snow was causing great confusion amongst his men, removing the advantage of their greater numbers.

He slashed again, and the rider fell away. Óengus

kicked his horse forward through the trees, seeking cover from the blinding snow. Warm blood flowed down his back from the new wound in his shoulder, saturating his uniform. More of his men screamed behind him.

While perhaps in that moment he should have been fearing for his life, all he could think was, *Keiren will not be pleased.*

## CHAPTER THIRTEEN

*K*ai flicked his eyes from side to side, one hand on his reins and the other on a dagger the Aos Sí had provided along with a horse. He wasn't sure if it was the unfamiliar weapon, the dark surrounding trees, the crispness to the air, or something else that made unease clench his gut like a fist. He and his remaining party, who'd also been supplied the same, had eventually reached the Sand Road, but had opted for riding on a parallel side path. That way, they would hopefully spot any travelers on the road before they themselves were spotted. While the Aos Sí had equipped their new mounts with everything they might need for their journey, they were still now only three, just he, Anna, and Sativola, none of them possessing magic like Finn or Ealasaid.

The fist around his gut dug its nails in at the thought of Finn. His only comfort was that he knew Iseult would take care of her, but . . . he wanted it to be *him*. *He* wanted to be the one to race back and protect her from Oighear, but what could he do? He was a weak human, utterly useless in a world that now seemed to be overrun by magic. He lifted his hand from his dagger to stare at the scar on his palm. Though the skin should have been slightly deadened to touch, it felt more . . . *alive* than the rest of the skin on his body. Right now it was *burning.*

Anna abruptly halted her horse. "Do either of you feel like we're riding into a trap?"

He turned and peered at her face, barely showing in the shadow of her hood. She rode with her back hunched, as if a great weight was on her shoulders.

"I've felt nervous since we reached Migris," Sativola grumbled from her other side. "And I'll continue to feel nervous until we reach a city where men still dwell. If we're walking into a trap, well, it wouldn't feel different than any other day."

"You'll learn to tell the different between nerves and traps," Anna snapped, "if you have a wise bone in your body."

Ignoring their bickering, Kai peered around at the surrounding trees. Though the air was chilly, there was no sign of snow. Still, he did feel an air of portent, and he could not decide if it meant something bad was coming, or if he simply expected something bad after everything else that had happened. He flexed his scarred hand uncomfortably.

They had ridden almost constantly since leaving

Oighear's domain, intent on reaching Garenoch. They didn't want Finn, Iseult, and Bedelia to reach the burgh before them, and leave once they saw they weren't there.

"Do you see that?" Anna hissed, pointing past Kai's face. "Is there a stream nearby?"

He looked in the direction she was pointing, noting the subtle mist gathering above the ground. While it wasn't an abnormal sight in their moist atmosphere, he was quite sure he'd never view acts of weather and nature as normal again.

"I say we take our chances on the road," Sativola said warily.

Kai wanted to agree, but part of him hoped the mist *was* unnatural. Not all magic beings they'd encountered had been malevolent. Perhaps if this was such a creature, it might have crossed paths with Finn. The Trow, for one, seemed to flock to her.

"Go to the road if you wish," he muttered. "I'd like to see what this is all about."

As he watched, the mist increased.

Without another word, Sativola turned his horse and trotted in the direction of the road. Kai supposed he couldn't blame him, especially after he'd been caught dancing half naked in the moonlight.

He startled as Anna stepped her horse up to his side.

He turned his gaze to her, though he still could hardly see her face. "You can wait on the road too," he advised. "I know you'd rather not see anything . . . *magical*, if you can help it."

Her shoulders slumped as she sighed. "Yes, the problem is, I *can* see such things, far better than you. I fear you won't know what to do without me."

He shrugged. "True."

He would have said more, but the mist had reached their horses' hooves, and had begun to climb upward. It hit his nostrils, and suddenly he felt overwhelmingly sleepy. He fought his eyes as they attempted to close. Perhaps this had not been such a wise choice after all. He slumped forward in his saddle, unable to remain erect, only vaguely aware of Anna slumping beside him, muttering, "You owe me for this."

As hard as he fought, his world went dark, then it was as if the strange trance had never happened. He sat upright, blinking at the misty woods around him in confusion. He felt alert and in control of his body. He turned to observe Anna in much the same state.

"What happened?" he whispered.

"The gray," she groaned. "We're part way between the gray place and reality."

He cringed at that revelation, but didn't have time to reply as a cloaked form stepped out of the mist.

"*You*," Anna gasped.

Kai peered at the cloaked figure. Its body was clearly feminine, draped in a silky black robe. Other than the determination of gender, he had no idea how Anna knew who it was. The face inside its hood was hidden from view.

"Yes, I," the woman replied. "Forgive me for not properly introducing myself before. I am Móirne."

Her voice sounded oddly familiar to Kai, yet he couldn't quite place it.

"I see you have lost track of my daughter," the woman continued. "Or perhaps you left her on purpose."

*Daughter?* Kai thought. Could it be . . .

Móirne pulled back her hood, revealing a face almost the twin of Finn's, save a more angular jaw, blue eyes instead of dark hazel, and brown hair instead of dirty blonde.

"Do you know where she is?" Anna bravely demanded.

Kai was glad that she did, as he was still too stunned to speak.

"She is safe," Móirne replied, "for now. She travels with some of the lesser denizens of our kind. They will aid in her journey for a time."

"Then why are you here?" Anna asked. "Or are you *really* here."

Móirne quirked the corner of her lips in a very un-Finn-like smile. Finn's smile was always broad and warm. This woman's was secretive. "I am not truly here, you are correct. I've come to ask a favor," she turned her gaze to Kai, "of *you*. You may not remember, but you owe me almost as much as you owe my daughter."

"You helped her save me," he recalled. "She told me what happened the next morning."

She nodded. "Yes, and now I need your help. I expect you will not refuse."

"If it will aid Finn, I will give you whatever you wish," he replied.

She smiled a little wider. "Perhaps she was right to save you, and it's actually quite convenient for me. I need you to draw the attention of my people. I've done my best to hide Finn from them, but her magic shines brighter every day. It draws our people to her like moths to a flame. Soon I will not be able to protect her, but I can still buy her time to finish what she started."

Kai's heart began to race. He'd heard enough of the Cavari to know drawing their attention was unwise. He couldn't let them find Finn. He might only be human, but if he could help, he would. "Tell me what to do."

"Kai, you cannot," Anna argued, placing a gloved hand on his arm.

He shook his head. "Tell me what to do," he asked again, his gaze remaining on Móirne.

She approached him and stood beside his horse, which remained eerily still, as if asleep. From the folds of her robe she withdrew a shiny gold locket, dangling from a fine gold chain. "This belonged to my daughter," she explained. "She left it with me before she-" she cut herself off, a sad look in her blue eyes.

Shaking her head, she held the locket up to him. He took it gently in his palm, trailing the chain across his fingers.

"Wear it," she instructed, "and along with her blood

running through your veins, it should draw their attention. Continue on your intended course, but keep to the woods. Once you make it to the next burgh, you should be safe for a short while. They are as of yet ghosts in this land, unable to fully enter the world of man, yet do not mistake me, if they catch you in the wilds, they *will* kill you. They will pull you into a place like this," she gestured to the surrounding mist, "and you will not leave alive. It is only the energy of so many humans in one place that disrupts their weakened magic."

He stared down at the locket thoughtfully, trying to commit every word she spoke to memory. "So make it to Garenoch, and they will not be able to harm us?"

She shrugged. "They may call other Faie to do their bidding, just as they have done in other cities and burghs, but it will take them time to muster such forces. Enough time for Finn to complete her task. After that, they will not be able to control her."

Kai draped the chain around his neck. "I will do as you say, but how will I find Finn afterward?"

She smiled sadly. "If she so desires, she will find you. Let us hope she will still be the same woman you remember."

He opened his mouth to ask what she meant, but suddenly she was gone, along with the mist.

Anna eyed him sternly from within the shadows of her hood. "You're a fool."

He grinned at her, elated with the small shred of hope

Móirne had given him. "I never claimed to be anything else."

$$\sim$$

"AND THEY'RE NOT afraid of you?" Corcra asked from her perch on Finn's shoulder.

The rest of her kin buzzed around them, occasionally alighting on Loinnir's fuzzy white head for a rest. For once, the sun was shining warmly on her face. Loinnir's gait was smooth and comfortable beneath her, her wound had been properly stitched with pixie thread, and she'd just eaten another portion of the honey bannocks provided by the Aos Sí.

She began to shrug her shoulders, then halted the gesture, not wanting to topple Corcra. "They're my friends," she explained, referring to her missing companions. "Why would they be afraid of me?"

"Your magic," Corcra replied. "All humans fear magic, except for the few who can wield it themselves, and those just fear being found out and associated with the Faie."

"Two of my friends have their own magic," Finn smirked, thinking of Anna, "though one doesn't like to admit it."

"Hmm," Corcra buzzed. "Be that as it may, I imagine they still fear the Faie."

Finn nodded. "I must admit, I fear some of the Faie myself. The Trow have been very kind to me, but others have not been as . . . pleasant."

Corcra hummed in agreement. "Yes, there are more violent, dark Faie, just as there are more violent, dark humans."

"I suppose that's true," Finn muttered, "but my friends are as light as they come."

Corcra chuckled. "I'll have to take you at your word, as I don't plan on conversing with any humans any time soon."

Finn laughed. "Well I appreciate you speaking with me. I feel hopeful now that there are other Faie as kind as you and the Trow."

A few of Corcra's people circled back from the path ahead, then came to buzz around them in a cacophony of tiny voices that Finn found difficult to decipher.

"The road you seek is just ahead," Corcra explained. "This is where we must part ways, and you must leave Loinnir behind."

At that moment Loinnir reared her head backward and shook out her mane, dislodging the few pixies who rested there.

"Hmm," Corcra murmured, maintaining her perch on Finn's shoulder. "It seems she would like to remain with you, but I do not know . . . " she trailed off as both her and Finn's attentions were drawn by Loinnir's horn.

The air around it seemed to shimmer, then it slowly faded from sight.

"Well that solves that, I suppose," Corcra mused.

"You mean she'll really stay with me?" Finn asked hopefully, feeling immense relief, not only that she wouldn't have to walk, but that she wouldn't have to be alone.

"She's chosen you," Corcra explained. "She says you are her new queen."

"Well she has my gratitude," Finn replied, "but as I've already explained, I am no queen."

Corcra simply shook her head and took flight. "We'll see, lass. We'll see. We'd appreciate it if you'd ride out on the road first. Draw the immediate attention of anyone who might be around to see, so that we might fly unnoticed high overhead."

"Of course," Finn replied. "And I hope to see you again."

Corcra hovered in front of her face and smiled. "Aye, lass. And we'll keep an eye out for your friends. If they are as friendly toward magic as you say, perhaps we can pass your message along to them."

Finn grinned. "I'd appreciate that. We cannot seem to stop losing each other. It would be nice, for once, if I were the one to do the finding."

Corcra gave her a little wave, then flew up high as Finn rode out onto the road.

Finn looked both ways to see a small caravan of travelers not far off. Quickly deciding that her promise to Corcra was worth the risk, she urged Loinnir to trot toward them, drawing their attention as the pixies flew high over the road to the relative safety of the woods beyond.

ANOTHER DAY CAME and went as Iseult and Bedelia waited in their cell. Apparently Oighear had defeated the contingent of men, as the occasional guards that passed by seemed unworried. Iseult had hoped the men would prove enough of a distraction for him to escape, but it seemed few were a true match for Oighear.

He stood at the sound of footsteps while Bedelia remained slumped against the wall on the stone floor. The slight illumination from the lanterns in the hall increased as someone approached with a torch. Iseult was surprised to see Oighear herself, in her glittering white gown. Normally, she had pairs of the Aos Sí bring either him or Bedelia up for questioning. She had never come down to them before.

She tugged at something on the end of a leather cord until a struggling Naoki came into view. Before Iseult could help himself, his eyes widened ever so slightly.

"Ah," Oighear observed, her eyes intent on his face. "So you've seen this creature before?"

A moment later his subtle giveaway wouldn't have mattered. Seeing him, Naoki rushed toward the bars of the cell, chittering frantically. There was a leather cord tied around her beak, and a few thicker ones around her wings, holding them down. Seeing the creature Finn dearly cared about in such a state filled him with rage.

"The men who encroached upon my lands were being led by this creature," Oighear explained. "We questioned one of the soldiers before he was killed. Apparently, their Captain was seeking out a girl with long blonde hair and dark eyes, along with a man fitting the description of your other companion with Dair blood. You can imagine why I found all of this wonderfully interesting."

Iseult glared at her. He could already guess her plan, but would let her say it first.

"The issue is," Oighear continued, "that this creature seems to fear my soldiers. She will not continue her tracking."

Relief flooded through Iseult, there was hope yet.

Finally Bedelia stood and staggered weakly to the cell bars. "So what do you want?" she growled. "Why are you telling us any of this?"

Oighear smiled wickedly. "I thought the creature might recognize you. Perhaps you can coax her to do her job."

"Never," Bedelia and Iseult said simultaneously.

"Forgive me," Oighear replied, demurely raising her free hand to her chest. "I was not asking your permission. You will accompany me, and a group of my most loyal followers. We will find the Cavari girl, and she will lead us to my shroud."

Iseult shook his head, having realized her plan after all. Though he had never been fond of magic, he wished for it in that moment, if only to strike Oighear dead. His hands flexed on the bars of his cell until his knuckles turned white.

Just before he would have made an attempt to grab

her and slam her against the iron bars, Oighear stepped back. Five Aos Sí warriors came into view, iron chains and other bindings in hand.

"Naturally, you'll be walking while we ride," Oighear explained. "Though the chains can be quite heavy, I expect they won't slow you down."

Iseult eyed the warriors approaching him. He could attempt escape now, but with Oighear standing out of reach, the odds were not in his favor. Perhaps once they were on the road, he and Bedelia could make their escape.

Oighear turned to one of the Aos Sí not holding manacles or chains. "Make sure my *horse* is well prepared," she ordered, "since my proper mount seems to have gone . . . *missing*."

The insight that Oighear's mount of choice was not available did little to comfort Iseult. One of the Aos Sí opened the barred door to his cell. He sighed and allowed the remaining warriors who entered the cell to thoroughly bind him. Following his lead, Bedelia did the same, though she eyed him curiously, as if hoping for a plan.

He subtly shook his head. He had nothing at the moment. Still, while Oighear's presence would complicate things, being out in the open was preferable to rotting away in a dungeon. The self-proclaimed queen had her weaknesses, and a long journey would only give him more time to find and exploit them.

Oighear turned her lilac gaze to him and smiled, as if challenging him.

He would do his best to not disappoint.

~

"You are such a fool!" Anna shouted over the thundering of their horse's hooves.

"Tell me something I'm not already aware of!" Kai shouted back.

Having caught up to Sativola, for a day and a night they had done as Móirne bade them, resting little while taking the most direct route toward Garenoch. Then, during one of their short rests, Anna had a vision. She'd woken with a start and urged them onto their horses.

Just as they departed, several cloaked figures came into view on horseback. They chased them now, on the final stretch toward Garenoch, though Kai feared they would not make it.

"You may be glad to die for her!" Anna shouted back. "But I am not!" She kicked her heels repeatedly against her horse's sides, but the animal clearly could not go any faster. As it was, their mounts were already frothing at the mouth from exhaustion, especially Sativola's from the extra weight of his massive rider.

"They're going to catch us!" Sativola shouted. "We should turn and fight."

"If we fight, we die!" Anna shouted back.

They could see Garenoch in the distance. If only they

could reach it, they would be safe, at least, according to Móirne. Some of the townsfolk had come out of their homes to behold the commotion. Kai's eyes squinted, then widened in surprise, recognizing a shock of blonde curls.

"Is that Ealasaid?" he shouted, shocked.

Anna didn't answer, too intent on the Cavari, now just a few paces behind them. Kai darted his attention away from their pursuers and back to where he'd seen Ealasaid, only to find a tall, black clad figure had herded her behind a building from the sight of the townsfolk.

Ealasaid raised her arms, and lightning crackled right behind Kai's mount, nearly throwing him from his seat. The horses of the Cavari shrieked, tossing a few of their riders. Kai glanced over his shoulder as lightning struck again, hitting a few of the Cavari directly.

The townsfolk in the distance were screaming in panic. Kai's horse began to slow, unable to go on any longer. He looked over his shoulder again and nearly toppled from his mount.

The Cavari were gone.

Badly shaken and hardly believing their eyes, Kai, Anna, and Sativola continued trotting forward. The townsfolk watched them in terror, as if they were questioning their own eyes as well. Kai began to wonder if they would even be allowed into the burgh, but slowly the crowd dissipated. Avoiding the remaining townsfolk's questioning gazes, they closed the final distance between them.

Kai had barely dismounted when Ealasaid sprinted toward them, practically knocking him to the ground with a hug. He patted her back, holding onto his reins with his free hand, and let out a shaky laugh. "I must say, I'm pleased to see you too."

"Who were those riders?" she asked breathily, pulling away. "I couldn't believe my eyes when they simply disappeared. It was like I blinked, then they just weren't there anymore."

Kai glanced warily about as Anna and Sativola dismounted and joined them, followed by Maarav, approaching from the cover of the nearby buildings.

"It's a very long tale," Kai explained, "one I'd rather tell from the relative safety of an inn."

"That is, if the townsfolk don't run us off for being in the proximity of magic," Sativola added.

"Oh they won't," Ealasaid said happily. "We have much to share with you too."

With his horse's reins in hand, Kai, Anna, and Sativola followed Ealasaid down the dirt road leading into the burgh. A few townsfolk remained outside their homes, watching the newcomers curiously, but to Kai's surprise, no one accused them of Faie mischief, nor did anyone try to chase them off.

He caught up to Ealasaid's side where she walked beside Maarav. "Am I to understand that the people here do not fear magic?"

"Quite the opposite," Ealasaid replied. "The Alderman has welcomed magic users to protect the burgh.

Although," she rolled her eyes at Maarav, "*someone* demands I keep my skills hidden."

Maarav rolled his eyes back. "You'll thank me for it later."

Kai observed the exchange curiously. He had definitely not forgotten the encounter with the assassins and their relation to Maarav, but he was also not going to turn down the friends who'd just saved his hide.

"We have a room at the inn," Ealasaid explained. "You can stable your horses there, and then tell us where the others are."

"Well that's a simple answer," Anna cut in. "We don't know."

"What?" Ealasaid gasped, suddenly halting.

Anna smirked and continued walking. Soon Ealasaid caught up, eager for an explanation.

Kai sighed and caught up himself. "Just know you were lucky to part from us when you did," he muttered, leaning close to Ealasaid's shoulder to prevent eavesdropping. "We ran afoul of Aos Sí, a Faie Queen, and now even more frightening pursuers are on our trail."

Anna snorted. "The latter part is thanks to *Kai*." She glared at him.

He scowled. "You would have done the same for me."

She laughed. "If you say so. Now let's find some fine wine, and agree to never leave civilization again."

"I'm with ye on that one," Sativola agreed.

Kai gripped the locket beneath his shirt with his free hand, wishing he could agree with them. Would the

Cavari still wait outside of Garenoch now that they'd seen he wasn't actually Finn, but a man with her blood, wearing her locket? They'd pursued them, sure, but now that they were within the town, would the Cavari not set their sights back on Finn?

The scent of baking bread hit him, making his stomach growl, but he feared he could not enjoy it. He couldn't let those fearsome riders seek out Finn instead. He needed a new plan.

# CHAPTER FOURTEEN

*B*edelia was not sure how much longer her legs would carry her. The heavy chains wrapped around her upper body, securing her arms, had fatigued her more than her injuries and restless nights spent in the cell with Iseult. They at least had left the deeper snow behind, though the ground was still icy. Around them lay numerous corpses, their frozen blood staining the ground in slick pools.

"An Fiach," Iseult muttered, his shoulder close to Bedelia's.

She nodded. She'd recognize the uniforms anywhere. Were these the same men from Port Ainfean, the ones who pursued Finn and Kai? Given their location, it would make sense, especially since Oighear now possessed Naoki. These men likely captured her when she protected Finn's escape from the port town.

Their Aos Sí minders, on horseback while Bedelia

and Iseult walked, cleared their throats in warning. Bedelia instantly moved forward, closer to the corpses, not wanting to incite another lashing. Her back was still damp with blood from the last. She looked down at the dead men's faces, most frozen in horror, or with blank open stares, their eyes iced over. She pitied them. Perhaps in some ways they'd been her enemies, but no one deserved to die in a battle they had no chance of winning. These men had been soldiers, and they'd been slaughtered like defenseless lambs.

Iseult reached her side once more, putting some distance between themselves and their captors. Oighear had dismounted with Naoki's leather cord in hand to let the little dragon sniff around. She'd layered a fluffy white fur cloak over her shimmering dress, though she didn't seem to truly feel the cold created by her own magic.

Bedelia turned her gaze away from Oighear and frowned down at the nearest corpse, its dark brown uniform soaked through with blood. "These are the men who attempted to delay us in Port Ainfean," she suggested, wanting to make sure Iseult had drawn the same conclusions as she. "That's why they had Naoki."

He nodded, observing their surroundings rather than the corpses.

"But doesn't that mean Naoki was leading them to Oighear's compound?" Bedelia whispered. "If she was following Finn's scent, that's where she'd go. So we'll just be backtracking."

"These men are far west of our previous trail," he

muttered. He gestured to the frozen hoof prints in the mud, several paces behind where the battle started. "If they continued on in the direction they were heading, they would have missed the compound entirely."

"I don't understand then," she whispered. "Were they not tracking Finn after all?"

She watched his expression as he stared coldly down at a corpse. Dried blood formed a messy pattern down his hairline, and she knew there was more on his back. She wasn't the only one who'd sustained beatings and lashes.

Iseult glanced back at their minders, then answered, "I believe the dragon tracks Finn by her magic, not her scent. They were likely heading toward the compound, but changed course when Finn escaped."

"Precisely," Oighear agreed, suddenly appearing behind them.

Bedelia nearly jumped out of her skin. Iseult did not. Instead, he turned his cool gaze to the Faie Queen.

Bedelia tried to quiet her breathing. Hadn't Oighear just been several paces away, over by the next group of corpses? She internally scolded herself. One would think after all her time with Keiren, she'd be used to magic. She turned to glare at Oighear, but the woman's eyes were all for Iseult.

"You don't seem to regret speaking your suspicions near me," Oighear commented. "That means you knew I'd already figured it out?" She raised her colorless brow.

Iseult nodded once, making Bedelia feel like a fool for not figuring things out as quickly.

"You would not return to this place for Naoki to find Finn's scent trail," he explained. "She would then only lead us back from whence we came. You knew Naoki had been tracking Finn's magic, not her scent. She'd last sensed her from this location, leading these men here, so it's a sensible area to begin anew."

Oighear reached down and stroked Naoki's bony head. "Dragons can sense magic better than any other creature, except unicorns, perhaps. Even a fledgling like our little friend can sense the magic of its familiar spirit across an entire ocean. *This* dragon has chosen the Cavari girl. We returned here because it is the border of my domain. Here ends my warding against foreign magic. It's as good a place as any to begin her tracking."

Bedelia began to sweat despite the cold. If what Oighear said was true, as long as she had Naoki, she'd always be able to find Finn. With her and Iseult along, Naoki seemed comfortable, as if believing her friends would never cause Finn harm.

Oighear smiled wickedly at Bedelia's expression. "I suppose you now realize I have nearly won this game."

Bedelia glared at her. "Perhaps, but the next time you meet Finn, it will not be in a room warded against her magic."

Oighear snorted and gave Naoki's tether a tug. "I am not afraid of a single Dair. An entire clan, perhaps, but one girl is no match for me. Now let us be off, we have much ground to cover."

She strode past them, tugging Naoki along, then mounted her gray dappled horse. From her perch, she cast a smug gaze upon Bedelia and Iseult as their keepers rode up behind them, prodding them forward.

"We have to do something," Bedelia whispered, leaning in toward Iseult's shoulder.

He did not meet her worried gaze, but answered with a slight nod, barely perceptible.

She could only hope he had more ideas than she, because if left up to her, they'd likely both die from exhaustion long before Oighear found Finn.

EALASAID COULD HARDLY BELIEVE her ears upon hearing Kai's story. Here she'd thought she would be the one with all of the information to share, but the Alderman of a small burgh like Garenoch gathering magic forces was but a trifle compared to encounters with the Faie Queen.

She took another sip of her hot tea, then pushed away her empty plate. They'd all had a hearty meal at their inn, an odd place called the *Sheep's Delight*, while Kai told his tale. Anna had remained mostly silent throughout, while Sativola drank more whiskey than Ealasaid thought possible for a single man.

"It's odd being back here," Anna muttered to Kai, staring down into her half empty mug of wine.

SARA C ROETHLE

"The place where it all began," he mused. "Think what might have happened had Anders and Branwen not recognized Àed."

Anna snorted half-heartedly. "We'd likely be much better off. Not chased by the Faie and An Fiach. Speaking of An Fiach," she continued, raising her gaze to Maarav and Ealasaid, "has there been any word of them this far south?"

Ealasaid shook her head, wishing she had known the group from the start. As it was, she'd always be an outsider, unable to reminisce about the past. "Only from travelers coming from the North," she explained. "The last we saw of them was in Badenmar." She turned a quick glare to Maarav, still angry that he'd refused to help the townsfolk . . . not that she'd been able to do any better. "Most have not even heard of them in these parts," she continued with a sigh. "These lands are still under the rule of the Gray City, or so I'm told, though most of the guard has withdrawn from the countryside, leaving the smaller burghs to fend for themselves."

"Hence the Alderman here welcoming magic users without drawing much notice," Maarav added. "Though I imagine it won't last for long."

Anna took a long swig of wine, then returned her mug to the table. "Yes, I imagine as soon as magic is used *against* the Alderman, all the magic users that have come to fight will be thrown to the dogs."

Maarav nudged her with his elbow. "I told you so."

She glared at him. She'd been arguing with him since

Badenmar about her magic. What was the point of having special gifts if she did not use them to help people? "Forgive me for wishing to use my gifts for good," she muttered.

He grinned. "And protecting *me* isn't any good?"

Sativola burst into drunken laughter at that and she tried not to blush. She *had* become rather protective of him, though she wasn't sure why. She knew full well that remaining by Maarav's side was not the most noble choice, but if she didn't, who would? Out of everyone, he was the one who'd remained by her side the most. What type of woman would she be if she didn't return the favor?

Anna sighed, not seeming to notice Ealasaid's embarrassment. "Well, regardless of magical acceptance, we're stuck here for the time being, thanks to Kai."

Suspicion twisting his features, Maarav drummed his fingers on the table. "Please explain to me again, why those dark riders will not come to find you within the burgh?"

"That is simply what we were told," Anna answered, "and it has fortunately proven to be true, at least thus far, seeing as we're still alive."

Ealasaid nodded. She'd seen the riders disappear with her own eyes, and she highly doubted it had anything to do with her lightning. She pursed her lips, looking at Kai. "So at what point will you be able to leave the burgh then?"

Kai shrugged. "The one who gave us this task simply said to get here, and to not leave."

Ealasaid noted Maarav's expression as it once again turned suspicious. Neither Kai nor Anna had divulged who'd sent them on their near-death mission, and it was clear Sativola knew little more than he or Ealasaid. She supposed she could not throw stones in any case. It wasn't like she'd been terribly forth coming with her own secrets all along.

"And what about Finn?" she asked, genuinely worried about her friend. She still felt the sting of the moment they'd parted, and the shocked look on Finn's face. "Why did you need to distract the riders from her? What task is she supposed to accomplish?"

Anna and Kai met each other's gazes for a brief moment, then Anna turned to Ealasaid and shook her head. "Please trust that you are better off not knowing. You do not want to be any more involved in this than necessary."

"Wise advice," Maarav concluded, emptying his dram of whiskey then thunking the empty container on the table. He stood, then offered Ealasaid a hand up. "Now if you do not mind, we have a task that needs tending."

Ealasaid let out a heavy sigh, her mind now turned toward their *task*. While she truly believed that Maarav cared for her, at least a hair, it didn't stop him from taking advantage of her magic for his own gain, even if it meant risking both their skins on a near constant basis.

All this, while cautioning her from helping people if it meant revealing herself.

Saying their temporary goodbyes to Kai, Anna, and Sativola, who would be staying at the inn that evening, Ealasaid allowed Maarav to lead her outside.

The sky was now dark, and she had to watch where she stepped on the rutted, muddy road, only sparsely illuminated by lantern light. Maarav removed a piece of parchment from his breeches pocket and looked it over, then pointed in the direction they were to go.

"Are you sure this is a wise idea?" she whispered as they began to trot along down the dark street.

"Now more than ever," he replied, his green-gray eyes scanning the road ahead, looking for the next landmark.

The directions they'd been given were confusing at best. If this was all a trap, she could only hope her lightning would save them.

She bit her lip and continued jogging forward, remembering the old woman they had met earlier. The gray-haired woman, Grelka, had known of her powers even though she hadn't used them in front of anyone in the burgh. Grelka had urged her to stop hiding, and to bring in a new era.

It had sounded like crazy ranting to her, but Maarav had become instantly intrigued. He'd seemed to sense an opportunity. Grelka had handed her a piece of parchment with a time and a place, instructing her to show up if she hoped to change her fate.

She lifted her skirts a little higher to avoid the mud as

they jogged on, rounding several more corners, until finally coming to a halt. The directions stopped there . . . in a dead end. The narrow space in between buildings ended in a solid wall, blocking passage back to the main thoroughfare.

"What do we do now?" she panted, lowering her skirts.

She and Maarav both jumped as a throat cleared behind them. They turned. Grelka was there, her sparse, white hair glinting in the moonlight. Warming her bony shoulders was a gray, heavy knit shawl, just as old and worn as her deeply lined face, and murky, puddle water colored eyes.

"This way," she instructed, gesturing behind them.

Ealasaid turned and gasped. Where before had been a solid wall, now stood a doorway. As she watched, the door creaked open, and a young man with sandy blond hair peeked his head outside.

"Are we ready, Grelka?" he asked.

"This is the last one, Ouve," Grelka answered.

Ouve turned wary eyes to Maarav. "And him?" he asked.

Maarav stepped forward as if to explain himself, but Grelka answered, "The soulless one may pass. The old blood runs through his veins."

Ealasaid noted how Maarav stiffened at being called, *soulless one*, and she wondered at the odd title. Before she could think further upon it, Grelka hobbled forward and hurried them inside.

Ouve moved out of the way as they entered, then shut the door behind himself. Ealasaid whirled on him, half expecting the doorway to be a solid wall again, but the door was still there, real as ever.

"Just an illusion," Grelka explained, taking in Ealasaid's wide-eyed expression.

Ealasaid turned to find Maarav had already moved further into the room, observing those already present. Candles bedecked every surface, though they illuminated nothing remarkable. Empty, dusty shelves lined most of the walls, interspersed between boarded up windows.

"An empty storeroom?" Ealasaid questioned to no one in particular.

"So it would seem," Maarav replied, moving to stand at her side.

Ealasaid scanned the other people in the room, noticing most faces were shadowed in the hoods of their cloaks. Patting her blonde curls self-consciously, she wondered if she should be hooded as well.

Ouve stepped into the center of the gathering, his lanky form towering over most in the room. He was almost as tall as Maarav, but with about half the muscle. His hood was off, readily showing his face, making her feel less conspicuous in showing hers.

"Here we begin the first meeting of *An Solas*, the light," he announced. "I thank you all for coming forward in trust."

Some of those gathered muttered and nodded their heads in understanding, while others made noises of confusion. It seemed about half of those present had been dropped into this situation without much explanation like she and Maarav had, though thinking of Maarav, he didn't seem terribly confused.

The boy continued to utter formalities, introducing the few who didn't wear hoods.

More curious about what her companion might have to say, she stood on tip-toe to hover near Maarav's ear. "Do you know something you're not telling me?"

He leaned down toward her so she could stand normally. "There have been a few whispers across the burgh of magic users banding together without an Alderman, or other magic-less official to rule them. I know you desire to do good, but I'd rather you not stick your neck out on your own. This seemed the perfect opportunity."

Her heart skipped a beat. After how dutifully he'd required her to hide her magic, now he wanted her to join some sort of secret resistance?

"You saw what happened up North," he whispered, "and what happened in Migris. We are at war, and the rulers of this time are powerless against what is to come. I, for one, would like to be part of the *new* leadership once everything comes to pass."

"And you think these people are it?" she gasped.

"They are the beginning," he replied. "Their forces will grow. Magic users are our only hope of standing against the Faie. Now pay attention." He pointed toward the center of the room.

Ealasaid turned her gaze to find Ouve looking at her. "Would you like to introduce yourself, my lady?"

She nervously shook her head, just as many of the others had done, and the boy moved on. "We must gather others to our cause," he continued. "Those that have been turned away from their homes, and who have been persecuted along with the Faie."

Ealasaid digested his words as he continued on. The great cities were falling. Migris lay in ruins. Their people would need them soon enough, and a new order would come to the land.

Her mind flitted to the ruined city in the North, and the Reiver, Conall, who had manipulated magic users to fight for him. What would it be like to have such a gathering *without* Conall? To be led by another magic user, perhaps with their best interests at heart?

The only relevant question was, who would be that leader?

Grelka ambled up to her side opposite Maarav, startling her. "Those riders," she whispered, "the ones who chased your friends near the burgh, do you know what they are?"

Her friends? Had Grelka been watching as she and Maarav were reunited with Kai and the others? There *had* been a crowd, but she hadn't noticed Grelka there.

Maarav leaned in front of her to quietly address Grelka. "Is it important?"

Ouve glanced at them, then continued his long address to the group.

Maarav placed a hand on Ealasaid's shoulder and guided her toward the nearest corner. Grelka followed.

Once they were out of earshot, Grelka began anew, "I've been seeing those riders in my dreams. They search for someone."

"Oh yes," Ealasaid began quietly, "They search for-"

Maarav gave her shoulder a painful squeeze, cutting her off.

She blushed, realizing she'd almost given away something Kai and Anna had asked her to keep private.

Grelka's gaze was intent on her, as if reading the thoughts she'd almost spoken.

Wanting to distract her, Ealasaid asked, "You said you saw them in your dreams?"

Grelka frowned, then nodded. "I am what the old clans call a seer. I saw the riders coming here, and I saw *you* stopping them."

Ealasaid's blush deepened. "I did what was needed," she explained simply.

Grelka shook her head. "I was not referring to your lightning today, I was referring to my dream. In my dream, you lead others to stop the riders." She gestured toward the others at the meeting, who were now all conversing amongst themselves. "You will lead *them*."

Ealasaid looked to Maarav, unsure what to think.

He stared at Grelka coolly. "I will not allow you to throw her into danger."

Grelka laughed, able to speak louder now that the

room was filling with conversation. "She will be fine. *You*, on the other hand, *your* fate has not been chosen."

"What do you mean?" Ealasaid gasped.

Grelka shook her head. "I can say no more. Meet me at the edge of town at dawn, and bring your hunted friends. Their task is not yet finished." With that, she ambled away to address others in the meeting.

Ealasaid turned her gaze up to Maarav. "Do you still believe this meeting was a good idea?" she asked caustically.

His eyes followed Grelka across the room. "I think I would like to know what else the seeress has to say," he muttered. He turned his gaze down to her. "Let's return to the inn and get some rest, then we'll speak with Kai and the others."

KAI TOSSED and turned in his bed at the inn. Anna seemed to be sleeping soundly in the bed beside his, divided by a narrow table. He expected Sativola to come crashing in at any moment, though he seemed intent on drinking his worries away.

Kai couldn't say he blamed him, and once would have been matching the man drink for drink. Not now. Finn had given up a portion of her power to save him. What type of man would he be if he didn't risk his life to save her?

His body erupted in goosebumps as he thought back

to the cloaked riders. He hadn't needed to see their faces to know there was something . . . off about them. Just like Moírne had said, they seemed almost like ghosts. Ghosts that could easily kill him.

He sat up, ignoring the cold sweat dripping down his back. He knew well enough where Finn would be heading if she happened to decide it unwise to enter Garenoch, or if the lurking riders blocked her way. He could go there, but would he simply be leading the riders right to her?

He stroked his fingers over the locket still dangling around his neck. Would the riders still sense it if he took it off and left it in the burgh with Anna so he could find Finn? Or, should he leave the burgh and ride far away from where Finn was heading, to once again lead them away?

He shook his head, truly wishing he could speak with Moírne again, but perhaps she could not enter the burgh, just like her kin.

Unable to quiet his mind, he silently crept out of bed and exited the room. He could still hear a measure of commotion below from the inn's patrons. Perhaps he could persuade Sativola to buy him a drink. Or two.

Or *three*.

## CHAPTER FIFTEEN

*F*inn crept back into the forest, away from the main road. She had almost reached Garenoch when she noticed the riders. Clouds obscured the moon, leaving her with little light to see by, but they were clearly watching Garenoch. The six figures, mounted on calm horses, stood side by side, observing the small burgh. For what, she did not know, but just seeing the riders filled her with overwhelming dread.

Loinnir stepped lightly behind her, following her into the cover of the trees. Once the riders were well out of sight, she climbed onto the unicorn's back, entwined her fingers with its mane, and took off at a gallop. She wanted as much distance between herself and the ominous riders as possible, and if she could not reach Garenoch, she would simply go to Greenswallow first. Perhaps she'd find Àed there, and if not, she'd retrieve the shroud then seek her friends.

Once she felt a safe distance had been gained, she asked Loinnir to slow. It wouldn't do to ride away from one danger, only to unwittingly ride into another. Her nervous breath fogged the air as they slowed. All was still.

They continued on throughout the night. Eventually the moon was replaced by the sun, and her surroundings began to feel familiar. She was close to her meadow.

"This was my home for a very long time," she explained to Loinnir, though she was still unsure if the unicorn actually understood her words, or somehow just sensed her desires. "I hope we can find the correct spot," she continued. "It might be a bit difficult to distinguish now that no tree stands there. We might be digging for quite a while."

Loinnir flicked her mane, but did not otherwise reply. Her ivory horn was still hidden by magic, so she just appeared a rather fine white horse. Neither of them should draw any extra attention as they passed the small farms leading to her previous home.

She was pleased to see the first stream of chimney smoke as they neared. These people, at least, were yet to be chased off by the Faie or An Fiach. A few moments later, an elderly farmer came into view, tending his crops, though the cold had withered them seemingly beyond repair.

The sight plucked at her heart. So many had been affected by the recent chaos, not just her. She'd venture to say they were affected even *more*, not less. She had never known a life of true peace, barring when she was a tree, and so, she had no true peace to lose.

She began to search her meadow as they neared, attempting to pinpoint the exact place she'd stood as a tree. Eventually her eyes found Àed's small stone hut. No smoke rose from its chimney, and the entrance was overgrown with vines. She tried not to cry. He might not be where she'd hoped, but she would find him. She *had* to.

Turning her gaze away from the hut, she thought back to her first walk there, just after she'd turned back into her current form. Àed had found her in the middle of the field, and had helped her hobble to his hut as she slowly learned how to use her legs.

Loinnir walked along unbidden, ambling serenely across the meadow. Finn observed each tree she passed, hoping for something familiar, then it hit her. As if sensing her revelation, Loinnir suddenly halted.

"This is it," Finn gasped. She turned her gaze to the distant mountains, then to a large boulder several paces away. Loinnir's hooves had landed on the exact soil where Finn had once taken root. She felt it with every nerve ending in her body.

She dismounted, then fell to her knees as Loinnir moved out of the way. Though rain and wind had mostly repacked the soil, it was still a little more loose in this area, with less yellow grass threatening to take hold.

Her entire body trembled with excitement as she began to dig.

∼

ISEULT SLUMPED IN THE SADDLE, defeated. Bedelia had been the first to fall, dropping to her knees, unable to move any further. He went not long after. Now, they were both too exhausted to put up any fight. Though their chains remained, they were finally allowed to ride.

Naoki had led them in a direct line southwest, no matter what lay in their path. Once they'd had to change course to walk around a wide lake, and for several hours after that fought their way through a forest thick with wild brambles.

They'd long since crossed the Sand Road, and continued on the other side. By Iseult's estimation, they'd bypassed Garenoch, which was further south. It was only a day's journey from Garenoch to Greenswallow, which meant Finn was not far off. He could only hope she would find the shroud and flee before Oighear reached her, but he knew it was unlikely. Once Finn found the shroud, she would try to find *him*, which meant either waiting in Greenswallow, or Garenoch.

In the state he was in now, he would only be able to watch on as Oighear confronted her. He honestly did not know which of them would win the battle, but Oighear had the upper hand. She was cruel and cunning, no stranger to using her powers for harm. Finn would hesitate to cause any damage, just as she had with the assassins.

He stiffened his back, realizing Oighear was watching him from her mount, smiling.

"Don't worry," she purred. "Once the Cavari girl is gone, you can follow a *real* queen."

Iseult simply stared at her, too tired to exchange insults, for what little good it would do.

"Watch him closely," she said to one of the Aos Sí. "He's bound to try something foolish."

The Aos Sí riding around them nodded. Iseult slumped forward in his saddle once more. Even if he could somehow defeat Oighear, he would then have to deal with ten Aos Sí warriors. Part of him wished they would just kill him now, as there was little hope of saving his soul, or Finn. Yet, he would not ask for death. He'd been on this journey his entire life, and he was about to see it through to the bitter end.

"ARE YOU SURE ABOUT THIS?" Kai asked, his heart thundering in anticipation.

Ealasaid nodded, her face grim. "If this will help Finn, we have to do it."

Anna, Sativola, and Maarav stood nearby, weapons ready.

Kai swallowed the lump in his throat. He'd only meant to tell Anna and Sativola that he was leaving to lead the riders astray. He couldn't risk Finn coming to Garenoch, unaware of what awaited her. He lifted his hand to the sore spot on his jaw where Anna had punched him for being a *fool*. She'd used many other choice descriptors, before Maarav and Ealasaid had interrupted. With little explanation, they'd urged Anna, Sativola, and himself to follow them to the edge of town where a group of magic users would be waiting. It had seemed utterly ridiculous at the time, yet here they all were.

Kai shuddered and brought himself back to the present, surrounded by strangers with a horse at his side. Anna and Sativola waited amongst the strangers, weapons gleaming in the early morning sun.

An old woman named Grelka, who he'd learned had orchestrated the early morning congregation, spoke in hushed tones to Ealasaid. Kai watched as Ealasaid frowned, then nodded to some quiet question. Both women turned then their gazes forward.

One by one, more townsfolk showed up to gather around Ealasaid and Grelka. As their presence grew, an odd tingle began to circulate through the air, or perhaps it was just Kai's imagination. They were all magic users, secretly banding together to protect not only themselves, but their kinsfolk.

"This will work," Ealasaid muttered, quietly reassuring herself as she moved to Kai's side, followed by Grelka. Ealasaid repeatedly clenched and unclenched her hands, as if warming up her magic.

A sandy-haired boy Kai had not met stepped out of the crowd, grinning from ear to ear. "I, for one, cannot think of a better way to recruit more members to *An Solas*. Once others see what we can do, they'll be flocking toward us in droves."

Grelka chuckled, then turned her gaze to Ealasaid. "Do not worry. This is the right choice. Everything will be as it's meant to be."

Kai frowned at them, not understanding half of what they were talking about.

"Grelka is a seer," Ealasaid explained.

Kai nodded in acceptance, though he didn't really see it as much of an explanation. Anna's visions of immediate danger were one thing, but no one could truly know the future. Still, Grelka thought his task of the utmost importance, and he wasn't sure why. Upon his arrival to the group, she'd said to him the same thing she'd just said to Ealasaid. "Everything will be as it's meant to be."

"It's time," Grelka suddenly snapped.

Ealasaid raised her arms skyward, along with the sandy-haired boy, and the other gathered townsfolk. Many more townsfolk lingered near the buildings at the edge of town, awaiting whatever spectacle was about to take place.

Anna met Kai's gaze and nodded. It was time for him to prepare as well.

He led his horse a few paces away from the group, then slung himself into the saddle. He lifted his free hand to grip the locket still at his throat and turned his gaze outward.

One of the townsfolk had spotted the riders early that morning, *waiting*. It had proven true that they would not, or *could* not enter the burgh, so the magic users would bring the fight to them.

As the final magic users raised their arms skyward, pressure began to build, like the eerie calm before the sky opened up to a massive storm. It continued to build for several heartbeats, then Ealasaid shouted, "Go!"

Kai jabbed his heels into his horse, then took of at a gallop. He glanced over his shoulder to see the distant riders launching into motion. The ground exploded all around, dirt flying everywhere. Lightning stabbed at what protruded, followed by waves of fire. Winds blew so powerfully that even from the distance, Kai was nearly swept from his mount.

Trusting in Ealasaid and the others, he leaned forward in the saddle and urged his horse into a full blown run, down the road toward Greenswallow.

"Again!" Ealasaid shouted.

Another wave of magic surrounded the Riders, who had not been slowed for long. Though impacted by the magic, injuries were not sustained as the Riders would fade from sight, avoiding peril, only to reappear in pursuit of Kai.

Ealasaid cried out, "We must stop them another way! Forward!"

Anna, Sativola, and Maarav, now on their horses, were the first to ride forward, prepared to intercept the Riders. The magic users were not far behind, some riding, some running at full speed.

Running as fast as she could, Ealasaid watched as those on horseback met the Riders, soon backed up by those on foot. Though their enemies numbered only six, the magic users began to fall beneath gleaming blades. Those still standing fought on. She knew they trusted Grelka's proclamation that the Riders must be stopped at all costs, even if it meant many would die.

Her lungs burning from exertion, Ealasaid reached the fight, then froze. She watched as Anna parried an attack from one of the dark Riders, then Sativola jumped in, sparing Anna injury. Ealasaid lifted her arms, but wasn't sure what to do. Some of the magic users could create fire, which could be aimed, but her lightning tended to be more erratic. Sure, she could hit one of the Riders, but there was nothing to prevent her from hitting one of her friends.

She screamed as a Rider slashed a short sword at Ouve, and her lightning came down almost unbidden, distracting Ouve's attacker. Seeming to sense an opportunity, Maarav darted in and slashed his blade deep into the attacker's leg, toppling the Rider to the ground.

Ealasaid gasped with momentary elation, before the Rider rolled to its feet and cut down the first magic user, a young woman, who got in its path. Ealasaid screamed, but it was too late. The woman fell in a bloody heap, her face in the dirt.

Ealasaid struck the offending Rider again with her lightning, but it was no use. The Riders seemed invincible. Grelka must have misjudged the situation. They would have to fall back to the safety of the burgh, lest they all lose their lives.

She was prepared to give the order, then her eyes nearly popped out of her skull at what she saw.

Black clad forms raced forward from the tree line, weapons raised high. She recognized Maarav's former mentor, Slàine, as she launched herself through the air and swiped her blade across the hooded neck of one of the riders. To Ealasaid's surprise, the rider toppled from its horse. It fell to the ground and was swarmed with black clad forms, like wolves piling on top of their prey. Weapons flashed, then the assassins fell away. Beneath them was an empty black cloak.

Hope renewed, Ealasaid flung lightning at another rider, distracting it for the split second it took for the assassins to attack. Seeming to catch on, the other magic users renewed their attacks, bathing the riders in flame and ice. One by one, they were taken down, by magic and blades alike, leaving behind empty cloaks. Their horses galloped away to disappear into the forest, as impervious to their wounds as the Riders.

Ealasaid rushed forward as Anna repeatedly stabbed the remaining form, even after it had turned into nothing more than a cloak.

"Where did they go?" one of the new members of An Solas asked, glancing around frantically.

"They are nothing more than ghosts," Slàine hissed, lowering her black cowl from her face as she stalked forward. "Overwhelm them with physical attacks and they cannot sustain themselves."

"We couldn't harm them with our magic," Ealasaid panted.

Slàine nodded. "They *are* magic. The best way to send them away is cold iron," she hesitated at the expression on Ealasaid's flushed, blood-flecked face, "but you at least proved a noble distraction," she added. She turned her attention away from Ealasaid and seemed to be counting her assassins. Several had fallen in the short, chaotic fight.

Ealasaid searched around the empty cloaks, assessing the casualties. A certain gray-haired lump caught her eye. She rushed forward toward Grelka, who clutched at her knit shawl, blood slowly blossoming across her chest.

Reaching her, Ealasaid dropped to her knees, placing a shaky hand gently on her shoulder. Grelka's face was ghostly pale, her eyes mere slits.

"I thought you said things were as they should be," Ealasaid cried, feeling like her heart was being torn in two. "I thought we would be victorious."

Grelka led out a gasping laugh that ended with her sputtering up blood. "We are," she hissed. "Kai will make it in time. His success is all that truly matters."

"But-" she hesitated, glancing at the fallen around her.

Too many corpses littered the battlefield, some even younger than she. "Was it worth so many lives?"

Grelka patted Ealasaid's hand weakly. "This had to happen . . . for us to stand a chance," she gasped. "In my dreams I saw two paths. One, where we would fight for our lives, but live free from hiding, and another, where we would cower and live as slaves." She smiled softly. "I've never backed down from a proper fight, and now it is your turn. Lead An Solas into a new age." Her eyes slowly fluttered shut.

Though she'd known Grelka a short time, her loss felt great, along with the others of An Solas that had fallen. Tears streamed down her face and plopped onto her bloody hands, still gripping Grelka's lifeless form. She could not bear to observe the other casualties. She'd seen that Anna was still alive, but many others had died. She struggled as arms wrapped around her from behind, lifting her to standing. She sensed her new captor was only trying to help, but she didn't want it. She didn't want to think. She clenched her eyes shut, unable to bear the sight of the maimed dead.

The arms around her resisted her struggles until she went limp and cracked open her teary eyes. She craned her neck to see a familiar blood-stained face next to hers. Maarav. She exhaled in relief, realizing the possibility of his death had been the one she feared most. She managed to smile up at him through her tears, but he was looking toward Slàine.

"I'd expected a dagger in the back the next time we crossed paths," he commented coolly.

Stepping away from the empty cloak she'd been examining, Slàine glared at him. "You always were a bit of a fool. I'd hoped to prevent any of this."

His arms still around Ealasaid, he waited for Slàine to explain herself.

Instead, she turned to her fellow assassins. "Help them burn their dead," she ordered, "then meet us at the inn." She turned back to Maarav. "We have much to discuss."

FINN SCRAPED FRANTICALLY at the earth. Her skin had long since been rubbed raw, her fingernails cracked and filled with black soil. She could feel power radiating from the earth below her, but it was still out of reach. Though Loinnir fidgeted with worry, Finn could not take the time to consider the cause. She just knew she had to reach the shroud before Oighear, the Cavari, or anyone else could show up to snatch it away from her.

Something cool touched her sweaty cheek, drawing her momentarily from her task. Snowflakes. Had Oighear's snow reached this far? Was she coming for her? Her fervor increasing, she turned back to her digging while Loinnir stomped in agitation beside her.

More snowflakes stung her face, and began sticking to

her tangled hair. She glanced again at the white flecks drifting in, then narrowed her eyes at something in the distance. Riders, six of them. The central rider wore a full, white fur coat, frothing up around her shoulders to meld with her white hair. Oighear. Near the hooves of Oighear's horse was a smaller white form, stooped low to the ground. She couldn't quite make out what it was. As she watched, several more riders moved into view to flank the others.

Fear exploding through her mind, she turned back to her digging. The shroud was her only hope. Perhaps with its added power, she might best Oighear. Just a little while longer, and the shroud would be hers. She frantically pushed her fingers through the soil and hit soft fabric. Her heart jumping in her throat, she wrapped her fingers around the silky textile and pulled upward. The shroud came free from the earth as she stood, littering the ground with specks of fresh soil. She stared awestruck at the magical garment dangling from her hand, not quite believing she'd actually found it.

She slowly turned her gaze away from the shroud, feeling like she was in a dream. The riders thundered toward her, their hoofbeats seeming louder than they really were. Loinnir stomped in agitation, but remained faithfully at her side. She stood with the tattered shroud in her hands, ready to protect herself, then dizziness hit her. Her breath slowed. She blinked as the riders came in and out of focus, moving impossibly slow. Suddenly she found herself in a different place. No, she wasn't in a new place. Her body had not left the meadow. She was only in a memory, sealed deep within her mind.

HER DAUGHTER'S SMALL BODY, *limp in her arms, covered in blood. She'd long since grown cold, but Finn refused to let her go. Finn's mother, Móirne, stood at her back in the windowless, candle-lit room, unspeaking.*

*Finn's entire body shook with tears. She had never wanted any part in the dealings of the Cavari, their treaties nor their wars. She did not care about her birthright, the Faie shroud, or the Aos Sí. The endless battles for power were futile.*

*Now, because of their wars, she'd lost the only thing she truly cared about. Those lowly sailors had killed her little girl to send a message to the Cavari. A message received solely by her. Her people cared not for her loss. It did not affect them.*

*She staggered to her feet, her lifeless child still in her arms, and moved toward her mother. Their eyes met.*

*"Tend to her," Finn ordered, forcing her tears to still.*

*"What will you do?" Móirne asked, taking the dead child from Finn's arms. Tears threatened her blue eyes. While Móirne held little love for their clan, she feared them. She had remained obedient, playing her part in their games while her own granddaughter paid the price.*

*"They have taken my heart," Finn heard herself say. "My soul. Now I'm going to take theirs."*

*She turned away from Móirne, still cradling Finn's lifeless daughter, and took the Faie Queen's shroud in her hands. The people of Uí Néid would pay for what they'd done, even if it killed her.*

~

"FINN!" Iseult shouted, arms chained to his sides. The Aos Sí rider holding the reins to his horse drew the animal to an abrupt halt, nearly dislodging him from the animal's back.

As soon as she'd stood with the shroud, she'd gone utterly still. Her gaze was distant, as if she wasn't really there.

Beside him, Oighear dismounted and handed Naoki's tether to one of the mounted Aos Sí. The dragon struggled against her tether, shrieking through the bindings on her beak, desperately clawing at the ground.

Two more Aos Sí approached on foot and pulled Iseult from his mount, throwing him to the hard soil, pressing his face in the dirt. He struggled, cutting his cheek on the rocky ground, turning his head just enough to see Finn. He heard another thump and a scream as the same treatment was given to Bedelia.

With a smirk back at him, Oighear began to sway toward Finn on foot. As Iseult watched, she extended her arms, dropping her white coat to the ground. Snow fell all around her, blending her into the scenery. She lifted her palms skyward like she'd summon the entire sky down upon them, her dress glittering in the odd mixture of sun and snow.

The ice increased, swirling around Finn while a white horse pranced back and forth behind her, clearly distressed

"Finn!" Iseult shouted again, only to get a boot to the side of his face, grinding his cheek into the dirt painfully. He grunted in agony as his vision went momentarily dark, but he refused to lose consciousness.

Slowly, his sight returned through the pain. The snow around Finn left her barely visible. She was still unmoving, clutching the shroud in both hands. Oighear was going to freeze her to death while she just stood there, deep in some sort of trance.

He struggled against his chains and captors as Oighear reached out her pale hand and placed it on the shroud, still in Finn's grasp. She began to tug, but Finn's hands gripped the fabric tightly. If Oighear managed to claim the shroud, it would all be over. Her magic was already the most frightening he had ever seen. With the extra power of the shroud, no one would be able to defeat her.

"Finn!" a voice called, drawing Iseult's limited gaze. A rider galloped toward them from the snowy road, bow raised. The Aos Sí turned to observe the new threat as one, releasing the pressure on Iseult's back. Half of the Aos Sí rushed toward the rider, but would be too late. Galloping at full speed, the rider let loose an arrow to slice through the air.

Oighear turned a moment before it struck her chest. She looked down at it in shock, dropping her hand from the shroud. With a furious growl, she wrapped one pale hand around the arrow's fletching and pulled, removing it from her chest with a gruesome spray of blood. Dropping the arrow to the ground, she reached for Finn.

As the first half of the Aos Sí intercepted Kai, those remaining rushed toward their queen, abandoning Iseult and Bedelia where they lay. Now free of her captor, Naoki rolled on the ground, attempting to remove the tether from her wings.

Iseult watched helplessly as Oighear renewed her grasp on the shroud, tugging hard despite her injuries. Her warriors neared her back cautiously, clearly unsure of what to do. Iseult's heart gave a nervous skip as Finn blinked several times, then finally came back into reality. Noticing Oighear, rage sparkled in her dark eyes, an emotion he thought to never see on her normally innocent face.

Maintaining her grip on the shroud with one hand, Finn held out the other. As one, the Aos Sí collapsed to the ground behind their queen, as if a giant hand had crushed them to the earth. Their bodies trembled as they struggled in vain to regain their footing, but could not. This time, neither roots, nor other forces of nature pinned the warriors, just sheer power. Iseult struggled to his feet, straining against the chains binding his arms to his body. Barely able to stand, he began to stumble toward the scene.

Glancing back at her felled warriors, Oighear gave another hearty tug to the shroud in Finn's grasp, but to no avail. She lifted her free arm skyward to mirror Finn. Hail suddenly pelleted the earth, pounding Iseult so powerfully he was forced back to the ground. Distantly he heard the Aos Sí detaining Kai cry out in pain. Somewhere behind him near Bedelia's grunts of agony, Naoki shrieked through her bound beak.

Flat on his chest, Iseult desperately wanted to stand and take action, but hammered with hail, he could not even lift his face to view the scene at hand.

A shrill scream pierced the air from Finn's direction. The hail suddenly stopped falling.

His heart in his throat, Iseult rolled to his shoulder and opened his eyes, dreading what he might find. As his vision cleared, he slumped in temporary relief. Finn had summoned her roots from the earth to snake around Oighear and suspend her in the air. Her warriors stumbled to their feet, battered and bruised from the unnatural hail.

Iseult forced himself to a seated position, but struggled to stand. All he could do was watch as the roots around Oighear became encased in ice. Oighear struggled, and all at once the roots shattered, dropping her to the ground on her side, tangled in her bloody gown. She unraveled herself and climbed to her feet, her angry eyes set on Finn.

Finn watched her warily, her shoulders hunched in residual pain from the unnatural hail.

Oighear staggered toward Finn. Her warriors watched on silently, awaiting their orders. Iseult could hardly breathe watching her snow white hand glide to her belt to withdraw a dagger.

"It seems we are evenly matched," Iseult heard her say, "and so, I will dispatch you through more mundane means."

Wet and shivering from the melting hail, Finn lifted the shroud in both hands. "Do not make me become who I once was," she growled. "If you will not desist, I will trap your soul with all the others."

Oighear continued to stagger toward her.

Iseult could barely force himself to watch. The last time Finn had stolen away someone's soul, she'd become a tree for one hundred years. He could not bear to consider what might happen now.

The Aos Sí warriors were utterly silent as Finn began to chant in a language unknown to Iseult, and he'd traveled enough to hear many. Oighear was only a few steps away, dagger raised desperately against Finn's magic.

"Hey Faie Queen!" someone called from the direction opposite the warriors.

Iseult turned to the voice. It was Kai, beaten badly by the Aos Sí warriors and missing his bow. He cocked back his arm, launching a large stone to sail through the air. It connected with Oighear's temple, just as she had turned to address the insolent disrupter.

She dropped to the ground and did not move.

Iseult finally managed to regain his feet and began stumbling forward once more through the remaining hail and snow, though his body was on the brink of collapse. Before he could reach the crumpled queen, Finn stepped toward her, eyes cast downward. He was just close enough to hear her shaky, breathless words.

"My quarrel was not with you, Oighear the White. You should have stayed in your forest."

Oighear did not reply, and instead remained deathly still. Stepping away from the Faie Queen, Finn turned an angry glare to the waiting Aos Sí.

"You're queen is dead," she announced. "I would advise against any further action."

As one, they dropped to their knees and bowed their heads to her.

Kai jogged toward Finn the same moment as Naoki, her wings now free. Iseult felt sick as he made slow progress toward them. Finn seemed . . . different. Had she been changed by the shroud? Had she regained her memories, recalling her lost child? Would she now lash out at her friends as she had the Aos Sí? She'd come so close to stealing Oighear's soul. If it weren't for Kai, Iseult was not sure what would have happened.

Finn gasped in surprise as she noticed Naoki. She crouched down, then lifted the dragon up in a loving embrace. She pulled the binding from her beak, and stroked the dragon's head to quiet its high pitched keening.

As the dragon quieted, Finn looked to Kai with a warm, open grin lighting up her bruised and bloody face, streaked by the tears pouring from her eyes. The shroud remained in her left hand where it clutched Naoki, all but forgotten.

Iseult nearly staggered, so relieved to see Finn as he knew her to be. Her smile for Kai hinted she had not been changed by her memories. She had not become like the other Cavari, but . . . would she have the same smile for him?

Kai knelt beside Oighear and placed two fingers at her throat, checking for her heartbeat. "Dead," he announced as he rose away from the corpse.

Finn smiled sadly at Kai. "It appears you were the ones to find me after all," she mused. She turned her smile to Iseult as he reached her. She removed one hand from Naoki to reach up and cradle his bloody cheek. "You'll always find me, won't you?"

"Always," he rasped, barely able to speak.

Observing his chains, and those on Bedelia, who was attempting to climb to her feet back where Iseult started, Finn turned to the silently waiting Aos Sí. "Remove their chains," she ordered.

"Yes, my queen," they said in unison. They stood, and two warriors branched off from the group, jogging toward their milling horses for the keys.

Soon enough, Iseult and Bedelia were both free, and the Aos Sí all knelt around Oighear's corpse, muttering in awe. They had likely thought their queen invincible. Iseult had almost agreed with them, before Kai and Finn had proven the notion incorrect.

The sun revealed itself fully, wiping away the last of

Oighear's snow and hail. Finn set Naoki on the ground to bounce around happily, then turned back to Iseult, her expression suddenly crumbling. "I remember everything," she breathed.

He couldn't imagine what she was feeling, remembering the death of her child. Overcome with emotion, he pulled her into an embrace, feeling her body tremble, and her tears wet on his shoulder. His embrace tightened, even in his weakened state. He longed to relieve her pain. He felt her arms slip around his lower back, with the shroud yet clutched in one hand. He soaked in her touch, easing the fear in his heart.

After a few moments she seemed to compose herself and pulled away. He reluctantly released her, then watched as she turned her attention to Bedelia, standing a few paces away.

At the loss of her touch, his shoulders slumped in an odd mixture of relief and sadness. He knew Finn needed her memories, but he had desperately wished she would not have to feel the pain of losing her child again.

While Finn fussed over Bedelia's injuries, Kai looked Iseult up and down with a wry grin. "It's killing you, isn't it?"

Iseult glared at him. "What?"

"That I was the one to save the day instead of you." He waggled his eyebrows.

Had he the energy, Iseult would have punched him.

Bedelia gave Finn a million assurances that she would

be fine, and finally, Finn walked a few steps toward Iseult and held out the shroud, still clutched in her left hand.

He found it odd, finally seeing it. After all that had happened, it seemed a simple, dirty piece of fabric. He looked up from the shroud and met her gaze, wanting to ask a million different questions.

She took a step toward him and forced the shroud into his hand.

He took it reluctantly.

Her lips curved into a small smile. "I realize now, my people are the ones to blame for my daughter's death. I will right my wrongs and fulfill my promise to you, then I will crush the Cavari."

He smiled, then took her hand, placing the edge of the shroud back in her grip. "There will be time to discuss that later." He glanced back at the ten Aos Sí warriors, now finished gawking at Oighear. "First, let us find an inn and a hot meal."

"One more thing," Kai interrupted from behind Finn. She turned as he lifted his hands to his throat, then removed a gold locket from around his neck. He held it out to her. "When you go about this *Cavari crushing*, perhaps go easy on your mother."

She took the locket in her free hand. Something about it brought her tears back to the surface, and she nodded, then pulled Kai into a hug. "I would never have gotten this far without you," she sobbed, then reached blindly back for Iseult. He went to her and took her hand. "I would never have made it without either of you." She sniffled, then pulled away from Kai to look between them. "Thank you."

Kai patted her shoulder, then laughed. "Don't worry about it. I needed a good adventure."

Iseult smirked, though it pained his face. "As did I," he consoled. "There are no thanks necessary."

She smiled, encompassing Bedelia in her gaze. "Where are Anna and Sativola?"

"Back in Garenoch with-" Kai cut himself off and glanced at Iseult. "Maarav and Ealasaid."

Finn grinned even wider, making Iseult decide against the venomous comment he had in mind for Maarav. Instead, they gathered their horses and prepared to depart. Finding no quarrel with the warriors, Finn sent the Aos Sí on their way. They did not carry their Snow Queen away for burial, a testament to their true feelings for her.

Iseult was glad to let her to rot just where she lay.

CHAPTER SIXTEEN

*K*ai was the first to notice the smoke as they approached Garenoch. Closer observation revealed funeral pyres. *Many* of them. With Bedelia and Iseult battered and sore, they'd taken their time on the return journey, allowing everyone to rest along the way. They'd stood no chance of returning in time to aid in the battle against the Cavari. It was long since over.

Now, the midday sun illuminated the burgh sharply. In addition to the pyres, the wide expanse of dead grass leading up to the town was interspersed with puddles of blood. There was no way of telling who had won the fight, and who had died, though the people still bustling around the streets of the distant burgh brought him a measure of comfort. Still, the amount of blood spilled was disconcerting. He needed to find Anna.

He glanced at his companions, feeling reluctant to

ride ahead. Every portion of Iseult's skin showing was black and blue. His clothes now seemed slightly too big for his hunched form. Bedelia was in much the same shape, her expression never shifting from a morose pout.

Yet, it was Finn who worried him the most. She hadn't divulged the memories she'd regained, but he had a feeling they were dark. She'd mentioned something to Iseult about the death of her daughter. She had to mean in her previous life, but that was the first he'd heard of it.

She now wore the gold locket her mother had given him, and reached up to rub her fingers across its face every so often. Naoki was curled up in her lap, wrapped in Kai's cloak, which he'd sacrificed to keep the dragon hidden. Though the Aos Sí had offered Finn one of their saddles and a bridle for her white horse, it didn't seem to need any guidance from her, which was fortunate, as she didn't seem entirely *there*. Her bruised hands didn't even touch the reins.

Seeming to startle into awareness, she glanced at Kai, then followed his gaze to the pyres. "Is this because of me?" she asked distantly.

Outwardly he replied, "It's because of the Cavari. They forced these deaths, not you." Inwardly, however, he thought *Please, oh please don't let Anna be among the dead.*

The townsfolk on the outskirts watched them warily as they approached. Fear that hadn't been there a day before now shone in their eyes. He wondered if the Alderman was now regretting the decision to allow magic users in his burgh. Magic always brought danger, no matter who wielded it. He'd learned from experience, traveling with Finn.

He exhaled in relief as a familiar figure came into view, twin daggers at her hips. Conversing with someone hidden by a market stall, she turned and spotted their group, then waved in greeting.

Kai waved back and laughed.

"There's Ealasaid," Finn pointed with her free hand, keeping the other arm firmly around Naoki to still her. Sure enough, Ealasaid had stepped out from behind the stall to peek in the direction Anna pointed.

Iseult grunted in acknowledgement. "And Maarav."

Feeling safe now that they'd crossed the boundary into the burgh, and anxious to hear just what had happened, Kai urged his horse to a trot. Soon enough, he reached Anna, waiting by the wide road intersecting the first rows of homes.

As he dismounted near Anna, Ealasaid and Maarav moved to surround him, along with a woman somewhere in her fifties, dressed in black, her gray hair pulled back in a tight braid. She was somewhat familiar, but Kai couldn't quite place her.

Ealasaid opened her mouth to ask a question, but stopped as Iseult, Finn, and Bedelia reached them.

Iseult dismounted, his gaze not on his brother, but on the gray-haired woman. He put a hand on Finn's leg to prevent her dismount. He eyed the older woman like she might bite. "Explain," he said simply, turning his gaze to Maarav.

"We intend to," Maarav replied, positioning himself between Iseult and the older woman, "in *private*. For now, you have nothing to fear from Slàine."

Iseult narrowed his eyes at Maarav, but stepped aside so Finn could dismount. With her arms around Naoki, she swung her right leg over the saddle. Iseult put his hands on her waist, easing her down without disturbing her bundle.

Together, they led the four horses down the main road toward the inn.

After the short walk, Kai and Iseult handed their reins to the stableman. Kai held out his hand for Finn's reins, but she seemed unsure. Clutching Naoki protectively, she turned and looked at her white horse, as if asking for permission. The animal flicked its mane from side to side, and Finn exhaled in relief. She handed her reins to Kai, who then handed them to the stablehand, along with a few coins. Bedelia passed her reins off behind them, remaining silent, as she had the entire ride from the meadow. Kai sensed something burdened her, but did not know her well enough to ask.

Soon enough, they were all inside the warm inn, sharing a table. Naoki had been left to rest in Anna's rented room, exhausted from her long journey, perhaps *longer*, than any of them had endured, due to lack of proper care. The dragon seemed more than content to curl up on the floor before the fire, judging by the way she began to snore within a few short moments.

Kai wouldn't have minded a proper room himself, but there were more pressing matters than rest, hence, his presence in the common room. They'd all had their wounds tended, and now he and Iseult sat on either side of Finn, like bookends sandwiching her to keep her in place. He knew Iseult was likely feeling the same as him, like Finn might suddenly disappear at any moment, or be taken away. They both guarded her with watchful eyes.

Across from them sat Slàine, Maarav, and Ealasaid, with Anna and Sativola positioned at the end of the table. Bedelia sat on her own at the other end. Tavish, Rae, and the other black clad assassins sat at a separate table, conversing quietly amongst themselves. Their presence made Kai uneasy, but he trusted Anna's judgement. If she felt they were safe from the assassins, then they were.

Slàine cleared her throat, calling the impromptu meeting to order. Kai turned his gaze to her, eager for an explanation.

"We tried to stop this from happening," she explained, her eyes intent on Iseult, as if he were the only one to whom she owed an explanation. "Not only the bloodshed that occurred outside of this town, but the bloodshed that will likely follow. As I already told Maarav, we wanted Finn not to turn her in for coin, but rather, to stop her from fulfilling her part in an ancient prophecy. We were the ones who put out the original bounty, simply as a means of finding her." She took a deep breath.

"This prophecy, passed down through generations, states that when the seasons change, growing unseasonably cold, magic will return to the land. The Faie will awaken from their long slumber, and three queens will seek the Faie Queen's Shroud in order to rule them all. Two queens will die. One will live. And the world as we know it, will end."

Kai shook his head in disbelief. This had all been because of a prophecy? "And you would have killed us all to prevent this prophecy from fulfilling?"

Slàine nodded. "My mother was a seer, as was her mother before her. While I lack such gifts," the edges of her mouth turned downward bitterly, "I made a vow at my mother's deathbed that I would continue her work. I would not allow this prophecy to come to pass, even if it meant cutting down everyone who stood in my way."

Kai could practically feel Finn's anxiety radiating from her small form. He turned to find her biting her lip, as if preventing the words threatening to escape.

Slàine smirked, seeming to know just what Finn was thinking. "*You* are one of the three queens. By birthright, you are Queen of the Dair, not just of your tribe, but of all. Oighear the White is Queen of the Aos Sí, and we do not know the name of the third queen, only that she is a magic wielding human."

Finn nodded, and Kai's eyes widened. Could it be true?

"Rulers among the Dair are not chosen by blood," Finn explained, her eyes flicking from Kai, to Iseult, then back to Slàine. "We're chosen by birth," she continued. "I was born during a rare alignment in the stars, placing me next in line to rule, but our previous queen, Maeveen, still lived until just before I-" she hesitated. "She was killed," she explained evenly, "and I was no longer around to take her place."

More confused than ever, Kai watched as Finn batted at the tears forming in her eyes. Iseult placed a comforting hand on her shoulder. She nodded and muttered, "I'm well, do not fret."

Still reeling from the news, Kai turned to Slàine. "So you went after Finn instead of Oighear, not bothering to figure out the third queen's identity?"

"We know only that she is human, and will reveal herself in time. That left us with two queens to choose from, and we knew Oighear would be difficult to reach once she resurfaced. Finn was the most practical choice."

"And you would have killed her," Iseult stated before Kai could, even though he'd been thinking the same thing. If Slàine wanted to prevent the prophecy at all costs, she would eventually resort to killing the three queens one by one.

Slàine shrugged. "If we had to. As you may recall, the bounty asked for her alive and unharmed. We were willing to negotiate."

"Hmf," Iseult replied. "I gather your presence here means you've reconsidered the power you hold in this situation?"

She nodded, pushing a stray lock of gray hair behind

her ear. "Yes, I know I cannot stop Finnur if she chooses to move forward. I now only hope to convince her of the truth."

Kai turned his gaze to Finn at the odd elongation of her name.

Not seeming to notice, she frowned so deeply it cut her face in half. "Well Oighear is already dead," she admitted, "and there was no third *queen* there when she was killed, unless you mean Bedelia."

All eyes turned to Bedelia, who shrunk like a black and blue flower wilting in the cold.

"Not her," Slàine confirmed. "The third queen is a magic wielding human. Each of the queens is," she hesitated, "or *was*, in Oighear's situation, capable of ruling over all with their innate powers. No matter which queen wins, the world will change, and countless lives will be lost. Such great change cannot come about without great tragedy. It does not matter who dies first or last. It is the claiming of the shroud we'd hoped to prevent."

Kai tensed. If that was the case . . .

"It is already done," Finn muttered, her gaze on Slàine. "I have claimed the shroud."

"Then it is finished," Slàine sighed. "One of the three queens has claimed the shroud. I have failed."

"I'll step down," Finn pleaded. "I was never officially acknowledged after Maeveen's death. If I refuse to claim my birthright, then the prophecy cannot come to pass."

Slàine shook her head. "That you are ruler by birth is

all that matters. It is the claiming of the shroud by a woman meant to rule that will set things in motion."

Finn looked like she might cry. Kai took her hand and gave it a squeeze, wanting only to offer comfort.

Her tears began to fall. "It's all my fault then. The world will end because of *me*."

Kai looked to Slàine hopefully. There had to be some sort of catch. Finn would never bring about the end of days.

Slàine simply stared back at him, her gaze unwavering.

He sighed. "What will happen now?"

She shrugged. "I do not know. The prophecy ended there. Regardless, we have failed."

Ealasaid, who had been hunched in her seat, making herself as small as possible, cleared her throat. "Forgive me, but didn't you say that two of the three queens must die for the prophecy to come to pass? From what you've explained, the shroud is only the first step. If Finn and this third queen are both still alive, perhaps not all is lost."

Slàine narrowed her eyes at her, then nodded. "Perhaps."

Finn exhaled in relief. "I will do whatever it takes to stop anything horrible from coming to pass. I will put an end to the Cavari, and any others who might threaten this land."

Slàine's eyes widened, then she bowed her head. "If that is truly your will, my people will aid you. If we cannot stop this budding war from occurring, we can only hope to end it quickly."

Kai watched, somewhat awestruck, as Finn nodded sharply. Something had changed in her demeanor. She was becoming the powerful woman she was always meant to be.

Slàine and the others continued to converse well into the evening, while Kai contented himself with a dram of whiskey, glad to at least be safe and warm with Finn by his side.

He knew, perhaps, he should fear her new role, and her magical capabilities. Only a fool would care more for the fate of the dangerous creature beside him, than for himself or his countrymen.

He sighed. So then he was a fool, but he'd never claimed to be anything else.

LATER THAT EVENING, Maarav finally found a moment to be alone with Slàine, while their respective companions rested from their long journeys.

"How could you not have told me?" he finally balked at her prolonged silence. "You practically *raised* me."

He looked to the woman he thought of as his mother in many ways. The woman who had taught him to fight. Taught him to *kill*. She was just as deadly now as ever.

Slàine smirked at his half-empty brandy mug, letting him know she'd been watching just how many times he'd had it refilled . . . which probably meant *too* many, though he'd long since lost count.

He followed her gaze as she glanced at Finn and the others, sharing drinks around a separate table, along with Tavish, who'd seemed glad to rejoin the group after having faced down the Cavari.

"I knew you might have conflicting interests," Slàine said distantly. She turned back to him. "Were you aware that I knew your mother before you were sent to us?"

His eyes widened. "I was aware she knew someone within *Áit I Bhfolach*. I did not know that it was *you*."

"You know better than to speak the name of our home out loud," she hissed, then hunched back into her seat, "but yes, it was I your mother made her bargain with. She wanted to take her sons to Migris, and I wanted one of her sons in return."

He pursed his lips in thought. Part of him felt like he should be angry, but the wounds of abandonment were so old, he could not muster any ire. "Why are you telling me this?"

She snatched his cup from his hand and emptied the rest of his brandy down her throat. Handing the empty mug back, she answered, "So that you will understand why I kept my secret from you. Your mother confided in me of your curse, and of her need to save her boys. I also knew that one of the three queens would be a Cavari woman who would spend a century melded with the earth as a mighty oak, after cursing *your* people. When the Faie sightings increased, I knew she was soon to return, and I spread word of the bounty."

Maarav nodded. "Yes, so you could have Finn brought to you, and you could decide what to do with her to stop the prophecy from being fulfilled. I still don't know what that has to do with *me*." He raised his empty mug to gain the barmaid's attention, but she seemed to be busy with their companions.

"Honestly," Slàine replied tiredly, "I had hoped to use you as a bargaining tool. If she agreed to my terms, I could hand over one of the last members of your clan. She cursed your people once. I thought maybe she'd hate the bloodline still."

His mouth fell open. "So you raised me up to be slaughtered? Am I nothing more than a tasty pig to you?"

Slàine scowled. "Why do you think I encouraged you to go off to Migris without any of our people? I changed my mind."

He leaned back against his chair. The room was spinning nicely, softening the blow of learning his adoptive mother had once thought to sacrifice him. At least she had changed her mind.

Slàine's features softened. He knew she would not apologize, nor would she ask for forgiveness. It was not her way. They were both here, alive, and that was what mattered.

"You like that girl," she observed with a suddenly smug grin, nodding in the direction of Ealasaid. "I'm not sure I've ever seen you so taken with someone."

He smirked. "The *girl* calls lightning from thin air and runs into battle without fear. The *girl*, is terrifying."

Slàine laughed, then lifted her hand to successfully catch the barmaid's attention. She pointed to Maarav's cup, then held up two fingers. Turning her gaze back to him, she taunted, "I didn't think you were the type of man to turn his back on danger and . . . *terror*."

The barmaid hurried over to them with her tray of fresh drinks in hand. He took two mugs of brandy from her as he stood, placing a few coins on her tray. He turned back to Slàine with a wink. "I'm not."

He sauntered across the room, then gestured for Tavish to move so he could resume his seat next to Ealasaid. He handed her the fresh brandy, then leaned in close to her ear. "You better drink up," he whispered. "Tomorrow you begin your leadership of An Solas, with *me* as your humble advisor."

She took a swig of the brandy, though she was clearly already a bit drunk. She quirked an eyebrow at him. "Why Maarav, I thought you'd *never* ask."

THOUGH THE WHISKEY before her soothed Bedelia's sore body, it did nothing to alleviate the weight on her mind. She watched Finn carefully, laughing with Kai and Sativola. She wished she could be part of the jovial scene, but she still needed to speak with Finn. She'd told Iseult all of her secrets, believing there was no way they'd survive Oighear's dungeon.

*No.* That wasn't right. She would have told him regardless. She had planned to do so in Badenmar, but lacked the courage. It was only with death staring her in the face that she'd been desperate enough to speak out.

Her gaze met Iseult's across the room. He sat near Finn and the others, but remained somehow *separate*. He gave her a small nod and she took a quavering breath. He believed Finn would forgive her. After all, she'd forgiven *him*.

She stood, brushing imaginary dust off her freshly cleaned breeches, then forced her feet to carry her across the room. Finn noticed her before the others and smiled.

"May we speak in private?" Bedelia asked sheepishly upon reaching her.

Kai looked at her questioningly, but did not object as Finn nodded and stood. "Of course."

The two women made their way across the common room toward the stone fireplace, blazing with a comforting fire, and an empty bench placed before it. Together they sat, and Finn waited patiently for her to speak.

"I have some things I need to tell you," she sighed, "but I do not know where to begin."

Finn smiled softly. "Does it have something to do with why you were in the woods the night we met, all alone as if waiting for me? And why you later conveniently waited on the Sand Road at the perfect time, even though I'd been out to sea for weeks?"

"D-did Iseult tell you?" she stammered. "I told him I would tell you myself!"

Finn raised her hands in a calming gesture. "He told me nothing!" she laughed. "Well," she began more sedately, "nothing except to be careful what I said around you, just in case. He thought it odd how you so conveniently happened upon us."

Her heart's nervous patter slowed. So Finn had suspected her all along? She was such a fool to believe she could have so easily deceived everyone. She was a warrior, not a trickster.

She took a shaky breath, then met Finn's earnest gaze. "I was sent by Keiren Deasmhumhain, daughter of Àed Deasmhumhain, to gain your trust."

Finn gasped. All humor suddenly drained from her face. "Àed? Do you know where he is?"

She nodded. "I will get to that soon. Keiren sent me to meet you in the woods that first night. I did not know her plans, nor do I now. All I knew was my quest, to gain your trust, and eventually lead you to Keiren. There was something or someone protecting you from her *sight*. I was there the night the Archtree burned. Well," she hesitated, feeling overwhelmingly guilty, "*I* burned it, upon Keiren's orders."

Finn was shaking her head over and over again. "I do not understand. Why would you burn the Archtree?"

"Keiren had hoped to stop you from finding

answers," she explained. "Now that I've heard Slàine's prophecy, I believe it has something to do with that. She wanted to manipulate you in some way. After you left the Island, she sent me to wait for you on the Sand Road."

"Were you truly never my friend?" Finn interrupted, heartbreak clear in her voice.

"I always was!" she quickly corrected. "Or at least, for the most part. After you saved me from the wolves, and didn't care if I told you why I wore armor or traveled through the woods alone, and especially after I learned you were the one who left the potion for me, my thoughts changed. I began to hope there was some way I could save you from Keiren, and she knew it. She knew my heart had changed, and I would never lead you to harm."

Finn took a deep, shaky breath, and was quiet for several seconds.

Bedelia was so overwhelmed with waiting for a reply, she had to resist the urge to reach out and shake her friend.

"And what of Àed?" Finn asked finally, not meeting her waiting gaze.

Bedelia closed her eyes for a moment. *This* was the hard part. The part Finn would never forgive. "Keiren turned him into a tree," she breathed. "He now stands where the Archtree once took root."

Finn blinked at her in shock. "So he's not dead?" she gasped.

"N-no, but-" she stammered, unable to interpret Finn's attitude.

"Well this is wonderful!" Finn exclaimed. "When he did not come to find me, I knew something terrible had happened. I couldn't help but fear the worst, that he'd been in Migris when it was attacked. But if he has simply been turned into a tree, there is still hope of saving him. I was a tree for a hundred years, after all, and it did not do me any harm." She frowned. "Well except for the loss of my memories, but those came back."

"But," Bedelia began again, totally taken aback.

Finn took both her hands in hers and eyed her intently. "Àed told me about his daughter, Keiren. That she was powerful, and cruel. Now I know it must be true if she would turn her own father into a tree. I will forgive you fully, if you promise to help me get him back."

Bedelia thought her heart might burst. She would forgive her, after everything she'd done? "I will give my life if that's what it takes. I swear it."

Finn released one of her hands to pat the other one. "Now now, if that's what it takes, we will find another way. Thank you for telling me."

She couldn't quite believe her ears. This had to be some sort of trick. "I don't understand," she blurted. "How can you forgive me so easily?"

Finn beamed at her. "I cannot claim to know much about the mortal realm, but one thing I've come to know quite intimately is friendship. My friends are not perfect, they have made mistakes, just as I have, but what makes a true friend is the ability to see beyond that. I see your heart, Bedelia, and that is all that matters."

Bedelia blinked rapidly as her tears began to fall, and foreign sensations overcame her. Sensations she had blocked out long ago. She never would have guessed that what it would take to bring her back to life was not a lord, not a lover, but a friend.

She pulled Finn into a fierce hug, which Finn happily returned. She did not care if half of those in the common room had turned to look at them, and could clearly see the tears on the warrior woman's face. All she cared about was that she finally had a friend.

Pulling away, Finn took her hand and stood, leading her back across the room. Kai and Iseult resumed their posts on either side of Finn while she told the rest of their party Àed's fate. The general consensus was joy that he was still living in some way, and could possibly be saved.

Bedelia shook her head in disbelief as her *friends* continued to drink and make merry. She couldn't help but feel that they were almost like a family. They might not all get along, and they might have their secrets, but they were there when it counted, and that was all that mattered.

# CHAPTER SEVENTEEN

*F*inn awoke, filled with sudden memory. The final pieces slowly coming back to her, bit by bit. The curtained window had darkened the room, though it was still night. Anna snored loudly in the bed next to hers.

Anna. Finn sighed. In the morning, she would attempt to use the shroud to remove her magic, but it seemed she still had several hours before she needed to figure *that* out.

The shroud was now tied around the waist of her breeches. After a much needed bath, she'd felt it best to keep it near. She didn't relish having the magical item so close to her skin, but she had listened closely to what Slàine had told them. She couldn't risk this third queen coming along and stealing it away from her, not when they didn't know what she'd do with it.

With a final glance at Anna, she donned her cloak and

boots, then let herself out into the hall, just like she'd done the night she'd stayed with Àed at this very inn. The same night Iseult tied a man up by his boot strings for accosting her.

The hall was dark, but lantern light could be seen from the common room below. She smirked. Would she have to jump out a window again? At least she was wearing boots this time so she wouldn't freeze her toes off.

She crept down the stairs, then halted at a sound. Someone setting a drink down on a table? Morning was just a few hours off. Who would be sitting in the common room at this time? Curiosity getting the better of her, she finished her journey down the stairs and peeked around the end of the bannister. A familiar shape sat alone at a table, his back toward the sole lantern.

"You should be resting," Iseult muttered, somehow sensing her presence.

She left the stairs and closed the distance between them. "As should you," she replied, reaching his side. She frowned at his visible bruises, sure that uglier ones hid beneath his clothing. Not that he would ever complain about either.

He did not look up, and her heart gave a nervous flutter. Refusing to back down, she lowered herself to the bench beside him. Finally, he met her gaze.

"I will keep my promise," she stated bluntly, having some idea what might be bothering him. "I will do my best to use the shroud to return your soul. Maarav's too."

He shook his head and smiled ruefully. "No, you will not."

"I will!" she gasped, holding a hand to her chest. "Would you doubt me after all this time?"

He shook his head. "It is not you that I doubt. I have failed you."

She frowned. "I don't understand."

He sighed and took another sip of his drink.

The smell of whiskey fluttered to Finn's nostrils.

"I had hoped to escape Oighear," he explained. "I knew she intended you harm, intent on possessing the shroud." He began to lower his gaze, then forced it upward. "I watched helplessly while she approached you. If it weren't for Kai . . . " he trailed off.

She smiled softly, now understanding his upset. "You know, I'm not entirely without defenses," she teased.

The barest hint of a smile crossed his lips. "Of that I have no doubt, but I swore I'd protect you."

She placed a hand gently on his arm, wishing she could somehow put every thought she was having into his mind. "You *have* protected me. I would never have gotten this far without you. I owe you *everything*, and I *will* be following through with my promise."

He took hold of her hand on his arm and gave it a squeeze. "Perhaps in time, but not yet."

She frowned, once again confused. "Why ever not?"

"I do not know what will happen," he explained. "I've always been unnaturally fast and resilient. I can blend into shadows, and often hide in plain sight. I always thought it was simply luck, but Maarav displays these same skills. I believe it's a product of our . . . condition."

"You don't want to lose those skills?" she questioned, even more confused. Iseult didn't seem the type to worry about such things.

He sighed again. "I previously would not have cared one way or another. I only cared about ridding myself of my curse. But now, you have a long road ahead of you. I cannot stand idly by, and I cannot allow myself to be weakened. Not now."

"But if I die," she began, "if the shroud is lost-"

He turned toward her abruptly, enfolding her hands in his. "If I stand any chance of preventing either, I must remain as I am. If you are killed, I will surely have gone down before you."

Her eyes welled with tears. She wasn't sure what she had done to earn such loyalty, but there it was. She searched every corner of her mind for some sort of argument. It wasn't fair for him to remain cursed, especially when she was the one who had cursed him. She opened her mouth to speak, but he shook his head.

"I will hear no more arguments," he said softly.

She closed her mouth.

"Tomorrow we will formulate a new plan," he continued. "We do not know what the Cavari will do now that you have the shroud, and there is still this third queen to worry about, and An Fiach. It seems there is no end to those who seek you."

She sniffled, still fighting tears. "My apologies," she chuckled. "You will likely soon be as notorious as I."

He gave her hands a final squeeze, then released her from his grip. "One can only hope," he teased, then stood, offering her his hand.

She looked up at him with a small smile.

"Am I mistaken, or were you going out for a walk? Perhaps to stick your toes in the cold soil?"

She grinned and took his hand, then stood and began to lead him across the common room. "This way," she instructed, "I know an excellent window we can depart through."

They both laughed as they wove their way through the smattering of tables, benches, and chairs, on their way to a moonlit walk. Although this time, they used the front door.

THOUGH FINN HAD INSISTED numerous times that Iseult get some rest, the next morning found the pair near the inn's front door, watching the sun rise, just like it did every day, though today was somehow different.

Though Finn worried about his health, her heart was full. All of her friends were back together, and now she knew where Àed was. Though she had many concerns, returning him to human form was her primary quest.

The inn doors creaked open. She turned to see Anna and Kai. Remembering her task, she fingered the shroud around her waist, barely visible beneath the edge of her loose blouse.

Anna's eyes followed her movement, then raised up to her face. "I've decided against removing my magic," she announced.

Gaining nothing from Anna's deadpan expression, Finn looked between Kai and Iseult. Kai didn't seem surprised, letting Finn know Anna had already discussed this with him. Iseult didn't seem surprised either, but then again, he never did.

She turned her gaze back to Anna. "Do you care to explain?"

She replied with a sharp nod. "After speaking to Ealasaid and her new . . . group, I've determined that it is in my best interest to remain," she hesitated, "*cursed.*"

Finn couldn't believe what she was hearing. After how set Anna had been on removing her magic, there was no way she would change her mind. Just as she'd said, she viewed her gift as a curse.

Anna glanced at Kai, who gestured for her to continue. She sighed. "*And*, I had a dream last night."

Kai gestured for her to elaborate, obviously growing impatient.

Iseult wandered off to check on the horses, disinterested in the entire scenario.

Anna glared at Kai, then stomped her foot in frustration. "*Fine*," she growled. "I had a *vision* that if I rid myself of my magic, I would not sense coming danger at the most important time. It would cost certain lives-" she hesitated. *"Lives* that I'm not willing to risk. That is the end of it." She turned on her heel and stomped back into the inn, leaving Finn and Kai alone.

Finn turned her confused gaze to Kai, who smiled and took a step closer to her.

"Do *you* care to explain?" she questioned, still confused.

He leaned in near her ear. "You were the one she dreamed about," he whispered conspiratorially. "She doesn't want you to die."

Finn's jaw gaped. Beyond her ability to remove Anna's magic, Anna never seemed to care if she lived or died.

At her stunned expression, Kai continued. "Anna does not give her friendship lightly, but once you have it, she will kill for you. I know she seems selfish at times, and in many ways she is, but loyalty is important to her. You have gained her trust, and that's something very few can say."

Still shocked, she leaned her back against the wall.

Kai mirrored her.

"And what of this danger she referenced?" she asked finally.

He shrugged. "She does not know. Her vision was vague."

They stood in silence as the sun slowly crept upward in the sky. Soon clanking and clomping could be heard within the inn, and patrons began to walk through the doors beside them, searching for a hot meal.

Ready for a meal herself, Finn began to push away from the wall, but Kai caught her eye before she finished the movement.

"Do you have something to say?" she questioned suspiciously.

He grinned. "I'm just wondering where we're going next."

She felt her mouth form an *oh* of surprise. "We?"

He rolled his eyes at her. "You didn't think you'd get rid of me that easily, did you?"

She smiled, relieved. She knew she had been a burden on Kai, and had nearly gotten him killed many times, but she selfishly didn't want to lose him. He seemed to understand her in certain ways others could not. "We're going to go find Àed," she explained happily.

Having heard Bedelia's tale, he groaned. "All the way back to that blasted island?"

Finn nodded, a mischievous grin on her face. "Don't worry, I'll keep you safe from the big scary Sirens."

He waggled his eyebrows at her. "If it means another kiss, I'll call out to them myself."

She laughed and punched his arm, then walked past him into the inn. She might be well on her way to fulfilling a dangerous prophecy, but her fear was far less than when she'd first set out. She was no longer a weak little tree girl. She was a queen. May the gods have mercy on any who dared to stand in her way.

~

"But I don't understand," Anders muttered, pacing around the expansive stone room. "What is she doing all of this for?"

He and Niklas both waited within the fortress while the angry red-haired woman ordered her troops. Anders had nearly run the other way when they'd gotten close enough to behold them. He'd had few encounters with Reivers, but he recognized their wild beards and black war paint. Even the painted women warriors among them were burly and fearsome.

Niklas smiled softly, drumming his fingers against the wooden bench on which he was seated. "Keiren Deasmhumhain longs to dissolve the barrier between the living and the dead," he explained. "The shroud of the Faie Queen can be used for this purpose, but few are strong enough to survive the ritual. As powerful as Keiren is, she was born to human parents. She is not immortal. She needs immortal blood if she hopes to survive her plan."

"And how would she obtain immortal blood?" Anders asked skeptically.

"Why, from an immortal being," Niklas replied, like it was obvious. "If an immortal being willingly gives away a portion of his or her life force, a measure of that being's blood can be shared. If someone were to share with Keiren in such a way, she could complete the ritual."

Anders frowned, then plopped down on the bench beside Niklas. "And what does any of this have to do with me?"

Niklas smiled. "Everything, dear lad. *Everything.*"

～

ÓENGUS SLUMPED FORWARD in his saddle, weak, and barely able to keep his seat. He'd made it to Garenoch just in time to witness the strange battle that had taken place there, and had seen Kai ride off in this direction. He had kept to the tree shadows as he journeyed onward, paralleling the only obvious path Kai could have taken. His horse, just as road weary as him, made painfully slow progress.

Yet, he could not give up. He'd lost the dragon, and his men, but if there was still some chance he could help Keiren enact her plan, he *had* to take it. She'd promised to give him back what she'd taken from him so many years before. Killing her would be the only other way to meet his goal, and he was not foolish enough to believe himself capable of succeeding.

Not that he wouldn't try if given the chance, but he knew he would likely be the one to die, and he couldn't do that. Not yet.

He'd reached the small meadow too late. Whatever action had taken place, had already happened. Remaining hidden in the trees, he spotted Finn, Iseult, Kai, and Bedelia as they prepared to depart. He considered following them, but found himself too weak. He lifted his hand to check the wound on the back of his shoulder.

He'd bandaged it the best he could, but it was in an awkward spot, and he'd lost too much blood.

This was the end for him.

He never thought he'd miss his shadow, but now he knew his true folly. It should not have been sent to the in between. It should be in reality with him. When he died, would he truly die, or would his shadow remain? Would he become little more than a specter?

Knowing he'd soon topple off his horse to the ground, he let the beast amble onward anyway. It didn't matter. The creature could soon go where it pleased.

He gazed off into the distance, catching a hint of something white. His life was truly leaving him. He was beginning to hallucinate. His horse seemed to be guiding him toward the object. Perhaps the white form would lead him to the underworld. Because it was a *form*. As he neared, he realized it was a woman, curled up in the dead grass. She was dressed in white, with perfectly white skin and hair to match. Crimson blood stained her chest, and speckled her peaceful features.

Utterly entranced, he barely noticed as he fell from his horse. He groaned as he hit the ground, then managed to roll onto his side. Opening his eyes, he nearly screamed at the visage before him. The white woman remained on her side, but her eyes had opened to regard him.

"A Gray Lord," she muttered. "How interesting. Yet, your shadow is stuck in the in between. You know, it's only supposed to go there when you dream?"

He blinked at her. Just a moment before, he'd been sure she was dead. "How?" he gasped.

Her cheek still in the rough grass, she smiled at him. "One of Clan Liath should know better. You cannot kill the winter. At least, not for long."

His heart thudded in his chest, and something cold and all too familiar hit his cheek.

Snow.

I hope you enjoyed the third installment in the Tree of Ages series! For news and updates, please sign up for my mailing list by visiting:

www.saracroethle.com

# GLOSSARY

## A

**Àed** (ay-add)- a conjurer of some renown, also known as "The Mountebank".

**Áit I Bhfolach** (aht uh wallach)- secret city in the North.

**Anders** (ahn-durs)- a young, archive scholar.

**Aonbheannach** (aen-vah-nach)- unicorn.

**Aos Sí** (A-ess she)- ancient humanoid Faie.

**Ar Marbhdhraíocht** (ur mab-dry-oh)- Volume on necromancy

**Arthryn** (are-thrin)- alleged Alderman of Sormyr. Seen by few.

## B

**Bannock**- unleavened loaf of bread, often sweetened with honey.

**Bladdered**- drunk

**Boobrie**- large, colorful, bird-like Faie that lures travelers away from the path.

**Branwen** (bran-win)- a young, archive scholar.

## C

**Cavari**- prominent clan of the *Dair Leanbh.*

**Ceàrdaman** (see-air-duh-maun)- The Craftspeople, often referred to as *Travelers.* Believed to be Faie in origin.

**À Choille Fala** (ah choi-le-uh fall-ah)- The Blood Forest. Either a refuge or prison for the Faie.

**Ceilidh** (kay-lee)- A festival, often involving dancing and a great deal of whiskey.

## D

**Dair Leanbh** (dare lan-ub)- Oak Child. Proper term for a race of beings with affinity for the earth. Origins unknown.

**Dram**- a small unit of liquid measure, often referring to whiskey.

**Dullahan** (doo-la-han)- Headless riders of the Faie. Harbingers of death.

### F

**Finnur** (fin-uh)- member of Clan Cavari.

### G

**Garenoch** (gare-en-och)- small, southern burgh. A well-used travel stop.

**Geancanach** (gan-can-och)- small, mischievous Faie with craggy skin and bat-like wings. Travel in Packs.

**Glen**- narrow, secluded valley.

**Gray City**- See *Sormyr*

**Grogoch** (grow-gok)- smelly Faie covered in red hair, roughly the size of a child. Impervious to heat and cold.

**Gwrtheryn** (gweir-thare-in)- Alderman of Garenoch. Deathly afraid of Faie.

### H

**Haudin** (hah-din)- roughly built homes, often seen in areas of lesser wealth.

*I*

**Iseult** (ee-sult)- allegedly the last living member of Uí Neíd.

*K*

**Kai**- escort of the Gray Lady.

    **Keiren** (kigh-rin)- daughter of the Mountebank. Whereabouts unknown.

*L*

**Liaden** (lee-ay-din)- the Gray Lady.

    **Loinnir** (lun-yer)- one of the last Unicorns.

*M*

**Meirleach** (myar-lukh)- word in the old tongue meaning *thief.*

**Merrows**- water dwelling Faie capable of taking the shape of sea creatures. Delight in luring humans to watery deaths.

**Midden**- garbage.

**Migris**- one of the Great Cities, and also a large trade port.

**Móirne** (morn-yeh)- member of Clan Cavari. Mother of Finnur.

**Muntjac**- small deer.

## N

**Neeps**- turnips.

## O

**Óengus** (on-gus)- a notorious bounty hunter.

**Oighear** (Ohg-hear)- Ruler of the Aos Sí, also known as Oighear the White, or the Snow Queen.

## P

**Pooks**- also known as Bucca, small Faie with both goat and human features. Nocturnal.

**Port Ainfean** (ine-feen)- a medium-sized fishing port along the River Cair, a rumored haven for smugglers.

*R*

**Reiver** (ree-vur)- borderland raiders.

*S*

**Sand Road**- travel road beginning in Felgram and spanning all the way to Migris.

**Scunner**- an insult referring to someone strongly disliked.

**Sgal** (skal)- a strong wind.

**Sgain Dubh** (skee-an-doo)- a small killing knife, carried by roguish characters.

**Slàinte** (slawn-cha)- a toast to good health.

**Sormyr** (sore-meer)- one of the Great Cities, also known as the Gray City.

*T*

**Travelers**- see *Ceàrdaman*.

**Trow**- large Faie resembling trees. Rumored to steal children.

## U

**Uí Néid** (ooh ned)- previously one of the great cities, now nothing more than a ruin.

# TREE OF AGES READING ORDER

*Tree of Ages*

*The Melted Sea*

*The Blood Forest*

*Queen of Wands*

*The Oaken Throne*

ALSO BY SARA C ROETHLE

**The Bitter Ashes Series**

*Death Cursed*

*Collide and Seek*

*Rock, Paper, Shivers*

*Duck, Duck, Noose*

*Shoots and Tatters*

**The Thief's Apprentice Series**

*Clockwork Alchemist*

*Clocks and Daggers*

*Under Clock and Key*

**The Xoe Meyers Series**

*Xoe*

*Accidental Ashes*

*Broken Beasts*

*Demon Down*

*Forgotten Fires*

*Minor Magics*

*Gone Ghost*

# SNEAK PEEK OF BOOK FOUR, QUEEN OF WANDS

# CHAPTER ONE

The small inn room felt hot. Bedelia shifted uncomfortably, wishing she could escape.

"Stop fidgeting," Anna snapped.

Bedelia shifted again in her seat, swiping her short, dark brown hair from her face using her good arm. She glanced at the aggravated wound on her other, high up on her shoulder. "Leave it alone, it's fine."

Anna grasped Bedelia's biceps firmly, forcing her back down into her chair as she tried to stand. "If you won't let me tend your wound, you could very well slow us down on the road. If you slow us down, you will be left behind."

Bedelia bristled at the threat, then relaxed. Finn wouldn't leave her behind just because Anna was being cranky. She attempted to tug the collar of her burgundy tunic back up over her bandage free wound. "It's fine, the Aos Sí already tended it."

"Yes," Anna sighed, moving back behind Bedelia's chair to peer at the arrow wound in her shoulder. "Then they whipped you and marched you through the muck until you were near death. It needs to be *re*tended."

She ground her teeth. The cursed wound hurt bad enough without Anna prodding at it. She heard dripping as Anna wrung out the cloth, soaking in scalding hot water. The water stung like hot coals, though Anna's hands seemed impervious.

Her breath hissed out as Anna placed the wet cloth on the edge of her shoulder wound and began to dab. She clenched her fingers around the base of her chair and accepted the treatment.

She became momentarily distracted from her pain as a soft chittering sound emanated from a lump of blankets on the bed behind them. Naoki, Finn's pet dragon, had been snuggled up there all morning. The creature had taken to spending most of its time in the woods surrounding the burgh, no longer in constant need of Finn's care, but would still sneak in through the inn's windows in the morning to lie in a cushy bed.

"You probably still have shards of wood in there from them breaking the arrow like that," Anna muttered, returning Bedelia's attention to her.

She grimaced, thinking back to the Aos Sí's surprise attack. They'd ended up tending her not long after they sent an arrow through her, but it hadn't been a very clean job. Being out in the woods, the quickest option was to break the arrow near her wound, then pull it through. She was quite sure she *did* have shards of wood in there, but she wasn't about to let Anna pick them out.

A knock on the door preceded Kai peeking his head in. His shoulder-length, chestnut colored hair fell to the side as he watched them. "Are you two done yet? We'd hoped to be on the road by sunrise."

Bedelia turned in time to see Anna scowl in his direction. "Yes," Anna snarled, "then Sativola had too much whiskey and couldn't find his boots, and Finn needed private time to commune with her blasted horse! *I'm* not the one preventing our departure."

Bedelia began to stand again, ready to use Kai's distraction to escape the room, but Anna gripped her arms, forcing her back down.

"Iseult put up less fuss than you!" Anna growled at her.

She ceased her struggles, genuinely surprised. "*Iseult* let you tend his wounds?"

"Yes," Anna said more calmly.

Kai left the door ajar as he moved into the room to hover over them.

"Apparently Finn cannot provide miraculous healing to us *all*," Anna added.

Bedelia turned to see her scowling at Kai again. She found herself once more wondering about the exact details of the night Kai almost died. All she knew was that Anna and Finn had stayed near his deathbed, and in the morning he was good as new. She'd also noticed large matching scars on Finn and Kai's palms, but could not say for sure if they'd been there before that night.

The hot cloth touched down again on her shoulder. "Curse you, woman!" she hissed. "You could at least let the rag cool a bit."

Anna very deliberately placed the rag back in the water, lifting it in and out a few times like a mop, then slapped it back on Bedelia's shoulder.

"Argh!" she groaned, but bit her tongue before she could make her situation any worse.

"I think I'll just go tend the horses," Kai muttered, slowly backing away from Anna.

As he retreated quietly to the door to let himself out, Bedelia glared in his direction. *Traitor.*

The rag slapped down again.

She gritted her jaw, refusing to complain any more.

"I see you've come to your senses," Anna said haughtily. She began to dab the rag more gently.

Bedelia sighed and allowed her thoughts to wander, hoping for a distraction from the pain. Her mind meandered to their first mission, a long way off from their current location. She wished she'd told Finn about Àed's location sooner. It would be a long journey back to the island where the Archtree once stood.

Finn stroked the flat-handled brush gently down the side of Loinnir's white neck, readying her for the long journey ahead. She hoped the unicorn would not mind carrying her all the way to find Àed.

The unicorn's horn had remained magically hidden since they reached civilization, long enough now that she sometimes questioned if she'd truly seen it at all.

Loinnir turned her neck to eye Finn with one sparkling blue orb, as if to say, *How dare you question my existence?*

She smiled encouragingly at the unicorn, then continued brushing.

The stable gate opened and shut behind her, drawing her attention. She turned to find Iseult approaching. He'd dressed in fresh clothing in his customary black, blending in with his shoulder-length black hair, flecked with white at his temples. To her, his eyes were almost as mesmerizing as Loinnir's, though instead of sparkling blue, they were a calm gray-green, like the eyes of a hunting cat. Though his brother, Maarav, had similar eyes, she only found them interesting on Iseult.

He approached her side, then ran his fingers down Loinnir's mane. "You know," he began, "Anna seems to believe your horse is actually a unicorn."

She gasped, then turned her face to hide her furious blush. Anna could see things that others could not. Had she been able to see Loinnir's horn despite the magic keeping it hidden?

Iseult chuckled at her reaction. He rarely laughed in front of others, really, he rarely even *spoke* in front of others, but when he was alone with Finn, it was as if he could finally relax.

"It seems to me the Aos Sí knew what they were doing when they gave her to you," he continued. "You make a good pair."

She smiled bashfully, resuming her brushing. "I apologize for not telling you the truth," she glanced around to make sure they were alone, then added in a whisper, "about her being a unicorn, I mean. It just seemed the sort of thing I should keep secret."

"I understand," he replied. "It's not as if I haven't hidden things from you in the past."

His tone drew her eye, but his face was, as always, unreadable. She considered reaching out to touch him, but hesitated, unsure if her touch would be welcome. Ever since he'd refused to let her return his soul, the topic had become a sore spot between them.

She had the Faie Queen's shroud now, the thing they had been questing for all along so she could undo the curse she, as Finnur, had placed upon Iseult's people so long ago. Now he wouldn't let her right the wrong, fearing it might weaken him, and he wanted to be able to protect her. She knew he was avoiding the subject for her own benefit, but it still hurt to have that tension between them.

Although, she could not blame him for avoiding the

subject, as she too had been unable to speak of her lost daughter now that her memories of the tragic death had returned. The loss felt like it had happened in a dream, or another far distant life. She feared that if she discussed it openly, it would become real once more, and she'd have to feel that pain all over again. She was already haunted by enough ghosts of the past. If she let this one in, it might break her.

"What are you thinking?" Iseult asked, shattering the silence.

She took a deep breath. "About Àed," she lied. "I hope we can find him."

He nodded, running his hand gently down Loinnir's neck. "It will be a long journey. One we can ill afford in these trying times."

"I know," she muttered, turning her gaze down to the brush clutched in her hands.

He was right. According to Sláine, Maarav's adoptive mother, she was part of an ancient prophecy. The lives of humans and Faie alike depended on her being the last of the three queens to survive. To risk everything to save the single life of an old conjurer was surely folly . . . but she was going to do it anyway. Àed was her friend. He'd taken her in when she had no clothes, no food, and no memories. She owed him her life.

Iseult gently laid his hand on her shoulder. "I'll stand with you, no matter which path you choose."

She removed one hand from the brush to place over

his, appreciating his presence, even though it was a constant reminder of what she'd done to his people.

He gave her shoulder a squeeze, then moved to tend his own horse, a dappled tan mare. He'd lost his warhorse when they'd been taken captive by the Aos Sí, but never once mentioned the loss afterward. It would have bothered Finn, but if it bothered Iseult, it did not show.

Stepping away from Loinnir, she dusted the fine white hairs from her charcoal gray breeches, then turned to watch Iseult sorting through the saddles draped on wooden bars against the stable wall near his tethered mount.

Leaving his horse for a moment, he approached with a saddle for her in hand, then looked a question at Finn. "Are you sure she's . . . what Anna thinks she is?"

Finn nodded, glad he hadn't said unicorn out loud. There was no telling what some of the townsfolk might do to get their hands on a creature that was supposedly no longer in existence.

"Then should we perhaps *not* saddle her?" He gestured toward her with the heavy saddle held effort-lessly in his grip.

Suddenly grasping his hesitation, her eyes widened. She glanced at Loinnir. Did being saddled like a common horse offend her? The unicorn had allowed the Aos Sí to saddle her. Perhaps she would not mind . . .

Reaching her conclusion, she nodded. A saddle was

more comfortable than riding bareback, and she'd need a place to affix her supplies atop Loinnir's back.

Taking her at her word, Iseult approached the unicorn and gently laid the cushioned saddle on her back. Loinnir did not protest, except to swing her neck far enough to eye Iseult as he affixed the straps beneath her belly.

Finn jumped as the stable door swung open and shut again, settling as Ealasaid approached her. Her curly blonde hair was damp from her bath, dripping rivulets of water down the shoulders of her gray corseted dress.

"I wish we were coming with you," she groaned, reaching her side. "I want to help rescue Àed too."

"An Solas needs you," Finn comforted, though she also wished Ealasaid was coming. "You cannot leave them now."

Ealasaid sighed. "But I never *wanted* to be their leader. I've never led anyone in my life. I'm a farmer's daughter, not some sort of princess."

Finn smiled at her, truly wishing Ealasaid could accompany them. "You know, I feel the same way."

Ealasaid turned her gray eyes up to her and cringed. "Sorry, I forgot that *you're* supposed to be a queen. You have it much worse."

Finished saddling Loinnir, Iseult breezed past them and muttered, "Keep your voices down."

Ealasaid paled at the warning, turning apologetic eyes to Finn.

Finn leaned in close to her shoulder. "Do you *still* want to come with us?"

She turned to watch Iseult's back as he left the stables, then moved her gaze back to Finn. "Now that you mention it, perhaps I am better off remaining here in Garenoch. At least Maarav never looks at me like he might want to run a sword through my belly."

Finn laughed, turning to leave the stable. "Iseult would never do that to you."

Ealasaid followed at her side. "No, he would never do that to *you*. The rest of us mean about as much to him as a meat pie."

Finn simply smiled in reply. She knew Iseult cared more than he let on. Well, at least she thought she knew. Truth be told, she never really knew what the man was thinking. Perhaps they were all just meat pies to him . . . but, she doubted it.

Kai leaned back in his chair, trying to ignore Sativola as he groaned about his aching head, drawing the eyes of those attempting to have breakfast in the common room.

"You knew we were departing today," he commented. "It was your choice to have so much whiskey."

Sativola groaned again, pushing his sweaty, golden curly locks back from his scarred face. "Having that much whiskey is never a choice. At a certain point, the whiskey gods just take over and have their way with you, whether you like it or not."

Kai smirked and shook his head, glancing around the common room for signs of their other companions. He was just about to get up and check on Finn in the stables, when she and Ealasaid walked through the inn's front double doors.

He waved them over, feeling a mixture of emotions as Finn spotted him and motioned for Ealasaid to approach. Finn was looking overly thin, almost sick. He'd tried to speak to her about her troubles on many occasions, but she always changed the subject back to him. He'd given up on trying.

"I'm going to look for Maarav," Ealasaid chimed as they reached the table. "Don't you dare leave without saying goodbye." She eyed Finn sternly, then Kai before turning away.

She crossed the inn and marched up the stairs to find Maarav, who was likely still in bed since he'd been the one to inspire the whiskey gods' takeover the previous night.

Finn took a seat across from Kai and peered into his eyes. "How are *you* feeling?" she asked pointedly.

He forced a smile, flexing his scarred palm beneath the table. Even though he was more worried about how *Finn* was feeling, he could admit, if only to himself, that he'd been feeling . . . odd, to say the least. Ever since Finn gave away a bit of her immortal blood to save him, he hadn't quite felt like himself. It wasn't necessarily a bad feeling, just different.

"I'm fine," he replied with a roll of his eyes. "Really, you have much more important things to worry about than my . . . condition." *If she could brush off speaking of her troubles, he could do the same,* he thought.

"Perhaps," she sighed, pawing nervously at her long, dirty blonde hair, "but I'm the one that did this to you. If you experience any more latent effects, I'd like you to let me know."

He nodded in agreement, though he had no intention of telling her next time something strange happened. It was only a small thing to begin with. He'd been out in the market procuring supplies for their journey, when the scar on his palm sent an odd tingle through his arm and down his spine. The feeling continued until he nearly fainted. Sativola had dragged him back to the inn, where he quickly recovered. That had been three days prior, and he'd had no odd experiences since.

He was saved from further questioning as Bedelia and Anna descended the stairs. He could see fresh bandages peeking out from the collar of Bedelia's burgundy tunic, and Anna was smiling, so he assumed Bedelia had finally allowed her wound to be thoroughly tended.

Silent until then, Sativola staggered up from his seat. "I'm going to see to me horse," he muttered, "before I have to hear from all these women a second time about making them late."

Anna approached, then her smile slipped into a scowl as she glared down at Kai and asked, "How's your hand?"

Finn and Bedelia both joined Anna's gaze on him as they waited for an answer, and suddenly he realized just how long their forthcoming journey would be.

He stood. "I believe Sativola needs my assistance," he muttered, then walked away. He could feel the eyes of the three women on his back as he exited the inn.

Yes, the forthcoming journey would be a long one indeed.